Shadowland

Shadowland

A Tale From The Dark Ages

C.M. Gray

Published 2015 by Creativia
Paperback design by Creativia (www.creativia.org)
ISBN: 978-1512023466
Cover art by Adriana Hanganu (http://www.adipixdesign.com/)

Contents

Prologue – The Storyteller

'My name is Usher Vance, and mine has been a long and interesting life, or so I've been told before in company such as this.' Brushing back a long strand of silver-grey hair, the old man gazed about at the small audience of expectant faces and settled himself more comfortably into the familiar leather chair. Over the years, he had come to regard the chair as his own and, like an old friend, was all too aware of its weaknesses and strengths. It creaked and sagged and he responded in a similar fashion, rearranging his somewhat considerable bulk as he fumbled for pipe and tobacco. His fingers began charging the clay bowl with motion requiring little thought and he smiled, relishing the delight of spinning yet another tale.

'I have lived more years than I can remember.' He leaned forward to better study a few of his nearest listeners. 'Probably more than the sum of all your years combined. Kings have called me friend and heathen warriors have sworn to burn the flesh from my bones, vowing to search all seven halls of Hell to find me.'

Several of the younger villagers in the room fidgeted and cast about for the reassuring sight of a parent or friend, but most simply stared at the old man with eager expressions, impatient for the tale, any tale, to begin.

As the summer had turned to autumn and, more recently, as the first cold days settled a wintry grip upon the land, the villagers had gossiped and speculated upon the subject of Usher's story for this year.

The night of Midwinter's Eve was a special night in the village and the event was celebrated with feasting, dancing, and one of Usher Vance's stories for as many years as anyone could remember. For most of the year, the old man kept to himself and was reluctant to part with any of his tales. Tales that when finally offered, were told as episodes of his life, although this was rarely held to be true amongst the villagers. Each year, after clearing the remains of the meal from the long communal table, they would drift towards the huge fireplace, each finding his own place on the assortment of mismatched chairs and benches, but leaving the old stuffed leather chair ready for the storyteller.

The clay pipe glowed as the storyteller drew heavily upon it, building the heat as he slowly allowed the atmosphere within the room to grow. At last, content that the pipe was good and lit, he blew out a long blue cloud of smoke, threw the taper into the fire, and pointed the stem towards several of the closest faces.

'I see some of our younger friends gathered here tonight, and as long as they care not for troubled sleep in the weeks to come, then a story I shall tell... but what part of this life shall I lay before you?' He sat back and sighed, bushy white eyebrows coming together in a thoughtful frown. 'A tale of treasure and treachery, or love and war, what shall it be? So many years I have lived and so many things I have seen. Yet we only have these hours of darkness this midwinter's eve, only enough time to fill the night with one true tale.' He pulled on his pipe once more, and then reached over to lift a leather tankard to his lips. The villagers watched silently as the old man drank, heedless of the ale that escaped to run through his beard onto his stained waistcoat. Wiping his mouth upon his sleeve, he gazed about and judged it was almost time to begin; he was almost ready to cast the spell of a master storyteller.

The innkeeper stepped forward and set another log upon the fire, the flames crackled and spat, drawing everyone's attention for a moment. A curl of smoke wafted out, escaping the confines of the chimney and filled the air with a sweet rich scent as the fire continued to crackle angrily. To minds freshly laid open, ready for a tale, it was as if a wild animal had been thrown a hunk of meat and was devouring it hungrily before them.

'I think I now have something in mind,' broke in the storyteller, reclaiming his audience. 'A tale I have that has been some time coming. Tis a tale of battle and of love, of rescue... and betrayal. So please, make yourselves comfortable and we can begin.'

'Once, when I was considerably younger than I am now, I met a king upon a hill. I knew him at once to be a king by the finery of his clothes and by his horse that was as white as the purest snow and as spirited as...' A sound broke the concentration of the room and the storyteller stopped and stared back towards the door. The latch was rattling as someone tried unsuccessfully to gain entrance; a murmur filled the room as the villagers bemoaned the untimely interruption. The sound continued and the grumbling quickly became calls for someone to aid the intruder so the storyteller could continue.

Muttering incoherently, the innkeeper tugged back the heavy curtain that covered the door, keeping at bay all but the most insistent of drafts, and the audience turned once more to Usher Vance who had taken the opportunity to drain his leather mug. He passed it over, and then smiled in thanks as a serving girl exchanged it for a fresh one. After taking a sip, he readied himself to continue.

The sound of the door opening and someone being invited in was accompanied by a gust of frigid air that chased about the room; however, it was all but lost on the audience as they settled once more, eager for the tale to go on. The door slammed and the heavy wooden bolts were drawn back into place, hopefully as a barrier to any further disturbance.

Usher Vance cleared his throat and continued. 'It was a fine day as I recall, with a sky of the deepest blue and a mere dusting of high cloud to offer some contrast to its perfection. The sun shone down upon us, as if it were a light cast from the heavens, purely to illuminate the splendour of this king and his noble mount. The rest of the king's party were some distance away. He must have ridden to the top of the hill alone to take in the view and was clearly as startled to see me, as I was to see him. I remember bowing low while the king attempted with little success to control his dancing horse, its nostrils flaring in agitation at finding me enjoying the beauty of the day, clearly both king and horse had thought, until I had disturbed them, that they were alone.

'Good day to you, sire,' I said, gazing up into a pair of icy blue eyes. 'My name is Usher Vance and I apologise for the fright I brought upon your horse.'

Before he could continue, a soft dry voice broke the spell of the tale, cutting into the concentration of the audience and causing Usher to falter.

'Still spouting stories of utter rubbish then, are you, Usher?'

The storyteller cast about the shadows, trying to see who had disturbed him. As he did, several in his audience spoke up, encouraging him to ignore the interruption and continue, while others hissed into the gloom in search of the unwelcome speaker. Somewhat unsettled, but seeing his audience still keen, Usher Vance drew upon his pipe and readied himself to go on, but the voice returned at the moment he opened his mouth.

'He makes them up, and for some reason, keeps the real history of his life a closely guarded secret. Do you think he has a greater story that he chooses to hide?'

A frown creased Usher's face as he sought out the heckler. Everyone had turned towards the door and as Usher looked over, he felt the first low feelings of a strange foreboding enter into the pit of his stomach. In the fireplace, another log burnt through and settled causing flames to leap up, brightening the faces of the villagers and revealing for the first time a stooped figure by the door.

The stranger, leaning heavily upon a thick staff, was cloaked from head to foot in a dark material that glistened with droplets of rain, freshly brought in from the cold winter's night.

'Why don't you tell them a real story, Usher? Why don't you tell them who Usher Vance really is, and where he came from, instead of prattling on like some old fool with no life worth the telling of?' The stranger took a step forward and, raising a cold white hand, drew the hood from his head. There were several drawn breaths and a whisper of speculation from the villagers as they watched this unexpected drama unfold before them.

The stranger pulled his eyes from Usher and gazed about him. 'You have a personality of sorts before you, but not the one you thought you had.' Usher felt the blood drain from his face as the shock of recognition crept upon him. He felt the clay pipe drop from his mouth but was only vaguely aware of the sound it made as it connected with the stone floor, breaking in two with the slightest of clinks.

'No welcome, Usher?' The stranger moved over to crouch down at the storyteller's feet. 'I have made a long and terrible journey to find you, old friend, one I shall reveal another time. For now though, I beg you tell us a real story, Usher Vance, not one of your fancies. Why not tell of how two boys chanced upon some wolves and saw the world they knew come to its end. Talk to us, Usher Vance. It's been so many years and my memories have all but deserted me.'

It took some moments while Usher considered the sparse white hair and the mottled, almost grey skin as the dancing flames of the fire revealed the stranger's features. Finally, it was the eyes, they spoke to him of another time and another person; they still blazed with an intensity that he had almost forgotten. Sighing, as he collected his wits from where they had deserted him to the furthest corners of his mind, he addressed the visitor.

'Good evening, Calvador. Forgive me for being somewhat bewildered; recognition was a little hard in coming after all these years. You always did like to make an entrance, didn't you?' He glanced around at the expectant faces and smiled as he accepted another clay pipe. Reaching out, he squeezed the shoulder of the kneeling figure and stared down into his cold, almost yellow eyes. 'It's good to see you, old friend. Will you stay to hear an old man's story?'

'I will stay to hear your story, Usher Vance, but the story is of two old men, not one. Two old men that were once boys, forced to grow up far too quickly, and I would also appreciate a chair and a mug of something warming, if that is not too much to ask.'

As one of the villagers helped him up into a chair by the fire, the innkeeper fetched mulled wine and a bowl of broth. 'Please begin, Usher. I hunger for memories of times past.' Accepting the broth, he blew steam from its surface before taking a tentative sip. After a moment, he looked up. 'It has been a long time since I tasted anything quite so good, thank you.' The innkeeper nodded and resumed his seat.

Seeing the room was at last settled, Usher gathered himself once more; ready to begin a tale he had not prepared, yet surely knew better than any other. 'My name is Usher Vance and this... this is my friend, Calvador Craen.' The old storyteller gazed at the small audience of expectant faces and then settled back. 'We have both lived long and somewhat interesting lives, a little of which I shall try to recall for you now.' He drew upon his newly lit pipe and nodded in appreciation. 'Between us we are very likely to be far older than you may think. Let me start at the beginning... at the end of a beautiful day... many, many years ago.'

Chapter 1

THE END OF A DAY

Edging his toes closer to the lip of the cliff, Usher peered down at the rock far below where Cal sat shivering in the lengthening shadows. If he didn't do it now, then it wasn't going to happen... he knew that. Biting back common sense and silently cursing himself, Usher stepped back and then committed himself to the jump that all summer he had felt destined to make.

'Cal, Cal. Watch me ... Cal!'

Running two steps forward he took a mighty leap, to gain some distance from the jagged belly of the cliff, and flew, rejoicing in the sudden rush of air as he tumbled, arms and legs waving wildly as he narrowly missed the rocky outcrop of the cliffs that they called The Tooth. 'Caaaaaaaaaaaaaaalll!'

As the dark water of the lake rushed towards him, he stole a moment of satisfaction from the shocked look on Cal's upturned face. He just caught his cry of *'Usher... You crazy fool! Ush...'* before he hit the cold water with an explosion that drove the air from his lungs and plunged him into a world of confusion.

The lake claimed him. A roaring sound filled his ears, and he struggled to control the panic that threatened to smother him. He gagged, and just managed to resist the impulse to draw a breath of ice-cold water into his aching lungs. The lake filled his senses, fizzing and swirling, smothering him as he kicked out, desperately seeking a direction for the surface with its promise of salvation and sweet warm air. At last, where he least expected it, sunlight revealed itself, dancing in patterns on the surface, and he kicked towards it, frantic in his need to breathe.

Slowly, very slowly, he closed in on the shimmering light, fighting the lake's reluctance to release him from its cold embrace. After an age of effort, he broke the surface, drew a great, gasping breath, and coughed. Then pain exploded in his hand as it struck a rock. Ignoring it, he stretched out struggling to claw himself onto the rock until there was one glorious moment where he relaxed and slowly brought his breathing under control.

'Usher? Usher?' Cal's cry brought him back to reality.

Looking up for the first time, he drew breath to call out in response, but then saw that he had surfaced some distance from where he had entered, and that Cal was standing with his back to him on the opposite side of the rock. Cal was frantically peering below into the depths of the lake, still searching for some sign of him. Very slowly, Usher climbed out and, taking care where he placed his feet, crept across the treacherous surface.

'Usher?' Cal was shivering, standing with his bare feet searching for grip as he edged closer to the water. 'Usher?... Hell's teeth Usher!... We never jump from the point, you crazy goat. Usher! Ush...'

Moving forward, Usher shoved him, silencing his friend's cries and sending him flying into the icy water, arms flapping for a hold on empty air.

He sat shivering and hugged his knees, and then grinned as moments later, Cal fought to the surface coughing and spluttering.

'*Usher, you...!*' screamed Cal, clearly annoyed as he splashed water up at his tormentor.

'Come on, Cal, stop playing about. You'll catch your death of cold in this water. Isn't that what your mum always says?' Usher drew his lips together and in a high-pitched voice, mimicked Cal's overbearing mother. '*Calvador, you wrap up warm and look after your sister. No swimming, climbing, hunting or having fun of any sort, do you hear me, young man!'* A stick came flying towards him and as he sidestepped to avoid it, he slipped then stumbled, scraping his back on the rock and sliding into the water once again. His face creased and his back arched in a spasm of pain and then the water abruptly cut off his cry as he slid below the still surface. Cal struck out, swimming around the rock in an effort to get to his friend as he came spluttering back to the surface. They helped each other up onto the rock, and it was all Usher could do to mumble his thanks with his face still reflecting the needles of pain in his back.

'I think it's about time we got back,' said Cal, as he clambered up and gathered their things. He sorted through until he found Usher's tunic and threw it over as Usher flopped down. 'Are you all right?' Usher nodded.

During the long hot days of summer, the lake was a favourite location for everyone at the village. The women washed clothes in it, most people chose to bathe there at least once a month, and many would use the shallows close to the wood to cool off or play once their work was done. The cliffs however, were a special place for the boys of the village. It was a tradition to challenge each other to climb ever higher before leaping down into the lake's icy waters far below. This late in the year, there were few other swimmers, especially as the chill air came in towards the end of the day. It was to be Usher and Cal's last swim of the summer and so Usher had made the one jump that no other boy from the village had made.

They were shivering as they hurried to pull on leggings and coarse linen tunics, exaggerating the chattering of their teeth and laughing at each other's efforts to dress. Usher fought with the unyielding material, trying to drag it down over his growing body. At fourteen years, he was growing fast, faster than his mother could stitch new clothes, and with a sound that made them both stop what they were doing, the linen ripped at the neckline.

'Oh, wick!' moaned Usher. Taking a deep breath, he slowly pulled the obstinate tunic into place before investigating the damage.

'It's only come away at the stitching,' observed Cal. 'Maybe Nineve will be able to fix it before your mother sees it.'

Usher shook his head. 'Nineve might try, but she only has eight summers. I doubt she can stitch any good yet, can she?' He didn't wait for an answer. 'Come on, let's get going, we're losing light.'

If it got too dark, the path would be treacherous. Both boys had finished the climb after sunset on several previous occasions, and been forced to make the last few spans in darkness, praying that they might find the next handhold and not become stuck clinging to the cliff until daybreak.

When they finally made it to the top, the sun was touching the horizon with the last of its light shimmering across the lake in a blinding show of colour. They sat and rested, watching entranced as the sun melted slowly below the far tree line, turning the sky blood red and painting the edge of a solitary cloud with a deep pink blush. Gazing upwards, they could see every shade of orange and yellow until it faded directly above them to a green and then blue, it was a worthy display for the last day of summer. The first few stars were already sparkling and a crescent moon sat high in the east. Far below, a commotion drew their attention towards the centre of the lake. A raft of ducks splashing across the smooth orange surface of the water came towards them, gaining speed in an effort to become airborne. The sudden movement jolted the boys into action, and had them untying slings from their waists before scrabbling around to find good rounded stones.

Cal was the first to stand ready. Whirling the sling around his head, he let fly, but then groaned as the stone missed, startling the ducks into veering away. When Usher rose a moment later, the opportunity had passed.

They walked back towards the trees in silence. Still damp from their swim, Usher's clothes were clinging to him. He felt a shiver run through him from the encroaching chill of the evening air and silently wished they were already back by the warmth of the fireside.

They made it to the forest where the path became darker, the moon offering just enough light as it filtered through the leafy canopy to see its foot-worn surface stretching ahead. The trail was familiar to both of them.

All around were the sounds of the forest, crickets, owls, frogs from the pond, and the occasional heavier footfalls of larger animals as they crept through the undergrowth. There were the sounds of both the hunters and the hunted. Something crashed through branches to the side of them and they picked up the pace again, ever more eager to be back in the village to warm up.

The smell of wood-smoke from the cooking fires was the first announcement that the village was not far ahead. It hung in the air, drifting through the trees, offering the occasional tantalising aroma of cooking meat, and roasting vegetables. Lost for a moment in the heady smells of the evening, they nearly didn't see what was standing in their path until it was almost too late.

Usher pulled Cal down into a crouch and clapped a hand across his mouth as a little way ahead, the black shapes of three wolves emerged from the trees to stand in the middle of the path, their noses held high, sorting through the unfamiliar smells around them.

'They won't attack,' Usher assured with a whisper, hoping he sounded more confident than he felt. He remained squatting down unsure of what to do. The wolves hadn't seen them yet, but they weren't moving away either.

Wolves normally stayed clear of people, and rarely attacked, especially at this time of year when there was still plenty of game. Their appearance this close to the village, was unusual to say the least. As the breeze changed, the biggest wolf's head swung towards them and bared its teeth, its eyes flashing silver in the low moonlight as it gave a low growl.

'Usher,' whispered Cal, but Usher didn't answer as he fumbled for his sling and searched for the stone he had found earlier. Too late to take a duck, but maybe it had been meant for a wolf instead. The wolf took a couple of steps forward as its two companions glanced across to see what had disturbed it, and then, without warning, a fourth wolf brushed through the bushes to join them from the darkness. Its arrival drew the attention of the others as it began licking at the muzzle of the big leader in a show of subservience. A moment later, the big wolf growled a stop and turned its attention back to the boys, but they had already slipped away.

'Keep moving,' Usher urged, pushing Cal on into the gloom.

'Are they after us?'

'Well, if they're not then they will be soon. We have to make our way around to the village. They won't dare follow us in there.' Behind them a wolf howled, breaking the silence of the night; a second howl joined it moments later and then a third. Abandoning all pretence at stealth, the boys set off through the darkness with the sounds of pursuit not far behind. Branches whipped and tore at them as they ran almost blindly; desperate for some sign of a way through the shapes and shadows that loomed ahead of them. They stumbled on, tripping and falling over unseen bushes and bounced into trees, holding their arms up as they tried to protect their faces.

'They're catching up to us,' shouted Cal, his voice both panicked and laboured from the exertion. 'I can hear them getting closer!'

'Here, climb.' Usher grabbed his friend and pushed him towards the shadowy form of a large tree, its branches barely visible but at least one hanging low enough to clamber up onto. Cal pulled himself up as Usher waited impatiently. 'Hurry!' he urged, and then followed quickly, the moment there was room. The wolves' excited cries sounded close behind as they caught sight of their prey. Ahead of him, Cal was having trouble moving up to the next branch.

'For the Spirit's sake, hurry, they're coming!' He pushed alongside Cal in an effort to get higher and had just managed to move up to the second branch, when there was an excited growl and then pain flared in his leg. He screamed as the wolf bit, and held on. It didn't have a good hold, but good enough for Usher to keep shrieking and for the wolf's huge weight to drag him back down to the branch below. The wolf growled and began to twist and swing, its legs kicking as it tried to dislodge its prey's hold on the tree. With another cry, Usher felt his grip on the branch slip and then felt Cal's hand seize his arm.

'Pull yourself up... quick!'

'I can't...' he let out another scream, his breath coming in sobs and gasps as he struggled to hold on. 'It's got me, Cal. I can't...'

'Kick it!' yelled Cal, desperately trying to haul his friend to safety. There were several jerks as Usher kicked with his free leg and the wolf swung. Then came a high-pitched yelp as he managed to land a solid kick on the wolf's snout and it dropped away whining.

In the darkness, Usher scuttled up out of reach. He couldn't tell how badly he was hurt, but could feel that his leggings were torn and when he glanced down, could see a dark stain of sticky, wet blood, flowing down his leg. Below them, the wolves scrabbled at the tree in frustration, whimpering and occasionally growling softly.

'We have to get higher,' urged Usher, feeling above for another branch. They made their way upwards and as they did, the leaves thinned, the light improving slightly, and in the highest branches with the tree swaying under their weight, the night sky finally opened up to them. They could see the village. Too far away to call for help but still not much more than a stone's throw distant. People were strolling about and the glow of cooking fires cast a warm light between the huts where chickens pecked at the ground and a goat was calling plaintively for its kid; it all looked so inviting.

Usher shivered and tried to get more comfortable. 'We might be here for a while. I think those wolves are still down there.' He peered below through the shadows. There was nothing to see in the darkness, but he could still sense the movements. He glanced across at Cal. 'Thanks for helping me. If you hadn't pulled me up, that wolf would have gotten me for sure.'

Cal smiled at him and nodded, then stared into the village. Old Jonkey, the hunter, had finished his day and was coming home on the southern path. His bow was over his shoulder, a string of three fat ducks hung at his side. His hunting dog, an old flea-bitten hound that had long seen its better years accompanied him, its tongue lolling happily. The pair stopped to talk to someone the boys couldn't see and

Jonkey handed over one of the ducks in exchange for a reed basket of vegetables.

'Jonkey!' shouted first Cal, and then Usher, trying to get the old hunter's attention. 'Jonkey, up here... Jonkey!' but the old man didn't as much as glance in their direction. With the various noises coming from closer in the village, it was obvious he couldn't hear them. They watched for a while as he chatted, then saw him turn abruptly as something caught his attention, then something strange happened. He dropped the ducks to the ground, brought up his bow and shot an arrow into the darkness of the trees. A moment later, as he was stringing another arrow, he fell to the ground clutching at his stomach with the old hound standing over him, hackles raised, barking angrily into the darkness.

Usher and Cal gazed transfixed as shadowy figures began to creep out of the forest into the light of the nearest fires. Warriors wearing rough leather kilts and loose-fitting shawls, their faces shadowed in a distinctive way that every village boy knew from fireside accounts to be painted blue.

'They're Picts,' hissed Usher, through clenched teeth, 'but they're meant to be way up in the north, what are they doing here in the village, so far south?'

The Picts began moving amongst the huts, breaking the calm of the night with howling war cries as, realising there were few warriors ready to confront them, they threw burning torches onto thatched roofs, driving the confused occupants shrieking outside, where they cut them down without thought or mercy. The fires spread quickly and the screams of the terrified villagers rose to join with the bloodlust-howls of the attacking warriors. It quickly deteriorated into a scene from some awful fevered nightmare.

'We have to get down there,' cried Cal, hysteria edging his voice. 'Those are our families!' He glanced below into the darkness, trying to decide if the wolves had gone but sounds of movement frustrated any question of descent. He grabbed at Usher's arm and began to sob.

14

'Usher, why are Picts attacking into the Weald? Surely, there must be a Roman villa to sack. Why an Iceni village? We have nothing!'

To sit in the tree, only able to watch their friends and family driven from their huts and murdered, was more than the boys could bear, but bear it they had to, as below them the wolves began to howl, confirming they were still trapped.

They watched as a young woman ran from a burning hut, her hair smoking from the intense heat, a baby clutched to her chest wrapped in a soft woollen fold. The woman was screaming hysterically, her baby wailing at being torn so rudely from its crib. As she ran, trying to find escape between the huts, two Picts saw her and gave chase. Catching up quickly they danced around her, hooting with glee as she continued to shriek, seeking desperately for some way to escape. With her baby clutched tightly, she kicked out, catching one of the Picts a glancing blow to the leg, which only increased their delight, then she tried to dash past. The closest Pict caught and spun her round. Both were shrieking, the woman in fear for her baby, which flew from her arms, and the Pict in excitement for the sport. Without warning, a spear took the Pict holding her throwing him back in a spray of blood. As he fell, the woman scrambled for her baby, picked it up, and dashed out of sight. The second Pict ignored the woman and ran towards the attackers that neither Usher nor Cal could see.

The round thatched huts of the village were burning fiercely now, flames and glowing embers clawing up at the cold night sky, dancing like great fire spirits celebrating their release from the depths of the earth to writhe in this orgy of madness. The roar of the blaze swept through the village moving from hut to hut, and then it began to spread into parts of the surrounding forest, illuminating every detail of the massacre and the warriors that delivered it.

Tears slid down Usher's cheeks, blurring his vision, but he wiped them away with a desperate need to witness every detail. The image of the Picts, screaming in an ecstasy of bloodletting as they chased down each fleeing villager would be, forever imprinted upon his mind.

A central figure directed the violence with a calm detached air from the back of a horse, almost as if he were overseeing the summer harvest rather than the annihilation of a people. He was dressed differently from the others, in black leather with a dark fur cloak draped across his shoulders. The horse tossed its head and one of its forelegs scrapped at the ground as if bored while the rider regarded the carnage around him through the protection of a conical helmet with burnished side plates and nasal guard.

Cal noticed him first and quickly pointed him out to Usher. They screamed out threats and curses, but of course, the rider couldn't hear anything above the noise of the slaughter surrounding him. After a while, they stopped and lapsed into an angry silence, watching as the warrior took the nose guard and lifted his helmet in one swift motion to consider the activity about him. It gave them their first opportunity to look upon the face of their enemy.

'Remember that face. He is the man doing all this,' muttered Cal.

'Remember, him? I doubt I shall ever be able to forget him,' hissed back Usher.

Everything about the rider appeared black. He had long black hair, gathered at the side of his head in a warriors' knot, and eyes that were merely dark hollows within the shadows of his skull. More black hair grew upon his upper lip that he now stroked and teased while directing his men at their deadly harvest. Even the rider's horse was black, and appeared blessed by the same disregard for mindless violence as its master. It stood unflinching while flames licked close to its haunches.

Turning in the saddle, the rider snapped out an order in the strange Pict tongue, directing three warriors towards the west of the village where he had seen something. To the observers in the tree it appeared he would not be satisfied until the whole village had been destroyed, his Picts working like a pack of dogs, picking off each running figure as they fled for the trees. Each figure a person that was a friend, neighbour or family member to Usher and Cal.

The largest beams of the huts began to give way. Loud cracks and crashes rendered the air, sending embers and sparks high into the night sky in great sparkling clouds as what was left of the roofs collapsed and the walls caved in.

Then in one glorious moment, the boy's spirits rose as three village men and one of the women came into view swinging swords and spears before them. As a group, they began beating back several of the attackers, however, the stand was short-lived. When the rider in the centre saw the threat, he simply directed more men to come in and attack the defenders from behind and they were swiftly overwhelmed and butchered.

The longhouse was now the only building still standing. It was the largest hut, the meeting hall of the village council, and the home of Elder Borin Torney. Its thatch was still blazing fiercely, and parts had dropped down setting the interior alight, the flames reaching out through the small shuttered windows and past Borin who now lay dead in the open doorway.

The Picts gathered around their leader's horse and roared their approval as the great central beam of the house finally gave way and the whole building collapsed in on itself.

Their task complete, the black warrior turned his horse and led his party out of the village by the southern path, herding a small group of wailing children ahead of them, leaving only the smoking deathly remains of the empty village to the spirits of the night.

The boys watched as the group strode out of sight. They heard their laughter echo through the forest as the Picts celebrated their venture, not realising they had left the cold heart of vengeance behind them seething in the heights of an old oak tree.

The remainder of their night passed sitting in silence; cold, uncomfortable and deeply shocked by what they had witnessed. Tears of sorrow, frustration and a deep sadness aided their survival, coupled with a burning anger and need for revenge.

Tentatively lowering themselves from the tree in the pre-dawn glow, they were relieved to find that the wolves had gone and they were able to push through the trees and find the path.

Walking into the village was like re-entering a nightmare. As dawn first painted the sky to the east with fingers of orange light, Usher and Calvador sought out the burnt husks of their family homes and wept.

A few barely recognisable family possessions were scattered amongst the smouldering ashes, things that by some turn of fate, had not burned. Blackened, trodden into the dirt and ash of the path, were items of clothing, some pots, and the remains of the harvest spirit Usher's mother had made from twisted barley stalks. She had made it several weeks prior, twisting the stalks into the shape of a man-spirit with barley heads as hair and then hung it by the entrance to their hut in celebration of a good harvest. Many of the villagers had commented about how fine it was and Usher remembered his mother's pride, now it lay broken and trodden into the blackened ground.

Tears streamed down Usher's face as he gazed upon the desolation, his mind still unable to really grasp that this was once the home he had grown up in and that his mother and father were no more. Unable to find their bodies, and unwilling to search too far, he gathered a few things into his bag and, still walking in somewhat of a daze, went in search of Cal.

He found him kneeling with his back to him in the ruins of his former home. His shoulders were moving and although silent, Usher could tell he was sobbing. He was staring at the remains of the fire as it still burnt in what would have been the middle of the house with two blackened bodies lying close together at its centre. They must have been Cal's parents but were unrecognisable as anything once human. Usher laid a hand on his friend's shoulder.

'Come away, Cal. We'll get whoever did this, even if it takes forever. We'll find them all and make them pay.'

Cal's hand covered Usher's as he fought to bring his tears under control. 'I don't see Nineve's body, maybe she was one of the children they took with them. There were several, remember? We have to go after them.' He climbed to his feet and angrily wiped the tears from his eyes. 'Why, Usher? Why would anyone come up here and...' he looked around, unable to finish. Usher shook his head, finding no other response.

They picked their way through the village in silence, their minds numb, unable to comprehend what their eyes were telling them. In a half-hearted effort to do something, they collected a few things that they felt might be useful and called out in the hope that someone had survived the madness and would come running out from the woods, but their cries went unanswered by the cold darkness between the trees.

Picking up the trail of the warrior band, they headed south. Two boys consumed with thoughts of revenge, and the need to know why their world had shattered and burned.

* * *

The storyteller coughed and reached for the pewter mug at his side, then glanced across at the tear-streaked face of Calvador Craen. His friend was still lost in the past, back at that burnt-out village, so far away and so long ago, with the flames from that fire still flickering in his eyes after all these years. Usher felt a shiver as the memories of that day crowded his mind. He leaned forward and placed a hand on his friend's knee. 'Are you all right, Cal?'

Cal turned his head as if waking from a dream. 'Why does it all seem like yesterday? Why can I still hear the wolves and see our village dying?' He shook his head in wonder. 'And why can I never get that stink out of my nose?' Taking a deep breath, he waved Usher to continue, and then resting his elbows on the arms of the chair and his chin on his hands, he returned to watching the fire.

Usher Vance took a fleeting look around the room at the silent faces, and then continued.

Chapter 2

A New Dawn

A soft warm light filtered through the trees, blessing the morning mist with an ethereal quality as the woodland birds welcomed the dawn with their chorus of celebration. It was cold. A breeze rustled through the leaves overhead, whispering a promise of rain later in the day, but for now, dawn had brought a sunrise. Down on the path, two boys plodded onwards, noticing little of the new day awakening as they dragged along confusion, despair and tired minds in an exhausted daze.

The tracks weren't hard to follow. The Picts travelled the main path without any fear of pursuit and had made their way through the woods and on into the lowlands; brazenly marking the trail with items they had looted, inspected and finally discarded. Each item serving as a stabbing reminder to the boys of the horrors visited the night before.

'What are we going to do if we catch up with them?' Cal asked. He kicked a stone and it bounced along the dry rutted path. It was the first thing either of them had said in some time and it brought Usher up with a start.

'What?' Usher's mind had been unconsciously reliving the terrible scenes of the previous night, leaving his feet to find their own direction as he tried to ignore the pain in his leg from the wolf bite. The wound wasn't too bad, they had managed to clean it in a stream and had bound it in torn cloth, but it still hurt and made him limp. He glanced about, surprised to find they had passed through the meadows and low brook and had now re-entered the woods.

He turned to look at Cal. 'It's when we catch up with them, not if and I'm not going to forget what the horseman looked like, and when we catch up with him...' he stopped for a moment, wondering what they would actually do when they caught up with the Picts. Neither of them had killed anything bigger than a deer, and they hadn't done that many times.

'We're not warriors,' broke in Cal. 'We can't fight those Picts, even if we do catch up with them.' He slumped down at the side of the path and lay back in a clump of bracken. 'What are we going to do?'

Usher looked down at his friend's face, and saw misery and fear staring back at him.

'We have each other, Cal, and when we catch up with the Picts we're going to find Nineve, and maybe some others from the village, and then... then we're going to get them to safety, somehow. After that... I don't know. We'll have to trust in the spirits and see what they offer us.'

They continued to walk until late afternoon, emerging once again from the trees of the Weald, the great rambling forest that stretched across the width of Britain. They must have been walking uphill for some time because the view that presented itself as they passed through the last few elm and beech trees was from high on a hill and breathtaking in the afternoon light. Grassland spread across a valley in a pattern of hedged cultivated fields, appearing before them like some huge sleeping-mat thrown down by a giant of legend. It wasn't a site they had seen before. The small fields planted by their village had been hard won from the forest and nothing compared to the scale of this area of sectioned and worked land. Usher took it all in, studying the small communities that dotted the valley. A Roman road ran straight and true from one end to the other, and smaller, local paths snaked between the settlements. He studied the road and surrounding land, eager for any sight of the Pict raiders, but could see little movement of any kind, and certainly no column of marching warriors. For Cal's sake, he suppressed his feelings of disappointment.

What looked like a Roman villa was dominating the far end of the valley and the closest settlement of tribal huts was just a short walk further down the path. Smoke trailed up from a group of familiar round dwellings and they could just make out a few cows grazing, with chickens pecking the ground round their legs. By the largest building was an old man was chopping wood, a halo of long grey hair billowing in the breeze as he raised and dropped his axe. The sound of each strike only reaching them up the hill as the axe lifted to the top of each stroke. With a sigh, they shouldered their packs and walked down into the valley.

The path from the forest was well trodden and led directly past the nearest settlement. It was only as they got closer that someone noticed them. 'Get away, leave my chickens alone!' The cries of a woman broke through the calm of the day as they neared the first hut. She was running towards them with skirts flying, bringing the boys up short, confused as to why she was screaming at them. A clod of mud landed close to Cal and they watched in amazement as she stooped to gather more stones and lumps of mud to throw at them.

'We're not after your chickens,' called Usher. Refusing to be intimidated, he turned to Cal. 'Maybe we should just move on, she doesn't seem too happy to see us.' The woman stopped running and began pelting them with anything she could lay her hands on. Finally, a stone hit Cal on the leg and he gave a cry.

'She's mad!' he yelled, clutching at his leg, but before they could either run or stop her from throwing anything else, another figure joined the exchange.

'You're not really after them chickens now, are you, boys?' The old woodcutter came out from between the huts and the woman halted her attack. Long past his fortieth summer, the man was breathing heavily and sweating from the exertion of chopping wood. The woman dropped her rocks to the floor and with a scowl towards Usher and Cal, she moved back to her chickens, apparently satisfied that another was dealing with the threat. Usher shifted his pack on his shoulder and tried to decide whether they should just turn and run, but then swallowed nervously, as he realised that running from the drawn bow that the old man was now holding wasn't really an option. It was no ordinary rough hunting bow either. Its dark wood gleamed in the warm afternoon light, hinting at a weapon built for more than merely hunting deer. Staring at the tip of the arrow aimed towards him, Usher decided he was as close to death as he had ever been. The old archer gradually eased the pressure off the bow; the hemp string singing softly as the strain released and the arrow pointed to the ground. With a hiss, Usher let go of the breath that he hadn't realised he had been holding.

'Well, you don't look much like raiders.' A slow grin crept across the man's grubby face. He was old, but not as old as they had first thought. The long grey hair had been hastily tied back from a heavily lined face; bushy eyebrows were exposed, drooping down over dark eyes that appeared to lay all the man's inner feelings bare. From scarcely restrained violence a moment before, they now reflected amusement. 'I see you wear Iceni colours, but you're not from round these parts, so where are you from?' He scanned the surrounding hedgerows and, seeing no others ready to pounce, unstrung the bow with a smooth practised motion.

'North ways,' said Usher, finding his voice and waving back towards the woods. 'We were just passing, we didn't mean any harm.' This brought another smile to the archer's face.

'I believe you didn't, boys. The name's, Meryn Link, and that over there,' he pointed towards the woman who was now crouched back down clucking at her chickens, 'that's my neighbour, Bretta. She don't mean no harm neither, just loves them chickens, is all. This has been a busy road over the last few weeks, an' any party of raiders that comes past here has seen fit to take a few of them chickens. Reckon she's just about had enough.' He gave a chuckle. 'Not the brightest of flames is Bretta, but she means well. Anyhow, tis late in the day and I can at least offer you shelter for the night, if you want it that is. I try to keep a traditional hearth of welcome in my home; an' if truth be told, I could do with the company. So please, be welcome.' He waved them towards the biggest of the huts then set off with the boys trailing behind.

When they entered, the hut was dark, warm, and clean, smelling of the fresh hay strewn across the floor and the smoke rising lazily from the low fire in the centre. It immediately reminded the boys of home and each choked back a momentary reminder of their loss. Meryn dropped some chopped wood onto the fire and it was soon crackling merrily, the glowing embers and flames bringing light into the dark space, showing few possessions, but a neat and tidy home. The boys slumped down and watched dreamily as the smoke rose, curling towards the thatched roof before escaping through the centre hole of the thatch of cut rushes. Usher hadn't realised until entering the warmth how utterly exhausted he was. The last day and a night without sleep had all but drained him of energy.

'Please... we're tracking a group of Picts, led by a horseman,' said Usher, rousing himself. 'They...'

'Picts? This far south?' The old man glanced across, and then smiled kindly when he saw their anguished expressions. 'Well anyway, there'll likely be plenty of time for questions and then maybe for answers later. Sit and rest or you'll not be tracking anything or anyone. You look bone tired, the pair of you.'

Meryn took his bow and placed it close to the door. As he did, Usher prodded Cal and motioned for him to look. The bow now leaned against the wall alongside a spear and sword. The sword was big, half as long again as any normal blade of the Iceni. They exchanged puzzled frowns and glanced up to see the archer smiling at their reaction.

'Tha's a warrior's blade.' Meryn went back and picked it up, pulling the blade from its sheath with a flourish that made them both draw back, suddenly unsure of their smiling host's intentions. The old man slammed the blade back into its polished black scabbard then held it up in a beam of sunlight that had found its way past the door. The sword's half-moon finger guard gleamed yellow as they all admired the weapon.

'How did you come by it?' Cal asked, in a hushed voice. 'Are you a warrior?' Meryn sighed and returned the sword to its place by the door, then stooped down to tend the fire.

'I once fought with a warrior band, yes, and soon I'll probably do so again. Unfortunately, I don't think my destiny lays in farming as I had hoped. There's an air of change about our land, causing many a man to pick up his sword. Word is, a king of the Britons has risen and like many others, I mean to join his army and fight the Saxon invaders. Fact is I've already delayed here too long.'

As the light of the day began to fade they helped Meryn gather in his animals and then watched with stomachs grumbling as he prepared a meal over the fire. While he worked, Usher described what had happened back in their village and that they were now in pursuit of the Picts and Cal's sister, Nineve.

Meryn had been slowly chopping a turnip while Usher was speaking. Once the tale had come to an end, he put the knife down and sighed. 'I'm sorry for the girl's plight, truly I am. What they want with a bunch of children I don't know, but you don't want to go chasing them Picts. They have a reputation as a cruel people, and a raiding party this far south would spare little time in killing you both before moving on. 'Tis a sign of the age we live in, now that our Roman masters are leaving us. Maybe you boys know, but before the Romans came, the tribes had a long history as warlike people. We were always fighting amongst ourselves or protecting our shores from ships filled with warriors that came from I don't know where. And then the Romans came and we fought them as well, turned them out a couple of times, so the storytellers have it.' Meryn poked at the fire and threw on a few more sticks, 'but they kept coming back and then stayed. A few of us still fought them, and when Boudicca's Iceni finally failed to drive them out, the land slowly settled and life for the tribes had changed. For over four hundred years, there has been relative peace in our land. The skirmishes between the tribes and raids from the Saxons and Angles have almost become a thing of history, almost. Now as the last of the Roman legions are departing, some say it's because their empire is crumbling, they leave behind their empty towns and their houses that no tribesman would wish to live in. Many believe those stone houses are still occupied by the spirits and ghosts of the past, and it is true that their stone and tile floors cut all connection to the earth, they just don't feel right.'

Meryn looked up at the boys again. 'Life is changing, lads. It's going unnoticed by most in the tribes, but a time of violence is fast returning.' Meryn spat into the fire as if the mention of the Romans had left a bad taste in his mouth. It hissed briefly in the hot embers, drawing their attention until he spoke again.

'They ruled here for a long time and brought much to this land, including some measure of peace; but that doesn't mean we had to like them. No man should be the slave of another, and we were all slaves to the Romans. They stole our lands, they stole hearts and they stole our identity. Well anyhow, now they've all but gone, and that means there's going to be a struggle for control. So beware of the Picts and any other warrior band you see. For there'll be more of them in the next short while, you mark my words.' He picked up the knife and continued his chopping, throwing the turnip pieces into a large iron pot suspended over the fire. It was bubbling and beginning to give off a tantalising aroma.

'We mean to catch them, and when we do, we'll free Nineve,' muttered Usher. 'We don't plan to attack the Picts. We're not fools, but we will get Nineve away... somehow.'

Meryn smiled. 'I like your attitude, boy and maybe you will get her away, but then what? Where will you go? What will you do? Your village is no more, your...'

'We can only live one day at a time,' broke in Usher, 'and trust in the spirits to guide us. The one thing we still have at this moment is hope, hope that Nineve is still alive. When we find her and free her, we'll seek a new direction. The spirits will guide us.' He glared at Meryn as if challenging him to find fault in his logic, but the old archer merely continued to smile, which Usher was beginning to find annoying.

'Well spoken, lad. It would seem you have a determination and strength beyond your years.'

They sat quietly, staring into the flickering flames for some time; each lost in his own thoughts. Finally, Meryn broke the silence. 'Do you know why they were after the children?' The boys shook their heads. 'Well, I was planning to leave for the west in another week or two, but maybe I'll leave a little earlier.' He stabbed the knife down into a log. 'A Pict warrior party did move through here late yesterday.' Usher glanced across to see Cal sit up and offer him the flicker of a smile before staring at the old man, willing him to go on.

'Did a horseman lead them? Tall? Dressed in black?' Cal asked, barely able to suppress his eagerness. Meryn looked up and seemed to study them both before answering.

'Aye, I believe there was a horseman.' He leaned forward and threw another log on the fire as he gathered his thoughts. 'They were keeping to the edge of the forest, but I saw them and marked their progress around the west side of the valley. Maybe we can help each other. I'll help you with your quest; maybe stop you from getting yourselves killed... but in turn you will be beholden to me. Do we have an agreement?'

'Yes!' agreed Cal readily, but Usher held up his hand and frowned at Meryn.

'What do you mean by beholden? What would you have of us?'

The old man's smile returned. 'Good question, young friend, a good question that deserves a good answer, and as soon as I have one to give, that answer shall be yours, but right now let me see that wound on your leg. We will clean and dress it and then it should be time to eat. A bite from a wolf can be a nasty thing if it isn't tended regular and properly... this is going to hurt.'

* * *

'Meryn was a good man,' said Calvador Craen breaking into the story. 'Was it really luck that we met him? He trained us well.' He looked at the villagers as if only just noticing them again, and then back to the seated figure of the storyteller. 'I seem to remember getting a few cracks on the head when we travelled with Meryn. We learned the sword, the spear, and the bow; and none of them were easy lessons.'

Usher nodded, and then searched the faces around him. 'May I get another of your excellent ales?' he asked, finding the face he was looking for and passing his empty tankard towards the innkeeper. The man beckoned for one of the serving girls to come and take it.

'Did you rescue Nineve?' asked a girl sitting close to his side.

'We may well have done, you shall have to wait and see,' he said with a smile '... you know, she would have been about your age at that time. Although for all the world, she seemed filled with a spirit far older than just those eight summers. She was a very special little girl; we just didn't know it at that time.

Can you imagine how she must have felt? A poor broken thing; seeing her family murdered, her village burned, and then she was dragged away by the Picts, they were all terrified when we finally tracked them down.' He turned to Calvador Craen. 'My friend Calvador here was very brave that day, as I remember; risking his life more than once trying to spirit his sister away.' He looked at Cal but his old friend had returned to staring at the fire, content to sup his mulled wine and allow the memories to wash over him. 'We'd been on their trail for almost a month, Meryn, Cal and I, and had practised weapons with Meryn almost every step of the way, not that we were very proficient at that point, but we knew which end of the sword to hold, and how to draw the longbow. We hunted a little on the way and scavenged some food when we came across a settlement or village. I remember always feeling cold and wet, and of course hungry. It was a miserable time.

'It was raining the night we caught up with them. A full moon was breaking through the clouds, and I remember how it was turning bitterly cold and we were so hungry... so hungry that we tried to catch fish.'

Chapter 3

The Shadows of the Night

Usher shivered, sneezed and then wiped a long smear of snot on the grass beside him before returning his attention to the hawthorn branch.

'It's going to rain again,' observed Cal, his voice as gloomy as the weather. 'Do you think we have enough dry wood for the fire later?'

'Wood we have. All we need is to catch something to cook over it and we'll be sorted for tonight.' Meryn pulled his line in, inspected the offered worm, and then cast it out into the pond again. Thunder rumbled in the distance and a breeze chased ripples across the surface of the pond.

'I don't remember the last time that I wasn't miserable,' said Cal, then sniffed loudly, 'my fingers are too cold to tie this stupid thing. Usher…'

'In a minute, I'm nearly done.' Usher sneezed again then dragged his sleeve across his nose.

'What are you messing about with, boy, didn't you ever fish before?'

Usher glanced up at the grinning face of Meryn Link and decided to ignore him. The knack of tying a hawthorn hook was firstly to cut the thorn from the branch properly, which he had now carefully done, and then to make sure that you tied not one, but two parts of the thorn securely, that way the fish wouldn't be able to pull free of the line when it was snagged. It wasn't easy, especially when the line you were using was a strip of thin bark plaited patiently by the light of a campfire. Of course, Meryn had produced a carefully rolled line of plaited horsehair for his own use, along with some well-carved bone hooks, which was the reason he was putting on that superior air. It was really beginning to annoy Usher.

'Pass me a worm,' he said, still concentrating on flattening his final knot.

Cal poked about in the muddy clay bowl and produced a fat worm that curled and rolled lazily in his fingers.

Usher glanced over. 'Do you have a smaller one, one of those red ones? They move a lot better.'

Cal sorted through; inspecting the various worms they had found and finally saw what Usher was looking for. He passed it over then returned to setting up his own line. The hawthorn kept pricking his fingers as he tried to tie it but his hands were so cold he couldn't feel a thing, anyway.

'You two really think you'll catch anything? I would have lent you one of my good bone hooks, but...'

'We'll be fine,' interrupted Usher. 'Why don't you just concentrate on your own line?' Satisfied the worm was firmly lodged on his thorn; he hefted the rolled line and swung the wriggling offering close to a patch of ragged lily pads, close to where a stream of bubbles had just broken the surface.

'You'll be into a tench if you put your worm there. Nasty taste, all mud 'n slime they are.'

Usher glanced across at Meryn, and then back at where his line was slowly disappearing below the cold green surface of the pond. He was too cold and despondent to answer.

'I'm so hungry,' muttered Cal, 'I'm sick of porridge and dry old oat cakes. We have to catch a fish.' He shivered and blew on his hands trying to revive some feeling so he could tie his line round the fiddly thorn.

'Don't eat them worms, boy.'

'I won't eat the worms, Meryn, but I'll eat a tench if Usher catches one.'

'Nasty muddy things, tench. They're a summer fish, sit at the bottom eating all the stuff other fish drop or can't get hold of... and they eat the stuff the other fish...'

'Well then catch something else. We've not eaten anything decent in days. If we catch a tench then Usher and I can...' Cal jumped up. 'Usher, your line!'

Usher's line pulled tight against his fingers and quickly began moving round to the left. He yanked it hard and felt the satisfying pumping of a fish fighting for its life on the other end. It was trying to get back into the lilies and he knew he had to turn it. Ignoring the pain as the line bit into his hand, he concentrated on trying to coax it out into open water.

'Don't let it get caught up.' Cal flung himself down flat in the mud and hung over the edge of the pond ready to help get the fish out.

'It'll only be a tench,' muttered Meryn. Usher continued to ignore him.

'Here it comes, Cal, get it,' cried Usher. He stood, careful not to slip down the bank into the icy water and drew more line in. With a flap that sent a spray of water up onto Meryn, the fish broke surface and rolled on its side; green, slimy and exhausted, one beady red eye looking up at him.

'Get it, Cal.'

Braving the cold water, Cal scooped the slippery green fish up and it flopped and flapped in his hands. For a moment, it looked like he was going to drop it, but then he turned away from the water hugging it to his chest and grinned up at Usher. Meryn peered across and shook his head. 'Tis a tench'

'We eat!' exclaimed Cal, smiling up at Usher.

'We eat, but maybe Meryn would rather eat more stone-hard oatcakes? Come on, Meryn, catch us something else.'

'I will boy, I'm not beaten yet.'

Sometime later, as the setting sun was making a brief appearance below gathering clouds, a tench stew was cooking over the fire. Three tench had been caught, two by Usher, the other by Cal. They had washed them of slime and then cleaned the flesh thoroughly before putting them in the pot. No other fish had been caught, and for once, Meryn had to grudgingly admit defeat, the stew was delicious.

It rained in the night but beneath a shelter of reeds, Usher slept with a full stomach and woke with enough energy to meet the day, even if it was a day that started with weapons training.

* * *

'Ouch!' Usher dropped the spear and brought his hands up, covering the sudden pain that had exploded on his head.

'Well look at me then, not the spear, you stupid boy.' Meryn tapped the spot between his eyes. 'Here. Keep your attention here and watch all of me at the same time. If you keep staring at the end of the spear, I'll just thump you on the head with the other end again! Your eyes are floating about like a bee searching for honey flowers.'

Usher stopped rubbing his head and picked up the spear, studying the archer intently as he did, lest the old man try to trick him as he had done several times before. Still glowering, he carefully assumed the guard position and watched as Meryn narrowed his eyes and smiled through his scraggy beard. His leg still hurt from the wolf bite, but it was healing and with Meryn insisting he clean and change the dressing every few days, it would be completely healed soon. Right now however, it was aching and making him limp. He wanted to rest, but when fighting Meryn, that wasn't an option. Breathing deeply to calm his emotions, he fixed his attention on the spot between Meryn's eyes, and tried to anticipate any movement his opponent might make. With only the slightest of warnings, the spear slashed round with a *whoosh* that Usher blocked successfully, the heavy clunk jarring through his arms.

'Better, boy, better, but pick up your feet; don't go tripping over yourself.' The spear flew around again, first on the left side, then quickly to the right and then with a flourish, it came back on the left side once more with Usher blocking each blow. 'Getting the hang of it?' questioned Meryn, dropping his stance to a more relaxed pose. Usher nodded, but as he let down his guard, the bottom of Meryn's spear came up from where it had rested against the floor, only narrowly missing his chin as he jumped back. The next few moments became a blur as Meryn pushed him with a flurry of heavy knocks and blows that jarred through him. 'Good, boy, good, keep your eyes focused on my whole body. It's an ability you'll have to develop quickly if you hope to survive long in battle. Only the best can do it, but then it's only the best that survive when the world turns to madness. Are you beginning to see the strikes coming before they land?' Usher nodded, then seeing an opening, tried a strike of his own. Meryn blocked it easily and then called a halt. Usher watched for a moment, unsure if it was just another trick.

Throwing back his head, Meryn's laughter exploded as he pointed to the expression on Usher's face. 'You look like you've been kissed by a fish... a tench at that, but we may make you a warrior yet. Take a rest, boy.' He turned to Cal who had been sitting cross-legged following the whole exchange. 'Swords, I think, Calvador.' Tossing the spear to the ground, Meryn unrolled the three wooden practice swords and Cal leaped in, snatching one up before Meryn could catch him out with a sneak attack. Meryn grinned. 'Very good, Calvador, don't ever trust me when we're practising and you need never trust an enemy.' He took up a sword and stepped back. 'There are no rules when two warriors face each other. One will live and, if he's lucky, the other may die. If he's unlucky, then he may live long enough to wish he were dead with some deep and 'orrible wound to remind him of his mistakes.' Then, with a two-handed grip, Meryn attacked.

The practice sessions had taken place first thing every morning, and then last thing every night while the porridge or stew was bubbling over the cooking fire. Meryn had pounded them with spears, bruised them with the practice swords, and made their fingers bleed from pulling back the bowstring, but they were improving, slowly. They both favoured the sword and Usher was proving to be more than competent with the bow; taking a rabbit three evenings running, much to his delight.

The tracks told them they were closing on the Picts and then, late one afternoon, an old woman gathering firewood at the edge of the forest gave them their first positive confirmation that they were on the right trail. She claimed a party of strange warriors had been camped close to an isolated spinney near the edge of the forest for the last two days. She had seen them coming and going several times. With a renewed sense of anticipation, they quickened their pace and as the light was fading towards the end of the day, they had finally seen the spinney in the distance. Thunder rumbled as they approached, and the rain, which had been drizzling all day began to fall with greater intensity.

The path quickly turned even muddier and they had to resort to wading through the long dying grass several times to circumvent especial boggy areas. By the time they had made it to the trees, the rain had been coming down in torrents for a while. Daylight dropped quickly as the clouds closed in, covering them in a chill-soaking blanket as they edged slowly forward. When it eventually began to ease some time later and the clouds began to part, moonlight broke through the canopy with a bright silvery light, at once transforming the freshly fallen raindrops into a myriad of tiny sparkles amid the shadows.

Usher huddled next to Cal on the edge of the spinney and shivered, he was soaked through and miserable. Cal sneezed and let out a dismal moan, and Usher laid a hand of comfort on his friend's shoulder. The only benefit of the awful weather was that it offered cover as they made their way across the moorland grass and now as they crept along the edge of the forest towards the Picts' camp. The smell of woodsmoke was the first indication they were getting closer. Thin ghostly wisps hanging between the trees showing up in the intermittent beams of moonlight as the clouds parted further and the rain began to ease at last.

Faster-moving clouds occasionally covered the moon, plunging the woodland back into darkness and it was in these moments that the three cautiously made their way forward, their feet silent upon the wet leaves. The boys were both shivering, but the tension of being so close to the Picts' camp meant they had all but forgotten how uncomfortable they were. At least it had finally stopped raining, leaving just the slower steady dripping from the trees all around them.

Meryn moved off, indicating silently that they should keep walking. He had warned them that the Picts were still a long way from their home and would have men stationed around the camp, so every shadow and every sound only increased their fear. Having left a trail of looted villages behind them, the Picts would no doubt be expecting some sort of attack from the tribes, so approaching them was never going to be easy.

Usher crouched quickly as an owl hooted, his senses stretching as he scanned the darkness to his right for some sign of Meryn. The archer had used the sound before to get their attention, but in the darkness, it was hard to see anything.

Moonlight broke through the clouds again and briefly lit Meryn as he stood about ten paces away beside a large tree. He made a quick signal for Usher and Cal to stay where they were and then melted back into the shadows once more. Usher turned to make sure his friend had seen and felt Cal move to crouch beside him. He instantly felt better with him this close as they waited.

A steady drizzle began to fall, caught on an easterly breeze, finding its way through the trees in a fine mist that coated everything in its path. Usher shivered again and wiped his hand down his face, then glanced across trying to make out Cal's features in the darkness. As the moonlight broke through the cloud once more, he grinned to see his friend wreathed in slowly rising haze and suppressed a laugh, his breath escaping in a small cloud in front of him.

Cal pushed him and he rolled over soundlessly in the wet leaves. 'I don't know what you're laughing at. Where's Meryn gone?' Cal's voice came as a whisper.

Usher sat back up brushing leaves from his tunic and shrugged, then pointed through the trees towards the faint glow of the Picts' fire, its crackling sounds just audible over the constant dripping of the wet forest around them.

'Gone to look at the camp, I suppose. I'm frozen, aren't you?'

'Mmm,' muttered Cal. 'I couldn't feel my hands back there so I'm warming them under my tunic.'

Usher glanced down and saw that Cal had his hands tucked under his arms. He tried the same thing, and then immediately regretted the sudden chill it brought to his bare skin.

Without warning, something moved in the trees to the side of them, and Meryn slipped out of the darkness and crouched down.

'There are ten of them, maybe twelve at the most,' said the old archer, drawing each breath in a suppressed ragged gasp. 'It's hard to see. I already dealt with the two sentries they had posted on this side, but there may well be more. They have a cart now and six or seven young captives, your sister may well be one of them.' He held out a hand to stop them as both boys made to stand up. 'We have to do this right, my young friends. They'll cut us down before you could even shout your sister's name if we just go charging in there. You.' He jabbed a finger at Usher. 'You have to lead as many of them away as you can. If you can manage that, then the two of us can go in and try to get them youngsters free. Hopefully, we'll find his sister amongst them.'

'And that's your plan?' Usher scowled at where he thought Meryn was in the darkness. 'What happens if they catch me?' The clouds parted again revealing Meryn's grinning face.

'They'll kill you, so don't get caught,' said Meryn, holding Usher's incredulous gaze until the clouds robbed them of light again.

'Don't get caught!' hissed Usher. 'Well that's good advice, I'll keep thinking that while...' He felt Cal grab his arm.

'I'll do it, Usher. I'm faster than you are, and you're the better fighter. We've only one chance to get Nineve away, so I'll get as many of them out of the camp as I can, I can do that. You go and find her, and get her out. Just don't get caught... all right?'

Usher nodded. 'Let's be sure none of us gets caught,' he whispered, as Cal slipped silently away.

Treading as quietly as possible, Cal crept through the wet under-growth, keeping the glow of the Picts' fire in sight until he found the well-trodden path that the warriors had been using. He waited a mo-ment, listening for signs of any sentries, and then hurried along it until he was well out of sight of the camp, and set his first trap. At least this was something he knew how to do. He knew he couldn't chance out-running his pursuers. However, with a few simple traps he could lead them far enough away, and then confuse them enough that they lost him with as little risk to himself as possible... or so he hoped.

Taking a length of platted straw rope from his pack, he tied half of it, knee-height between two trees, then carefully marked where it was by dragging out a branch, partway onto the path. Thirty paces further he did the same thing with the other half length. Then, with his breath rasping and his heart hammering loud in his ears, he retraced his steps towards the camp.

As Usher followed Meryn forward, he was experiencing similar fin-gers of fear creeping up from his stomach. Just a few nights ago, he had been sitting round the fire in his family home with a full stom-ach, listening to his parents' talk of the harvest stores and the up-coming winter solstice celebrations, and thinking of little more than sleep. Now here he was, cold, hungry, and about to enter the camp of his parents' murderers. Choking back a sob, he stumbled and forced himself upright, trying to see something, anything, in the near utter darkness of the forest. All thoughts of the cold had gone. If anything, he now felt hot and there was a rising fluttering of panic in his chest as the images of these same warriors burning his village and murdering the fleeing people came uncalled from his memory. He thought of his parents, his poor mother...

Something thumped against his chest and he stopped. Meryn had thrust out an arm to stop him from blundering into a dead body lying against a tree, and his mind cleared with a jolt. The moon, as if by design, chose that moment to make its appearance and he stared down into the sightless eyes of a fallen Pict warrior. Usher felt the sudden jolt of terrible reality, and everything began to spiral out of control... then Meryn's hand clamped over his mouth and his voice hissed into his ear.

'He's dead, boy! As dead as the friends and family he killed back in your village, and there'll be a few more of them before we're done here, so get used to it.'

Usher felt his cheeks glow as he realised how he must appear to the old archer. He drew in a deep breath, and then mumbled, 'I'm sorry.'

'Shh,' Meryn silenced him, and then cautiously waved him forward to the tree line around the camp.

Eight children were huddled close to the wagon with just one Pict warrior standing guard over them. They looked cold, wet, and bereft of any life; Usher recognised several. Crouched together, they were silently staring towards the warmth of the distant fire where the majority of the Picts were eating and relaxing. Usher counted them, quietly mumbling the numbers, ten. There were ten of them including the one guarding the children.

It suddenly became utterly apparent to Usher, the enormity of the task ahead of them. Even if they did manage, by some miracle of the spirits, to get the captives away, how long would they be able to evade the Picts who would be sure to follow? He glanced at Meryn, sensing he must have come to the same conclusion long ago, yet here he was still helping them. Usher only hoped he had a plan. If they survived, then beholden to him they certainly would be.

As he studied the Picts, one of them got to his feet swaying happily, tipped up a clay jug, and emptied it in a series of greedy gulps. Usher felt a wave of relief as he realised the man was drunk. The warrior tipped the last of the ale into his open mouth then hurled the jug into the forest, swaying slightly as he listened to the sound of it falling through the branches. He belched loudly, and then shouted something in the Pictish tongue, which brought laughter from the others. With another happy belch, he turned and started into the forest, probably seeking a little privacy to relieve himself.

Indicating Usher should stay where he was, Meryn slipped away towards the disappearing warrior.

Moments later, he returned. 'Nine' was all he said before continuing his vigil of the camp.

'Will you be able to kill a man?' The question came as a warm breath, whispered into Usher's ear. It took him with such surprise that he pulled sharply away; rubbing furiously at the tickle the words had left. Meryn chuckled softly in the darkness. It was something he had been asking himself since first seeing the Picts at camp and he honestly didn't know the answer.

Meryn thrust his polished bow into Usher's cold hands. 'Here, when the shouting starts, kill him first.' He pointed to the guard standing over the children. 'Then turn and kill any of the others that you can.' Wordlessly Usher accepted the quiver of arrows and, with fumbling fingers, placed one ready against the bowstring.

It wasn't long before the Picts around the fire were calling out to their missing friend, his absence finally noticed. The calls quickly went from laughing taunts to cries of concern and as two warriors stood up to investigate, Meryn bent to whisper, 'Good luck, my young friend, the game is about to commence.' He then crept soundlessly away to intercept them. Now alone, Usher watched and waited for the scene to unfold as the wind whistled through the branches above him and he tried to ignore the shiver of apprehension that he felt run through him.

It had taken Cal some time to work out how best to get the warriors angry enough to follow him. He had skirted the path on either side, gathering moss and wet leaves until he had a good armful, and then crept as close as he could to the camp. With a silent prayer to the spirits of the forest, he ran towards the fire and, dashing between two lounging Picts, dumped the soggy mass into the flames, plunging the campsite into near darkness. He leaped, cleared a sleeping warrior, and began hollering and screaming as he ran before stopping at the edge of the path. Being drunk, the Picts were slow in reacting, but a few well-aimed rocks brought four of them up on their feet, and they lurched after him while two others spluttered and cursed as they tried to pull the moss and leaves from the now heavily smoking fire.

Cal set off, running as fast as he could, with the moon making brief appearances from its cloak of clouds. Behind him, he could hear the Picts shouting their challenges already close on his heels. His heart was beating so hard it felt as if it were a bird trying to burst free from his chest and he had the insane wish to laugh out loud, which he did, hooting and calling to urge the angry warriors on.

The first branch marker showed up briefly upon the moonlit path, and then the clouds shrouded it in darkness once again. Judging where the rope was, he took the biggest jump he could and prayed he would clear it. He landed, and then ran on, thanking the spirits for providing the cover of darkness. He was at the second trip-line when he heard the shouts and curses of the Picts falling heavily over the first.

He gave a loud laugh and screamed out. 'Come on, you smelly blue pigs, try and catch me!' Their answer came to him as a renewed chorus of angry yells and, using this noise to disguise his own flight, Cal made his way off the path into the trees and doubled back towards the camp.

When Cal came dashing into the camp to dump leaves on the fire, Usher let the arrow fly. It was something he hadn't wanted to think about too much beforehand, but when he needed the shot, his instincts took over. The bow came up, the startled face of the Pict warrior appeared along the arrow, and he let go. Time seemed to slow down as he watched the arrow travel the short distance, spinning in the air. He saw it connect with the Pict's temple with a hollow *thunk,* collapsing him to the floor.

Part of Usher fell with him. He wanted to continue standing in the shadows, staring at the fallen man surrounded by crying youngsters, now up and screaming. However, there was another part of his mind that took over, stirring him into action, forcing him out of the trees towards the now hysterical children. He deliberately didn't look at the fallen Pict, but concentrated on searching the grubby familiar faces for Nineve.

Finding her at last, he held his hand out towards her. 'Nin, it's me, Usher. Come on, we have to leave here. All of you... come on!' He grabbed Nineve by the hand and herded them all towards the gap in the trees and the path that lay beyond. As they got there Meryn emerged, blood soaking the sleeve of his tunic and dripping from his sword. His appearance brought renewed screaming from the children.

'It's all right, he's with us, just keep going!' insisted Usher. With Meryn's help, he began shepherding the children into the forest and away from the madness of the camp.

'There are more of them... we didn't get them all,' hissed Meryn as they hurried on, scanning the shadows around them. 'Four went after Cal, I killed three, and you killed one.' He grabbed Usher's arm and spun him around in the darkness. 'You did kill the one guarding this lot, didn't you?'

'Yes!' said Usher, maybe a little more roughly than he should have. The moment would live with him for the rest of his life. The drawn bow, the flight of the arrow, the look on the man's face as he...

Falling to his knees, Usher emptied the contents of his stomach and fought to bring himself under control. He didn't need Meryn to tell him this wasn't the time so he pushed himself up onto unsteady legs and ran on to catch the others.

Standing on either side of the four girls and two young boys, they walked further away towards the edge of the forest. They were quieter now, but were still sobbing enough to draw attention.

'There are still two around here, someplace,' muttered Meryn, 'I don't like it when we can't see them. They have the element of surprise and that's not good.' Without warning, the sound of someone or something crashing through the trees came from their right and they dropped, pulling the children down with them.

'Shh,' hissed Meryn. 'Be silent now or they'll find us.' The sobbing became quieter as the noise got nearer. When the clouds parted, the moon shone down into the wood to reveal Cal standing in front of them gazing about with a look of fear and panic.

'Whaaa!' he shrieked as he saw them and fell back into a bush.

'Shh,' cautioned Meryn. 'They're still here.' Cal nodded and clambered to his feet, then smiled as Nineve came running into his arms. As the clouds once more cloaked their progress, Meryn led them through the trees and away, the sounds of the Picts searching behind them fading into the night.

* * *

The fire crackled and, for a moment, it was the only sound in the room. 'You know, I still have a problem with the colour blue,' said Usher Vance, breaking the silence. 'Sometimes it need only be a clear summer sky, or just the right shade of blue on a milk jug that brings it all back, and then I feel the weight of fear descend upon me once again, eating into me like a... like a ...' He shook his head. 'Like I don't know what!'

'Weren't the bad men following you?' Usher stopped his line of thought and looked down at the boy sitting cross-legged on the floor with two of his friends. All three had the rapt expression of complete belief in his story that he so often craved when spinning a tale. He smiled.

'Oh, they came after us, tracking us from the moment we started running they were. We had a good start, thanks to Calvador here, but they weren't happy and wanted the children back. What they wanted them for, we didn't know at the time, but we knew it was for some reason bad enough to burn villages to get them.' He took the opportunity to have a drink of ale and filled his pipe afresh.

'I remember being scared of the Picts as they hunted us, but I also remember being mighty scared of the one who hadn't been there that night, the rider… the man in black.'

'Horsa,' muttered Calvador, scowling into the fire.

'Now, Cal, don't go spoiling my tale. Yes, it was Horsa. We learnt his name later, but he wasn't in the camp that night, thank the spirits, just the Picts, and now six of them were hunting us. It was around dawn that we heard them catching up to us… calling out and shrieking they were, trying to scare us into running and giving ourselves away.

Chapter 4

THE SOUND OF FALLING LEAVES

Meryn spun towards Cal. 'Keep the girls quiet, the Picts are getting close.' The four girls cast tear-filled eyes towards the old archer and stifled their sobs as Cal whispered quietly to them. The two boys were also scared, but were trying their best to be brave and follow Cal's example.

Meryn shook his head and sighed. 'This isn't going to turn out good if we stick together. I'm going to try and lead them in another direction, maybe pick a few off if I'm lucky.' He pulled Usher away a few steps, and then lowered his voice even further. 'Listen, lad, we have to put some distance between those Picts and these children. Hide here for a while until you hear them going after me, then I'll lose them and swing back to join you later.' His grip on Usher's shoulders became tighter. 'We've now entered the tribal land of the Trinovante. Keep to this path and don't leave it. If you keep a good pace, you'll come to a settlement called Witney before sunset, rest there. Man named Egan is the local reeve. You can trust him. He's an old friend and the Trinovante are fine people if you don't mind their ways.' Meryn looked up as a long drawn-out call echoed through the still forest. Another cry answered it, much closer than the first. 'Stay low until they're gone.' With that, he was away, darting through the undergrowth, already notching an arrow as he ran.

Usher glanced across at the tangle of bushes where Cal crouched with the others. The children all looked scared and he offered a smile of encouragement before creeping over to them.

'Don't worry; everything will be fine as long as we can stay as quiet as mice. Meryn will lead them away from here and then we can get moving.' He glanced round as a sharp scream of pain sounded close by; a moment later it was followed by the sound of a body falling to the leafy forest floor. A low moan came from somewhere through the bushes about twenty paces away. Usher glanced at the girls and held a finger to his lips to make sure they remained silent, large eyes stared back at him. They scuttled back further into the bushes and huddled together, shivering. Cal held his arms protectively around his sister and motioned for the others to come close, and then he nodded for Usher to go and see what was happening.

Moving with all the silence he had learnt from the hunters of his village, Usher crept through the thick forest growth in the direction of the sounds. It didn't take long to find the man who had cried out. A Pict warrior, lying eyes closed with his face wracked in pain, one of Meryn's arrows protruded from his chest. The Pict was clutching it, blood oozing between his fingers. From the pained rasping noises the man was making, Usher guessed he wasn't going to live much longer. That would leave only five, as long as others hadn't joined them.

Sounds of approach broke the silence. Someone was pushing cautiously through the bushes, each footstep a soft rustle in the dead leaves. Usher shrank back, trying to lose himself in the shadows beneath a large blackthorn bush. He held his breath, not daring to move. The dying Pict's eyes fluttered open as he realised someone was coming. Usher was surprised to see that, as one of the other Picts came into view, the dying man appeared to be more fearful than relieved. The reason soon became apparent. Instead of helping him in any way, the newcomer ignored him and carefully scanned the area, then roughly pulled off the fallen warrior's pack and, without any ceremony or kindness, searched him, paying no heed to the grunts of pain or words of apparent appeal spat out in the rough Pict tongue. Taking a knife and a few coins, the newcomer threw the pack to the side, muttered something that Usher couldn't understand, and then swiftly severed the dying man's throat with a sharp, violent cut. Without another thought, he turned his back upon his fallen companion and began studying the forest floor. Usher wanted to scream and run, but willed himself to lie quiet and not breathe. He couldn't take his eyes from the Pict.

Dark intense eyes stared out from a face that glistened wet with patches of blue mud. Usher had heard tales of the Picts and their blue-painted faces. Indeed, he knew that many of the tribes painted designs on their skin with the same type of mud made from crushed woad plants, but nobody did it in Usher's village, and to be near this one was terrifying. The smell of the man reached out towards Usher. It was stale and musky, reminding him more of the smell of an animal, mixed together with something altogether more acrid. Usher covered his nose and continued to stare out through the thin cover of black-thorn branches. The Pict was squatting down no more than five paces away. The warrior's hair hung in thick greasy clumps, like so many lamb's tails hanging from his scalp, held back from his face by a band of rough hide. A heavy beard thick with blue mud caked his cheeks making his face appear twisted and misshapen, Usher shuddered and forced back an overwhelming impulse to simply turn and flee.

Snorting noisily, the Pict continued to study the ground and then moved closer; following something that only he could see in the fallen leaves. Usher listened to his heart beating and offered up a silent prayer to the spirits of the woods.

A shout and then a scream from some way off made the Pict look up, but he didn't run, or turn away as Usher had prayed. Instead, he looked into Usher's eyes and smiled.

* * *

Driven by a stiff easterly wind, rain was falling in a constant misery from a thick covering of cloud. Unseen in the early evening light, eight Saxon longboats, each holding over sixty warriors, cautiously approached the coast of Britain. The laboured rowing of the oars, dipping to each low beat of a drum, the sound that had held them together, and brought them so far.

Their journey had taken many days of battling through rough seas and bad weather without any luxury of shelter or rest. Hugging the continental coastline, their passage had led them south from their home, lured by tales of a rich land newly deserted by its Roman masters; it was an invitation they could not resist.

Once far enough south, and at a point that they judged was the narrowest divide, they had gathered their courage and turned away from the security of the coast. The sight of land was gradually lost behind them, and they ventured across an open, hostile sea, in search of the fabled kingdom hidden behind curtains of cloud. Floating above deep water, their superstitions and beliefs set fear in their hearts but gave strength to their arms, for they faced far more than mere stormy weather. Every hardened warrior amongst them had set out from land with the sure and certain knowledge that below their small boat, when they ventured into deep water, was an ocean filled with giant sea creatures that would hunt them and surely devour them. If they should manage to pass quickly enough and not attract the attention of one of these monsters, then they still sailed at the mercy of angry gods that entertained themselves in the torment of man and were given to unleashing their wrath at the slightest of whims.

Now across the expanse of water and with land in sight once more, their journey had been blessed with survival, and the voyage was near its end. The boats, high prows carved and painted to depict roaring mythical beasts, followed the sullen coastline until they finally bit into the shingle of the eastern shore of Britain. The long oars were silently stowed, the large square sails lowered, and the first Saxon warriors jumped down into the shallow water and ran up the beach; their feet crunching heavily in the loose stones. It was the task of these brave few to defend their brethren from any foes concealed within the tree line at this, their ships most vulnerable time, it was an honour granted only to the battle-tested elite. Behind them, others dropped down, gripping ropes of twisted flax and hemp, and began pulling the boats higher, beyond the clawing reach of the breaking waves.

The lead boat stopped moving, a rough plank appeared over the side, and a single Saxon warrior, ignoring the frenzied activity around him, descended onto the beach. As soon as he felt land beneath his feet, he stooped, picked up a handful of stones and, drawing in a deep breath, let them drop slowly through the fingers of his clenched fist. Raising his huge head, he cast about the beach and nodded in satisfaction.

His size easily set him apart from his men. His arms were thick with heavy bands of silver and gold, and he carried the scars of countless battles, worn with pride as his right to rule over others and marking him as a mighty warrior. He scanned the beach through heavy, sunken eyes that squinted out beneath bushy eyebrows and around a thick and pitted nose. A strong jaw was concealed beneath a dark beard, broken at its centre by thick fleshy lips that were drawn in a smile of anticipation for what was to come. It was a collection of features that made a particularly unpleasant face.

As with most of his men, a conical helmet with decorated nose guard protected his head but his had the addition of a layer of chainmail falling behind to shield his neck. A woollen tunic fell past knee level, covering thin linen britches that were bound around the calves with leather strapping for ease of movement. At his belt hung a sword, a pouch holding a few personal possessions, and a seax, the long single-bladed knife favoured by all Saxons.

Taking a deep breath, he removed his helmet and allowed the cold wind to tug his long hair loose as he surveyed the coast with a critical eye. The wind felt good, the chill causing little discomfort. The country they had journeyed from was also one of biting cold and if anything, the weather on this new land felt like home.

'Britain. I have waited a long time to greet you, and now at last I have arrived.' His voice was deep and carried an undercurrent of anger as he surveyed the land he had come to conquer. He glanced up as one of his men emerged from the trees and ran down the beach towards him, coming to a stop in a spray of stones.

The warrior slapped an arm against his round wooden shield, a greeting returned by the slightest of gestures. 'We are close to a small village,' the warrior pointed to the south, 'and there's a large stone building some distance inland. There is no one here to greet us.'

'He will be here; we are of one blood, and one bone. Burn the village, and then follow us inland. I shall take this building of stone and await my brother and the others there.' Dismissing the man, Hengist returned to his vigil, scanning the beach and trees, his brow creased in thought. *Where are you Horsa? We have journeyed to the right place and I hunger for the sight of you.* Sighing once more, he looked back to where the boats lay on their sides, unloaded and secure above the surf. Instructing three men to watch over them, he turned and started up the beach, already impatient to leave. His thoughts turned back to the task at hand, the conquering of these British Isles that cried out for a new ruler now that the Romans had deserted it. This would be *his* land.

'Now our day has come,' he murmured to himself, as he drew in the deep sweet air of Britain. 'This land will soon tremble at the news of our coming, and the names of Hengist and Horsa shall be sung in the mead halls here for all eternity, for the Saxons have now truly arrived.'

* * *

The Pict leaped forward with a shriek of triumph, arms outstretched, reaching for Usher to pull him from the security of the bush towards a certain death. Scrabbling back, Usher dug his heels in and then desperately tried to turn around and get away, but he wasn't fast enough. He felt the Pict's hand wrap around his ankle and begin to drag him out, jabbering incoherently and cackling with delight as he did so. Spinning back around, he stared into the ugly blue face that loomed above him and felt a cold rush of panic overwhelm him. A moan escaped his lips and he thrashed about, trying to hold onto the bush, a root, anything, but nothing came to hand. In an act of desperation, he dug his fingers into the forest floor and threw a handful of dirt and leaves up into the grinning face and the warrior jumped back with a piercing scream, his hands immediately going to his eyes where he rubbed furiously trying to clear them, shouting and screaming in pain and frustration.

It had been instinct, rather than fighting tactics that had saved Usher, but for the moment, he was free and the Pict was blind. He gazed up and stared for a moment as the Pict clawed frantically at his eyes, blinking back tears, peering about, searching the shadows blindly. The eyes were red in the blue face and the warrior began rolling them erratically and cursed in the strange, coarse Pict tongue before rubbing at them again, which only seemed to be adding more dirt and blue woad, which in turn made him even madder. Then his head snapped up and, blinking rapidly, his watery gaze turned in Usher's direction once more. Usher stopped breathing, only exhaling when the sightless eyes moved past him.

Throwing back his head, the warrior let out a shrill undulating cry and several birds erupted in an explosion of feathers from the branches high above. Usher knew the cry would bring the other Picts to them and began to scan the surrounding trees fearing the first would soon arrive. He had to silence him.

Edging forward, his eyes never left the Pict who continued to mutter and rub at his face. For a moment, Usher contemplated getting back to the others and running as far and fast as they could. But the Pict would keep calling, the other Picts would find him, and then they would know which direction to search for them.

He managed to move three steps but then his foot came down on a branch and the sound of it snapping echoed through the trees. The Pict spun and stared right at him, and Usher felt panic rise again. Taking another careful step, he realised the Pict wasn't looking directly at him, he had been drawn to the breaking stick and was still blind but now moving cautiously in the direction of the sound, hands outstretched, shouting challenges as he came. The warrior's face was a mask of hatred and contempt as tears, dirt, blue woad and now blood, all smeared together making him appear like some kind of evil spirit. Fear threatened to loosen Usher's bladder, but he raised a foot and stepped cautiously to his left, watching as the Pict drew his sword and stabbed forward and then to the sides in a vain attempt to skewer him. Dragging his gaze from the Pict for a moment, he scanned the ground ahead and carefully circled further around, searching the Pict's movements for an opening. Seeing a branch, he stooped to pick it up, along with a smaller one that he tossed to the other side to distract the circling man.

'Yaaahhhh!' With a cry, the Pict leapt forward and slashed his sword in a vicious arc, lopping a branch from the bush close to where the stick had landed. When it met no more resistance than the bush, he sprang back and began turning about in a slow circle, head cocked to one side, listening intently.

He continued to circle, but this time, when his back was turned, Usher dashed forward and brought the branch down hard onto the back of the sticky blue head. He watched in relief as the man collapsed soundlessly into the dead leaves.

Edging closer, Usher kicked his arm, the warrior groaned and made to rise, and with a sob of dismay, Usher brought the branch down once more and then again even harder. A wave of nausea rolled over him but at least that time, the Pict stayed down.

Cal appeared and glanced from the downed Pict to the branch in Usher's hand. 'Did you kill him?'

'I don't know... I don't think so.' Usher stared down at the fallen man and felt an urge to throw up; but his stomach was empty and he only succeeded in making a hollow retching sound. Wiping saliva from his chin, he gazed transfixed as blood trickled down the man's face, mingling with the blue mud. His eyes fluttered for a moment and Usher felt a sense of relief flood through him, he hadn't killed him. 'Quick, help me pull him into the bushes.' He bent down and took the man's arm and, with Cal's help, they set about dragging him into the shadows.

'He's heavy,' remarked Cal, as he strained to move the dead weight of the Pict through the leaves.

'Well, the other's going to be heavy as well, but we have to get them out of sight. There could be more along any moment.'

'Usher?' hissed Cal, stopping for a moment. 'If he's still alive... do you think we should kill him?' He stared into his friend's eyes, clearly unhappy at the thought of any more killing.

'I... I don't think I could,' said Usher at last. 'Could you?' Cal shook his head with obvious relief. They went back out to the clearing for the dead Pict with the arrow in him, creeping silently, listening and straining their senses for any sounds of others approaching. When they got to him, they roughly grabbed him by the feet and dragged him back through the bushes and lay him alongside the first, and then ran back out to cover their tracks and the bloodstains.

Once back alongside the two Picts, Usher pulled away the long strips of leather the fallen warriors used to hold swords and packs, and then tied up the unconscious one, binding his hands and feet then gagging his mouth so he couldn't cry out.

'This sort of feels worse than killing him,' murmured Cal, staring down when they had finished. 'If his friends don't find him, he could die like this out here in the forest.'

Usher shrugged. 'He was going to kill me; I saw it in his eyes just before I threw the dirt into them. This is better than he would have done for any of us. Anyhow, he's now in the hands of the spirits or whatever gods he has looking out for him. We have to get out of here.' Picking up the Pict's short sword and bow, he moved off through the bushes back to where the others still waited.

Keeping off the path, the little group made its way through the forest with the occasional sounds of the remaining Picts fading behind them. Twice they heard distant cries of pain and hoped that it was a Pict warrior and not Meryn. The archer had managed to give them the opportunity of escape, but they hoped he hadn't paid for it with his life.

The middle of the day came and went without the opportunity to eat, and it was late in the afternoon when they finally emerged from

The Weald, their bellies aching with hunger. Despite their misery, the children were silent, having given up their sobbing much earlier in the day.

They made their way along the path as it crossed a shallow river and then meandered close to the forest without ever entering it again. When later they came across a blackberry bush, it proved a good distraction as, happy for a while, they picked the few overripe berries left by the birds, and crammed them into their mouths, grinning blackberry grins. Nevertheless, both Usher and Cal knew they had to find more substantial food and shelter before nightfall. The thought of another night exposed to the weather without any proper hot food was not something either wanted to face.

They finally moved on, entering open, rolling meadowland with a small herd of deer grazing about two hundred paces away, next to an isolated clump of trees. The largest stag had already seen them and was watching them warily with head held high.

'Don't even think about it,' said Cal, smiling at the way Usher was fingering the bow he had taken from the fallen Pict. 'We don't have the time or energy for a chase. Anyway, the village must be close and Meryn seemed sure we would receive a warm welcome there.'

'All right,' said Usher, a little reluctantly, 'but I'm sure if I got closer through the trees, then we could have taken one of the deer into the village as an offering.'

'Just how do you think we would carry it?' asked Cal, with a grin. He slapped Usher on the back and, taking Nineve's hand, encouraged the others on once more with promises of warm fires, food, and the chance to sleep on soft furs.

They trudged on through the remainder of the afternoon and finally arrived at the village as the sun was dipping low on the horizon. It was larger than they had expected and surrounded by a newly built palisade of timber. Several men were erecting the last few heavy tree trunks, standing them upright into holes dug in the ground, and then trimming the sides to fit close to the next before pointing the tops to discourage anyone from climbing over.

'It looks like they're expecting trouble,' said Cal, eyeing the workers. Usher nodded, then wondered at how distrustful the world had become in such a short time. Just a few weeks ago, they would have entered a strange village secure in the knowledge that shelter and food would always be offered to strangers, no matter from what tribe they came. Now here they were, wondering if the reception they might receive would be hostile.

As they approached, one of the men looked up and waved to them, then spoke to someone they couldn't see on the other side of the wall. They stopped where they were and a woman came out wiping her hands on a large cloth. Smiling, she beckoned them over.

'Come in, 't'aint nothing to be feared of here in Witney, not for children that is, anyhow. Come... come.'

Usher bit back the retort that they weren't all children and pushed the others forward.

'Let's go in, she seems friendly enough,' he muttered. As they walked forward, he offered a smile to the woman and raised his voice. 'We were told by Meryn Link to come here, and then to ask for the Reeve who is known to him, a man named Egan? We...' He didn't get a chance to finish as the woman came forward and gathered the small group of children into her arms; the girls immediately began sobbing again.

'Oh, you poor little things, where did you come from?' She looked up at Usher. 'My name is Bell, and I'm wife to Egan who is indeed the Reeve here. I also know Meryn Link well enough; too well, I'm afraid. Where is the old rogue?' Without waiting for an answer, she started into the village past the workers, guiding the girls protectively in front of her. 'We can speak once we have some food inside you, but for now, welcome to Witney.'

Chapter 5

WITNEY

'Nooooo! No... no... please, it hurts!'

'Oh, keep still, boy! You act like you've never suffered a haircut before!' Bell pushed the wooden bowl back onto Cal's head and continued cutting at the hair sprouting out at the sides.

Witney had offered the security they needed and now, after three days, they were rested and well fed. Bell had stitched the tear that the wolf had made in Usher's trousers, and offered a replacement for his tunic. They were now comfortable enough with Bell and her family that Bell had insisted on them bathing and having haircuts. The bathing had been cold but fun as the boys splashed about in the river, rubbing off the worst of the dirt that covered them with handfuls of fine sand. The haircut was the last of her demands and wasn't so welcome.

'Keep it washed and short and you'll attract fewer lice,' she had advised them, and, reluctantly, they felt obliged to comply. It was too dark in the longhouse to cut hair, so they had all trooped outside where there was plenty of light. As the stool was placed ready and the knives sharpened, the people of the village realised there was entertainment to be had, and a large group began to gather, eager to witness the spectacle, and of course to offer advice and comments.

'Owwww!' Cal tried to pull away again but Bell placed a firm grip on his shoulder to restrain him. He turned around and glared at her and then across at Usher as he sat grinning close-by. 'It isn't even a sharp knife,' he moaned. 'Owww, that hurts, Bell!'

'Spirits, boy, you complain worse than anyone I've ever met. Hold still and it will be over... all the... quicker... there!' She pulled the bowl away from Cal's head and stood back to regard her handiwork. 'A good straight line all round, and now your hair won't bother your eyes none... next!' Cal leapt from the stool and smiled as a slightly less cheerful Usher shuffled forward.

'That knife will be all the blunter now,' muttered Cal, with a grin. 'It's going to hurt worse than a sore tooth!' Usher sat on the stool and watched nervously as Bell drew nearer with the bowl, then brightened at the sound of voices approaching.

'Well, it looks like that old rascal Meryn Link has finally found his way out of the forest,' said Bell, peering between the huts. Usher leapt up, knocking the bowl to the floor, and followed by an angry shout from Bell, dashed towards the old archer who had just appeared accompanied by Eden.

'Meryn! You made it out of the forest. What happened? Did you get the Picts? Are they chasing you? Are you...'

'Slow down, boy. Give yourself a chance to draw breath and me the chance to greet my friends.' Meryn ruffled Usher's untidy mop of hair, unaware it had just been granted a temporary reprieve from Bell's bowl and knife. 'Ah, and there she is, one of my dearest friends, Goodwife Bell. Why, Bell, you look younger than ever. One day you shall have to tell us what spirit you keep trapped in your pocket that grants you...'

'Oh, be still with that chatter, you old fool,' chided Bell. 'Bring yourself inside and we'll try and put some meat on those sorry bones... and you,' she wagged a finger at Usher, 'don't you think you've missed out on a haircut. We'll be getting round to you soon enough.' They all trailed inside the longhouse with Cal shaking his head at the luck of Usher's escape.

Inside, as the boys pushed past the door-skin, a large group of villagers were already settling themselves about the central fire, eager to hear Meryn's news. Bell passed Meryn a hunk of rough bread and set a bowl of barley porridge in front of him. The porridge had been cooking for some time and was thick and steaming. Everyone in the room heard Meryn's stomach growling as he cupped the bowl in his hands, closed his eyes, and savoured the heavy aroma appreciatively. There was a respectful silence as the old archer dipped in his bread and used it to scoop some of the mixture into his mouth. Then he smiled his thanks at Bell who merely nodded and took her place next to her husband.

'Well, I led them Picts a merry dance,' began Meryn, after a few moments and a second mouthful of porridge. 'Killed two others, but there's still a few of them out there. Don't think they'll be coming this way though.' He wiped the back of his hand across his mouth and belched softly. 'I led them south.' He glanced over at Eden. 'The lads told you what happened to their village, and about the Picts, didn't they?'

Eden nodded. 'Aye, they did, but they had no idea why any of it took place. Do you?'

Meryn shook his head, his mouth too full to answer. 'What news do you have of Vortigern?' he asked eventually. 'Is it true he's gathering the tribes to keep back the invaders?' He quickly scooped up more porridge as the village reeve glanced across at Usher and Cal.

'Before I go into news of Vortigern, maybe I should ask our young friends if they know anything of what's happening in our land. I suppose you know that the Romans have all but gone?'

Usher nodded. 'We rarely saw Romans in our village, it was too remote, but we heard they were leaving. Then we saw signs of deserted buildings close to where Meryn was living, but we don't really know much of what's happening.'

'I can't say anyone really knows much,' said Eden, 'except that the Romans have been slowly leaving for years. They've been keeping their local governors in place as long as they can, but the last Roman troops marched out of this area around the time we were sowing crops and celebrating the Beltane festival. Since then we've been hearing of Saxon raiding parties attacking the coastal villages. Word is that they're daring to come further inland.' He nodded towards the door. 'That's why we've been building the wall; just in case they take a fancy to raiding Witney.'

'They'll not get in here,' said someone from the back. Other comments followed and Eden had to stand after a few moments to appeal for quiet.

'Anyhow, we have the Saxons, and now it would appear Picts as well, troubling our people.' He turned his attention back to the boys. 'For many years, our leader under the Romans was King Constantine. Constantine was a good and fair man that had the following of most of the tribes until he died a few years ago. Actually, word has it, he was murdered by a Pict assassin.'

Usher and Cal exchanged glances at the mention of another murdering Pict, and there were more angry comments thrown about in the room. Eden raised a hand in another appeal for quiet before continuing.

'In the place of King Constantine, Vortigern took power in the name of Constantine's sons, which many thought a little strange seeing as the druids were accusing him at the time of arranging poor Constantine's death. Anyhow, as a king, Vortigern is neither liked nor trusted, and most that go to join him do so for our land, not for the man claiming to be its ruler.'

'What of others with more of a right to be called king?' Cal asked, and Eden smiled.

'A good question, young Cal, and that honour would go to King Constantine's oldest son, Ambrosius. He would have grown to be a man now, but the druids spirited him away just as Vortigern took the throne. We know not where he is, nor if he would ever come to lead us. In the absence of Ambrosius, most agree that Vortigern is leader of the tribes, and however reluctantly, it is to him that we must rally if we want to rid our land of the Saxons.'

The discussion continued until long after dark. The current problems were presented and debated, and opinions discussed on everything from the possible locations of Ambrosius, to the truth behind the reports of invasion and, of course, the murderous nature of Picts was considered and what they were doing so far south.

Nineve and the other young ones had retired to their sleeping furs and Cal and Usher were both yawning when Meryn finally declared his intention to join Vortigern despite believing him the wrong man.

'His is the only force being formed to push these invaders back into the sea, and hopefully trying to keep those blue-painted murderers back behind their wall. I'll be leaving in the morning to lend my bow and do what I can.'

'You could stay here and help defend Witney,' said Eden, and there were several calls for him to do exactly that, but Meryn shook his head.

'The problem is bigger than just Witney. I'll go to find Vortigern and take the fight to the Saxons.'

Later, as Usher huddled next to Cal in their pile of sleeping furs, they listened to the conversations that continued by the fire. The stories of battle and daring becoming more and more unbelievable as the mead and ale jugs emptied. The calls of disbelief and laughter that followed each tale got louder with each telling. They heard several of the men claim they would be leaving with Meryn to join with Vortigern and it appeared that quite a band would be heading out the next day.

'What are *we* going to do, Usher?' Cal asked, in a whisper. 'We could go with Meryn, but what about Nineve?'

'I'm sure she could stay here with Bell,' replied Usher. 'But for us, I agree, it's going to be more fun going with Meryn, don't you think?'

'Yeah,' said Cal, in a sleepy voice, 'much more fun.' They continued listening to the men's conversation until their dreams placed a blanket on their minds.

* * *

The tall Briton walked through the crowd of children, stopping from time to time to peer down at a frightened snotty face, his expression holding a growing look of disgust and irritation. He was clutching his long brown robe about him, clearly concerned that it might become soiled should it touch any of the young captives.

When he had first entered the large room, several of the smaller children had seen he was neither Saxon nor Pict, and had run over to him, wailing and sobbing, begging him to help take them back to their families. However, as they swarmed forward, the two Saxon warriors who accompanied him had beaten them back with sticks and the Briton had done nothing to stop them. The children now realised that this man was as evil as the others were and they were keeping their distance.

'No, no, no!' spat the Briton. 'None of these is child to Constantine. Are you people listening to the descriptions given to you? Are you? A boy of some fifteen summers? Half of these little rodents are girls.' He stepped back as the Saxon warrior he had been addressing moved towards him threateningly. 'Very well, I'm sure you are… really,' he blurted hurriedly, holding a pale hand against the warrior's chest. 'Take me to Hengist, this is a waste of my time and we have plans to discuss. None of these is the child we seek. Get rid of them all.'

'Get rid of them?' questioned the warrior looking confused. 'Kill them, you mean, or let them go?'

For a moment, the Briton appeared almost as puzzled as the Saxon. 'I don't care *what* you do with them,' he spat the words with distaste. 'I don't want them, do whatever you wish!' Wrapping his robes even tighter about him, he pushed past to the door into the blessed relief of fresh air.

Once outside he took a deep cleansing breath and walked away from the villa, glad to have the feel of earth beneath his feet once more.

Walking through overgrown gardens that until recently would have been lovingly tended by Roman-trained gardeners, he was escorted away from the buildings towards a hastily erected roundhouse. However, just as he was about to enter, he was rudely shoved aside as someone from inside made to leave. A protest for this rough behaviour had just formed on his tongue, when he saw who had shoved him, and he thought better of it. The warrior leaving, dressed from head to foot in black, was the unmistakable figure of Horsa, brother to Hengist the leader of the invading Saxons and a man whose reputation for violence was enough to cause most men to avoid him.

Laughter from within the building followed the huge warrior, and Horsa turned back with an angry glare towards those inside. The Briton stood back and tried to blend in with the scenery.

'Do not mock me, brother. I round up your children and bring them in, so this... creature,' his gaze flicked across to the Briton then back inside the hut, '... can pick them over. Nobody escapes me for long. My Pict dogs are plentiful and I shall unleash more into the Weald to track down these puppies, but first, I will find this archer and kill him myself, and then... then I want to make war, not hunt children. I tire of playing these games.'

The Briton took a further step back as Hengist emerged from the hut to tower over them both.

'I do not mock you, brother. I pity anyone foolish enough ever to mock you. Go now... hunt. Kill; and find Constantine's brats.' He slapped a hand down on Horsa's shoulder and the two brothers embraced, then Horsa turned and strode across to his horse, mounted, and rode out of the Saxon camp. Hengist turned to the Briton. 'Come, Silus, we have much to discuss before I meet with your master.'

* * *

So far, the morning had been a pleasant one for Usher and Cal. Meryn, in contrast, had remained sullen and silent since they had left Witney at first light. The archer had drunk his fair share of mead and ale the previous night and was obviously feeling the worse for it.

When Meryn had risen to a sober dawn, and realised none of the others that had sworn their allegiance to fight the Saxons were coming, he became moody and resigned to going alone. Then, when the boys had asked to join him, he reasoned they would at least be company, and agreed to their plan. They were, after all, old enough to make their own decisions.

They had said their goodbyes to Witney, with Bell gathering the children for a tearful farewell. Cal had promised Nineve he would return for her, and that this was the best place for her until he did; she had reluctantly agreed.

The weather was pleasant, with no sign of the previous week's rain clouds; instead, by mid-morning, a warm sun was blessing their journey and the boys, at least, were in good spirits. They were making their way along one of the main Roman roads that stretched west across Britain, all the way to holy Glastenning, which was close to where Meryn believed Vortigern was assembling the tribes. Usher and Cal were trailing behind, practicing their sword play, lopping the heads from dandelions and stabbing out at unarmed bushes, which they imagined were murdering Picts, when the sound of running feet made them both turn around.

'Cal! Cal, Usher, wait for me!'

'Oh no, it's Nineve!' cried Cal, crestfallen, as his younger sister bounded along the lane towards them wearing a big grin. 'Nin, go back! You can't come with us.' He spun around to appeal to the only adult in the group. 'Tell her, Meryn, tell her to go back.' Meryn cast bleary eyes to the boys, and then at Nineve, and shrugged. Dropping his pack, he slumped down beside the road, clearly uninterested in offering any assistance while the boys dealt with Nineve.

'I'm not going back,' said Nineve, her lower lip quivering.

Usher put his hand out to stop her. 'Nineve, you really can't come. We're going to…' Nineve glared up at Usher, and, before he could finish speaking, she kicked him, hard, in the shin. 'Oww! You little…' Usher spun around clutching at his leg.

'I'm not talking to you, Usher Vance.' She turned to Cal and her face resumed its soft, pleading look. 'Please, Calvador. You can't make me stay back in that boring village. *We're* the family now. I miss Mamma and Papa and I don't want to lose you as well. I'm meant to be going with you, I know I am.' She continued to look defiant but her lip was trembling. Cal opened his arms and she ran to him, sniffing back a tear. 'Let me stay, Cal. I won't be any trouble.'

Cal sighed. 'Oh, Nin.' He glanced across at Usher but he was busy rubbing some life back into his bruised shinbone.

They stopped at mid-day for a light meal of dried fruit, bread and hard cheese, and then continued walking until late into the afternoon. Meryn had fallen back, still sullen and non-talkative, while Usher was ahead, leaving Cal and Nineve time to talk.

The Weald was to the south of them with open grassland to the north and the Roman road continuing to run ahead, straight and true into the distance. Like all Britons, they walked the well-trodden path at its side whenever possible. The feel of cut-stone setts underfoot was an unwelcome disconnection from the earth and, therefore, the spirits it was home to. It was also the major reason the Roman villas continued to remain vacant long after any claim to them had passed.

It was as they were approaching a part of the road where the trees were growing thick to either side around a large muddy puddle, that their journey took a sudden halt.

'At last! Thou hast arrived!'

Usher jumped back into Cal, as the cackling voice came from the shadows, and they collapsed on the road, both scrabbling to get away from the strange little man who had leaped out at them. Meryn, awoken from the depths of his sore head, dashed forward but quickly sheathed his sword when he saw the only threat might be the ripe smell emanating from the unwashed druid. For his part, the druid didn't seem the least perturbed by their reactions. He jumped about in great excitement, waving a branch of mistletoe above his head with one hand as he leaped from one bare foot to the other. The other hand was wildly swinging a staff about; flicking mud into Usher's shocked face in the process. He suddenly stopped and offered a toothless grin to each in turn.

'Thou art most welcome to my grove. I have waited for thee most patiently.'

Chapter 6

THAT'S THE TROUBLE WITH DRUIDS

The branch of mistletoe flicked towards Meryn. 'Thou' - the druid's voice was shrill and dry, like the screech of a crow at the moment it took flight - 'shall remember who thou are and save a king!

Thou, ' hopping from one foot to the other, the druid's branch swished across to Nineve, who let out a squeal and hid behind Meryn's legs, 'will one day lead the druids.' The strange old man stopped, smiled, then popped an acorn into his mouth, and for a few moments, as they watched in dumbfounded amazement, he went into facial contortions manoeuvring the nut towards his few remaining teeth.

'Is he a bit...?' began Cal, in a whisper, but Meryn hushed him before he could finish.

Crunching the acorn happily, the druid turned towards Usher and, with dirty robes flapping, sprang high into the air. As he landed, he flicked out the mistletoe and cried. 'Thou,' a spray of half-chewed acorn splattered Usher, 'shall become a dragon! And thou,' Cal drew back, 'will walk the halls of death!' The old druid smiled, nodding around at them, clearly delighted to have delivered his prophecy.

'Is that it? Is he done?' Cal asked, helping Usher up from the mud. 'I don't like the sound of the halls of death much. I wonder what type of dragon you'll become?'

Usher smeared a muddy hand down Cal's grinning face. 'I am *not* going to turn into a dragon!'

'I don't like him,' said Nineve, with a whimper, 'he's scary.' She gazed around Meryn's legs at the druid who was once again chewing acorns and beaming happily. 'And he smells funny.'

'We thank you for your prophecy, Oh... wise druid,' began Meryn, 'but ask for some clarity on your...' He let out a cry of exasperation as the druid emitted a screech and scampered back into the trees.

'This may take some time,' he explained in a tired voice. 'That's the trouble with druids. They give you a small piece of utter nonsense, then you have to coax them into unravelling what it might possibly mean. It's like trying to milk sense from a talking goat!' He shouldered his pack and set off after the old man.

'A smelly goat,' added Nineve, as she took Cal's hand. They followed Meryn who was already disappearing into the trees.

The druid had hunkered down next to a path that led into, what appeared to be, the gloom of a deep hole. Trees and bushes crowded close to the top, while above floated a halo of flittering butterflies.

'This is a druids' well,' muttered Meryn, as they approached. 'It will be strong with the spirits.' Usher drew in a deep breath and placed a protective hand upon Nineve's shoulder as she edged closer pushing between him and her brother.

The druid was humming and chatting happily to himself, squatting down with his bony knees sticking out to either side of his filthy robes, casting rune stones into the dirt between his feet. The thirteen bone knuckles, each carved with a different symbol, bounced across the ground and landed in patterns through which the druids could unravel the mysteries of life, or so they claimed.

Approaching cautiously, Usher glanced about, taking in his surroundings as the others gathered around him.

From what he could see, it appeared the druid had called the grove home for a number of years. A shallow cave in a rock appeared to be his sleeping shelter. There was a small pile of tiny animal bones lying next to the ashes of a fire as evidence that he ate more than just acorns.

While the worn area where he now squatted was obviously a location long favoured for casting his runes. Tied into the trees on either side of the path were small pieces of cloth fluttering in the breeze.

'I think these must be his offerings left for the spirits,' muttered Meryn, as he tore a piece of cloth from his tunic and tied it amongst the others. Hoping he was doing the right thing, Usher did the same. The druid glanced up, beamed at him, and then continued his incomprehensible chatter.

'Well, we know why his clothes are rags now,' said Cal, studying the trees in wonder. 'Most of his stuff must be up there.' Meryn frowned at him and was about to address the druid when the old man leapt up and landed in front of Cal.

'Thou dost dream of wolves… thou have…' he leaned in, peering deeply into Cal's eyes and didn't seem to notice when Cal pulled back, wafting his hand in front of his face after smelling the druid's breath, 'the affinity.'

'No I do not! I don't have any such thing.' As if challenging his denial, the howl of a wolf came from the distant forest. The druid beamed as Cal's mouth opened in shock, then held up a dirty hand and shook his head before Cal could dispute the claim any further.

'They follow after thou, waiting for thy dreams,' keened the druid happily.

'Please,' broke in Meryn. 'We are unused to the druid ways. Do you have some guidance for us?'

'Unused to the druid ways!' the druid burbled happily, and then wiggled his branch of mistletoe at Meryn. 'I have told thou much, if thou would but listen.' He rummaged in the folds of his cloak. 'Though there is more to tell. Thou, for instance, hast healing hands. Though thou art also a fine warrior; brave, loyal, courageous, yet kind and somewhat… stupid at the moment.' He chuckled as Meryn's face flushed red and his hand twitched towards his sword.

'Take no offence, thou dost not remember thy true self, and all are necessary attributes for a warrior such as thou. Here,' he reached back and, as if from nowhere, produced a cloth bag, which he tossed to the startled Meryn, 'a gift.' The druid watched, but went back to cracking acorns, as Meryn reached into the bag and pulled out a silvery, shining helmet.

'I hope we all get one of those,' said Cal, gazing at the helm as it sparkled and glimmered in the sunlight as if the druid had spent all his life shinning it for this one moment.

The druid cackled merrily. 'Thou hast thy wolves... walker of death!'

'Lucky old me,' muttered Cal.

Meryn carefully tried the helmet on. It covered his head well; had a nose-guard of bronze and ear-plates hinged with more bronze, each cast in the image of a boar.

'The boar is thy companion, warrior. Its spirit walks with thou, and like thou, it is ... somewhat stupid and forgetful.' His face split into a near toothless grin. 'But loyal to its own, brave, and when cornered... *deadly*. Wear it well. For it is made to be worn by thou and thou only... until its true owner is finally recognised.'

'What of me, druid?' Usher asked. 'You said I would become a dragon. How can that be?'

'I have nothing more I can tell thou, nor the nice young lady.' He smiled at Nineve and then bowed low, but she hid her face behind Cal, which was where the druid's eyes now settled. 'Remember thy dreams, Calvador. The wolves are with thou - on both sides of death.' With that, he dropped Cal's startled gaze and dusted down his rags. 'Visit the well, drink deeply, and return to me when thou are complete. The spirits of the well wait to bless thee.' With that, he settled back to his rune stones and Meryn led the group past him and down the path.

The well, as they descended the twisting path, was bigger than it had appeared at the top. At the overgrown entrance where the narrow path disappeared, there had been little to indicate that this strange place even existed. Now, as they descended below ground level, they could see it was about forty paces across and gloomy. Motes of dust and pollen floated in shafts of fading light and air rich with the heady aromas of earth and decay. The path had become slick and muddy in places as it continued down, passing through a thin mist that hung across the deep hole about half way down, like a veil between two worlds. A steady dripping was all that disturbed the silence, along with the occasional soft whimpering of Nineve and Cal's incessant muttering.

'Shhh.' Meryn held a finger to his lips as the sound travelled slowly around the well, then smiled at Nineve. 'This is a holy place,' he whispered. 'There is nothing here that will harm you. Come...' He held out his hand in the half-light, and Nineve took it, still staring wide-eyed as they descended further to the base of the well. There was a wide shelved area next to the black stillness of the water and they gathered there to gaze about.

'What do we do?' Usher asked. 'It's cold down here. I think we should leave as soon as we can.' The mist moved and swirled as Meryn bade them all to crouch down. Cupping his hands, he scooped up some water and drank, then indicated they should do the same.

The water was chill but refreshing and tasted good. Usher dipped his hands a second time, not realising how thirsty he had become. It had been a long, strange day and he felt the need to sleep begin to overwhelm him. He was comfortable here. Why he had thought the well cold and scary, he couldn't remember. Now it seemed warm and welcoming. Glancing across, he saw Cal, yawning, already leaning back on his pack. Then, as Nineve went over and cuddled-up next to her brother, Usher lay down as well.

Meryn remained unmoving, kneeling at the side of the well, staring into the deep dark water.

Usher would later recall that just before sleep overcame him, he looked past Meryn and saw three women walking towards them through the mist. Two were beautiful and bore smiles that reminded him of his mother, the last was a hag, bent and hideously ugly, and it looked to him like she was scowling.

* * *

Horses and men screaming surrounded him. The sound of metal clashing against metal... the sickening sound of edged steel biting into flesh. Fear, panic, breathless and tired, a desperate desire to go on, must not fall, searching... but for what?

Chariots amid a sea of fighting warriors, cutting, slashing, screaming; winning through to the side of another chariot....

A blinding light crossing the sky, chanting, cheering; a funeral pyre...

* * *

Nineve snuggled against her older brother... wandering happily through a warm summer meadow filled with flowers and butterflies... a stream with someone lying on the ground next to it, it was Calvador. Reaching down to roll him over, he rises from death; a wolf walking at his side... they slowly fade away.

A standing stone, tall and ancient, a garland of flowers, druids, Meryn smiling down, a blinding light travelling across the sky; the dragon, a celebration.

A final battle, a bargain made... a crossroads in the shadowland, the mists once more surround her...

* * *

Meryn felt the cool touch of a hand on his cheek and knew comfort, his mind feeling as if it had finally awoken. He watched detached, as visions of battle moved about him, knowing no blade could reach him as warriors fought and died all around... a flock of ravens disturbed from their feast rising into the air.

The familiar feel of his bow in his hand but now hung with shells and ribbons.

Images changing faster, faster, apple trees, a setting sun, flashing blades, chariots...

* * *

The smell of blood was thick in his nostrils, movement close by, men approaching, moving away into the shadows where the men will fear to follow. Listening, sensing the movements of the others as they travelled... a stag, sick, old, tired... tracking the herd, separating the sick one... at one with the pack, with his family... the excitement of the chase, the kill, the taste of blood, food...

Men screaming. Writhing in the agonies of battle as, all around, fear, panic, pain, the agony of loss, and then... death.

Trapped... the mists surround everything, no way out, white; all is white, no place to turn, panic, feelings of terror and fear... a primal scream...

'Cal!'

Cal's eyes flashed open and he drew a breath into his lungs, gasping as the remnants of the dream faded. 'Nineve?' Tears were running down Nineve's face and he pulled her into a hug. 'It's all right, Nineve.' Looking over, he saw Usher standing alone, gazing across the well, his face set in a stubborn frown.

'Come.' Meryn strode past them towards the path. Picking themselves up, the others followed, retracing their earlier steps upwards towards the light to emerge into a day fast fading into evening.

The druid was waiting for them, squatting at the top of the well, swaying from side to side and grinning happily.

'The sisters came. The weird sisters revealed thy dreams, remember them well. Ye must go now. Do not tarry, there is much for thou to do. Abandon thy journey west and turn to the south. Thy destiny is to greet and support a man thou't will meet on the southern road, two days journey away in the tribal lands of Ceint. Thou will know each other, fear not for that. Now go... go, go... go!' He waved them on, flapping his arms and, still muddled somewhat by their dreams, they moved on without a word.

As they rejoined the road, Usher glanced back. The druid had returned to his rune stones, crouched down with his back to them, chattering quietly to himself as if they had never been there to disturb his madness.

* * *

Usher Vance stopped speaking and fumbled for his pipe. The circle of villagers remained silent and expectant, waiting for the story to continue.

Fearing the old storyteller was about to have another turn, one of the serving girls placed a hand upon his arm and softly asked if she could fetch him anything. He shook his head, but then changing his mind, reached out towards her. 'Some ale... please. I just need a little ale, and perhaps a moment to collect my thoughts.' Wiping his brow on his sleeve, he glanced across at Calvador Craen, who had taken the opportunity to stand and stretch.

Realising there was now an unmistakable halt in the tale, several listeners excused themselves and hurried away to the privy, while others called to the serving-maids for ale and mead.

'I'm beginning to think you know more details of this tale than I do,' said Usher, as the murmur of voices allowed him a quiet moment with his old friend. He blew out a stream of blue smoke and offered the tobacco pouch to Calvador Craen who had turned to regard him. 'I remembered meeting the druid right enough, but what happened in the well was lost to me until I started to speak of it.'

Calvador Craen accepted the tobacco pouch, sniffed at it suspiciously, tasted a little then spat it into the fire with a look of distaste, and then nodded. 'It has indeed been many years, old friend. Look at us.' He held out a wrinkled hand that trembled in front of him, and shook his head. 'We changed our direction after meeting the druid and the sisters in the well. It was then that things really started to get strange... do you remember?'

Seeing that most of the villagers had returned, Usher nodded, took a drink of water and another thoughtful pull on his pipe, then continued. His face once again creased in concentration as he fought to summon his memories.

'We had no real idea who we were meant to be meeting. Our dreams in the well had given us no clues, as to who he was or where we should find him. Only that we should be heading south...'

Chapter 7

The Southern Road

'I'm cold,' murmured Nineve. She snuggled closer to Cal, and he wrapped his arm tighter about her. Usher glanced at them and tried not to think of how cold, wet and miserable he was also feeling.

'Shhhh, go to sleep,' he heard Cal mutter. 'You'll soon forget about the cold.' They pulled the wet fur higher around themselves and Cal glanced up as Usher threw more sticks onto the fire. It crackled and spat as the flames took a reluctant hold on the wet wood.

Above them, wind gusted, moaning and whistling through branches that creaked unseen in the inky blackness of the night. They huddled down, waiting for the rush of cold air to reach them beside the fallen oak that was their only shelter, and resigned themselves to a night of discomfort and torment.

After leaving the druid's grove they had walked in silence, each still caught-up in the strangeness of their experience. When they arrived at a crossroads they hesitated, unable to make a decision on which direction to take. It was almost as if some part of each of them remained at the well. A spark of their life held within the dream and unable to wake properly into the world they could see around them. The road south, the way the druid had urged them to take, led directly into the immense dark forest of the Weald. With the daylight fading, it appeared murky and foreboding. Eventually, Meryn summoned enough clarity to make a decision and they headed towards the trees, searching for somewhere to make camp.

At first, all had gone well. They walked a short way into the forest, found shelter by the fallen oak and lit a fire. Dry, sweet-smelling bracken was plentiful so they pulled together rough piles as sleeping pallets and slumped down while the evening light faded around them. However, soon after darkness claimed the forest, the weather began to turn. A cold wind picked up, bringing with it a wet and thoroughly miserable night that only seemed to be getting worse. Meryn was the only one apparently unaffected by the rain falling on his face, having fallen into a deep untroubled sleep soon after arriving.

'I don't know how he does it,' remarked Usher, staring over at Meryn's sleeping form. 'He's getting as wet as we are, but he hasn't woken since he first put his head down. Surely he can't be comfortable?'

'He's not asleep; he's unconscious. He's making up for too little sleep and too much ale last night,' observed Cal. Lightning flashed and they tensed, each counting softly until an ear-splitting crack of thunder rent the darkness. 'It's getting closer,' he mumbled. The rain intensified, and he hugged Nineve. She let out a small sob and shivered against him.

With no dry wood and the rain falling even heavier, the fire soon died, and as it did, the sounds and fears that only complete darkness can bring crowded in to surround them. It was an awful feeling, to be robbed of sight. Not even a small spark of light to cling on to as the forest and storm did their best to unnerve them. Usher closed his eyes tight and willed himself to endure it. When exhaustion did eventually force sleep upon him, it was fleeting, uncomfortable, and filled with images drawn from the memories of the druid's well.

Sometime in the early hours, the rain stopped and as the first glow of dawn filtered through the trees, it revealed a forest wreathed in a white cloak of mist, drifting like ghostly wraiths amongst the shadows. Usher helped the others, listening to Cal's mumbled complaints of aches and pains, and of how wet and cold he was. Usher tried to respond but he was too tired and cold to summon the words. Nineve was also silent, moving woodenly as she rose to stare about at the wakening forest.

They rolled their wet sleeping furs and made ready to depart, their movements leaden and stiff reflecting how tired and unhappy they were. Meryn, as he woke, appeared refreshed from his night and was in a far better mood than the day before. He hefted himself up and smiled around at the others. Upon seeing their lifeless faces and how wet they were, the smile quickly dropped as he scanned the forest and saw the remains of the rain dripping from the branches all around them.

'Oh, so it rained a bit, did it? Well all right... last night we didn't have the time, but if we're still in the forest tonight, we'll be sure to construct a proper shelter, give you youngsters a better chance of getting some rest.' Usher stared at him then shook his head, silently wishing he were back at home, waking in his parents hut with the normal sounds of morning rather than here in this wet forest with... Nineve began to cry and he watched as Cal hugged her and hid his face in her hair. Usher shook his head and took a deep breath, then turned away without saying a word.

'What?' said Meryn. 'What did I say?'

They pulled pieces from the loaf of hard bread that Meryn produced from his pack, and then trailed off, munching silently as they searched for the southern road, leaving the archer looking bewildered.

Although the rain had stopped, the mist was getting thicker. The well-trodden path was easy enough to follow, even if it offered little hint of their surroundings. It was a strange feeling, walking through a world of white. Usher kept close to Meryn with Cal and Nineve trailing along close behind. Dark shapes loomed through the dripping whiteness. Each strange apparition first appearing like a monster set to pounce, before revealing itself as no more than a tree or bush. By midday, the mist still hadn't lifted. It continued to cover them in its cold embrace, chilling them and fraying tired nerves even further as it became harder and harder to keep to the path.

A pheasant exploded into flight close by, shattering the silence of the forest and shocking them with its warning screech. However, it wasn't a pheasant that made the noise that followed, and it scared them even more.

'What was that?' hissed Usher. They stopped where they were, searching through the white cloak of their surroundings.

'I'm not sure... what did you hear?' whispered Meryn. He pulled out a knife and moved it from one side to the other, ready for combat as his eyes searched the mist for whatever the threat might be.

Usher didn't answer. He stood; head to one side, straining his hearing to confirm or deny what he thought might be there.

Meryn nudged him urgently. 'Talk to me.' But Usher didn't have time to answer as a sharp crack came from close in front of them. It sounded like a small branch breaking under something heavy... like a foot.

Meryn tugged on Usher's sleeve and, drawing Nineve and Cal after him, quickly backed away from whatever was coming down the path towards them.

'I heard someone cough... or thought I did,' whispered Usher, after they had retreated a few paces. 'Maybe it was a deer? They sometimes...'

'Shhhh,' warned Meryn. Still backing further, he passed the knife to Usher and carefully drew his sword from its sheath. As they reached the side of a large tree, Meryn saw what he had been looking for and was about to lead them down a small animal track when the sound of running feet came pounding towards them. Without warning, two Picts burst from the mist, swords swinging, and blue-painted faces registering a sudden shock at seeing them.

'Run!' yelled Meryn, as he thrust out his sword. The blade took the first Pict in the stomach, his face creasing in an agony of surprise as he fell. Nineve began screaming. Pulling her behind him, Meryn drew his sword and slashed across at the other attacker, who was yelling something in the strange Pict tongue. 'If we get split up, we meet at the end of the path,' urged Meryn, 'on the southern road.' Blocking a savage cut, he threw his sack at the Pict to distract him, and stabbed out with the sword, plunging it into the warrior's throat, abruptly cutting off his undulating cry. Without further discussion, the archer turned and dragged the now hysterical Nineve down into the trees.

For a moment, Usher and Cal stood alone, staring down at the two Picts as they gurgled and thrashed through their death throes. The sound of angry voices got closer. With a quick glance at Cal, Usher pushed past after Meryn and Nineve.

The nervous cry of horses and shouting followed them as the dead Picts were discovered. Then, as they crashed blindly through the undergrowth, came the sounds of pursuit.

'Move... quickly, we need to get going.' Usher urged Cal on, fending off the branches that sprang back at him from where Cal let them go.

'Hey be careful,' said Usher, but Cal had his own problems.

'Ahhh,' Cal slipped down a small incline and then, as Usher tried to step to the side, he tripped over a tree root and fell down onto Cal.

'Shhhh. They're going to hear us.' Usher began rubbing at his bruised shin and they lay panting for a moment, before getting gingerly to their feet.

'It's not my fault, I can't see anything,' said Cal, 'you try... you go first.' They got up and moved a little slower, but it was tricky in the mist and they continued to trip over branches and unseen obstacles, still trying to follow Meryn's trail, but it was impossible to see where they were going. The mist still covered everything, revealing only shapes and shades of light and shadows. Usher could hear his heart beating loud in his ears and felt panic rising as he frantically sought some route of escape or sign of Meryn. Then, as they trotted cautiously on, a large hawthorn bush loomed up out of the mist and he ran straight into it. He struggled, badly scratching his face and arms. Stifling a cry of pain, he untangled himself, went down onto his hands and knees and crawled further into the bush. Cal followed, ignoring the thorns as best he could. Once hidden at the centre, they collapsed, panting. Usher tried to bring his breathing under control as he strained his ears for any indication that they might have been seen.

The main path must have been close because they could hear horses snorting and stomping, and harnesses rattling. There were voices, although the boys couldn't make out what they were saying. On the other side came the sounds of men calling to each other as they moved through the trees, beating the bushes, as they searched for them.

'We've lost Meryn and Nineve,' whispered Usher. He wiped the sheen of mist from his face. 'We have to get around the Picts and back onto the path, then catch up with Meryn and Nineve later on. If we run into the forest the wrong way, we could be lost for days.'

'I hope Nineve is all right,' murmured Cal. 'I wish we were all together still. Come on. Let's get out of here while we still can.'

'Slowly and quietly as possible,' cautioned Usher as he followed his friend.

* * *

Meryn stopped, hardly daring to move a muscle or even draw breath as he felt the sharp edge of a blade press against his throat. If the Pict had wanted to kill him, he would have done so with a quick savage cut. He waited, felt his hair grabbed, and then his head was jerked back exposing his throat even further. His eyes watered with pain and frustration and he cursed himself for not paying enough attention to where they were going. He'd been too absorbed with hurrying the sobbing Nineve away from the path. The sudden bloodshed had shocked her and she had been doing her best to hold back, insisting he wait for the boys to catch up. Believing the threat was behind them, he tugged her along, concentrating on keeping her moving rather than watching their surroundings, when the knife whipped around a tree and the Pict had drawn him into this painful embrace.

'You are a breath away from death,' hissed a heavily accented voice. 'Drop your weapon and do not call out.' Realising he had little option but to comply, Meryn dropped his sword and shrugged the bow from his shoulder, allowing Nineve's fingers to slip from his grasp as he did so. If she hadn't noticed the Pict yet, he could still hope she might run back the way they had come in search of her brother.

She did take a few steps, but then realised he wasn't following and turned back. When she saw the knife and the blue face, leering at her over Meryn's shoulder, she gave a small cry and then a second Pict emerged from the mist and clamped a hand over her mouth, stifling the scream before it could leave her throat.

Nineve struggled as a foul-tasting cloth gag was jammed into her mouth, but it did no good. Forcing her facedown onto the ground beside Meryn, a Pict knelt with his knee in her back to stop her moving, and then tied her arms back with tough hide. Meryn glanced across at her as the hide bit painfully into her flesh bringing tears but she knew there was nothing he could do. Once they were satisfied, the Picts dragged them to their feet and guided them out towards the path. They stumbled on as the voices echoed through the trees around them and the search continued.

When they reached a small group of horses, they were pushed roughly down beside a tree. A brief argument flared up between the Picts then one remained to guard over them, while the other ran back into the mist to help with the ongoing hunt.

Meryn glanced to Nineve and she saw the terrible sadness and frustration in his eyes. There was nothing either could do but wait and hope that the boys had fared better than they had.

* * *

It was late in the morning when the mist finally began to lift. Bright shafts of sunlight, striking through the treetops, banishing the confusion of the forest floor. They had managed to find the path while the mist had still covered everything, and the sounds of the search were growing fainter in the distance. As the morning wore on and they remained alone, they slowed their flight to a plodding walk.

'Maybe we should go back?' muttered Cal, glancing around. 'They can't be ahead of us; we would have caught up with them by now. They have to be back there somewhere. Maybe the Picts caught them... I'm worried about Nineve.'

Usher shook his head. 'Meryn told us to meet at the far end of the path if we got split up. Maybe they went by a different route and that's why we haven't seen them. We don't want to go back and get captured only to find out they got away!' Usher slapped his friend on the back. 'Come on, Meryn knows what he's doing. They're probably waiting for us with a cooking fire already lit and wondering where we are.'

The path through the trees wound on and on, seemingly without an end, and they were becoming aware of just how big the Weald really was. There was no sign of pursuit, but also no trace of Meryn and Nineve. Twice they came to crossroads where paths led off in other directions, but on each occasion, they saw no other travellers and trudged wearily on.

The sounds of the forest accompanied them. Birds sang, squirrels chattered, and larger animals like boar and deer, occasionally passed, noisily but unseen through the undergrowth, causing the boys to quicken their pace, in fear it was the Picts about to jump out at them.

Day turned to evening and the light began to fade. Reluctantly, they resigned themselves to spending another night in the forest. They turned from the path and searched for a place to make camp.

They used what light remained to construct a shelter in case it rained again, but, although dry and more comfortable than the previous night, and travel-weary as they were, they still endured a night of troubled sleep, their dreams filled with strange images and fears for Meryn and Nineve. When the first light of a watery dawn found its way into the forest, both boys were already awake and although cold and stiff, were ready to move on.

The morning went by in an uneventful blur of exhaustion, neither of them having much to say. It was early afternoon when they finally left the forest and emerged into a meadow filled with bleating sheep.

'They're not here!' Cal cried, throwing down his pack in frustration. 'This is it! The end of the path and they're not here!' At the sound of his raised voice, a dozen rooks took flight from a dead tree as it stood sentinel beside the path and screamed obscenities while circling overhead. Their cries echoed round the meadow, causing several sheep to move hurriedly away before raising their heads inquisitively, their jaws still chewing methodically as they contemplated the new arrivals.

'There must be a village close to here, maybe they'll be there.' Usher gazed across the meadow where the path crossed through the long grass before disappearing into a hedgerow. In the far distance, smoke was rising from an unseen fire, hopefully a sign of habitation.

Cal gave a deep sigh and nodded. 'What if something happened to Nineve? I should be looking after her. We shouldn't have left her.' With little choice, they set out across the meadow into the warmth of the late afternoon.

At least it was pleasant to be out of the forest, to feel the warm sun on their backs once more, and despite their worries for Nineve, they began to relax, it didn't last long. They were about half way across the meadow when a galloping horse burst from the trees behind them and reined in, scaring the rooks back into flight in a cacophony of irritation. Usher recognised the rider immediately. The last time they had seen him he had led a party of Picts to burn their village. The moment he saw them, his face split into an evil smile, and then he kicked his horse back into a gallop with a yell and came thundering towards them.

'Run!' screamed Usher, but Cal was already running.

Fear and panic drove fatigue from their legs and sent them sprinting towards the hedgerow with the rhythmic drumming of the horse's hooves and the manic screaming of the rider loud in their ears.

Usher was first to reach the apparent safety of the hedge, and slipped through a gap only to hear Cal let out a scream behind him. Spinning round, he saw the rider had leaped from his horse, knocked Cal to the ground, and was now triumphantly dragging a stunned Cal to his feet.

The warrior was a big man with black hair, and a black beard. He was armoured in black leather with a sword hanging at his side and wearing a helmet of the same colour. In fact, everything about him was black, from his clothes, right through to the aura of evil that surrounded him.

'Get up, boy, or I'll cut your throat and watch you die slowly here and now; either way I get to bring you in. What by thunder...!' Maybe he thought Usher had run on or that he simply wasn't a threat, but he was unprepared to defend himself as Usher charged in to help his friend, screaming out his fear and hatred.

Slashing his sword in a way that would have made Meryn shake his head at the total lack of any technique, Usher attacked, and as he attacked, he screamed. 'Get away from him! Get away!' He slashed left then right, forcing the Saxon to drop Cal and fall backwards, narrowly escaping the swing of Usher's blade as he did so. Unfortunately, with one quick roll, the Saxon was back on his feet and blocking the next blow with a resounding clang that sent a shudder up Usher's arm and it was all he could do to keep hold of the sword.

'Two puppies, and this one has teeth!' The Saxon laughed as he drove Usher back with a flurry of well-executed jabs and cuts. 'You'd like to slice me up, eh, boy?' The Saxon's sword jabbed out, forcing Usher back into the hedgerow.

'You killed my family,' screamed Usher, 'and his!' He leapt forward and struck wildly, but the Saxon easily deflected the blow, throwing back his head, laughing as he did so, clearly enjoying the sport.

'Well, if I killed your family, it's surely only right that I send you to the shadowland so you can see them again.' He leaned forward and rubbed the corner of his eye with his free hand, imitating a crying child. 'Boo-hoo, maybe they're all missing you?'

Usher ran forward, exactly as the Saxon had anticipated, but at the same time, Cal leaped on the warrior's back, driving him to the ground with enough force to empty the air from his lungs.

All Cal's anger and grief at losing his parents and being parted from Nineve exploded; he ripped away the warrior's helmet, and then slammed it down repeatedly on the unprotected head. The Saxon screamed and struggled to his feet, easily throwing Cal to the ground, but by then Usher had closed in enough to swing his sword, driving it on with every fibre of his being at the back of the warrior's head.

At the last moment, something within Usher made him turn the blade, making the flat of the metal strike the Saxon's head, not the sharp edge. The blade snapped in two, the warrior dropped to his knees, and then slowly collapsed face down into the grass.

'Oh spirits… I killed him.' Usher stepped closer, drawing in a breath when he saw the blood running freely through the thick black hair. However, he was spared any further uncertainties over the Saxon's condition when Cal strode in and gave the fallen man a vicious kick to the side; the Saxon groaned but didn't try to get up.

'No, Usher, unfortunately he's still alive. This man killed our families! I think we could kill him right now and have no worries about the ill of it.' He kicked the warrior in the leg, eliciting a further groan and the man made a weak attempt to rise before collapsing unconscious.

'Quickly, Cal, let's get out of here,' urged Usher, glancing round. The black horse was standing close by cropping the grass, apparently unaffected by the whole spectacle. Throwing down all that remained of his broken sword, Usher swept up the Saxon's blade and tentatively approached the horse. It lifted its head and regarded him thoughtfully as it chewed, then bent down again to tug on another mouthful. As it did, Usher took its reins and clambered up into the saddle.

'Come on; climb up… before he wakes.'

Cal picked the helmet up and, with a yell, threw it as far into the meadow as he could. He walked past, but then couldn't resist one last kick at the fallen man. His foot came in and the warrior's hand stabbed out, catching Cal's ankle in a strong grip before twisting him to the ground.

Cal stared into the warrior's open staring eyes. 'Whaaaa, Usher!' He kicked out with his free leg, catching the man on the side of the head and the grip slackened. Scrambling up, he dashed to the horse and jumped up behind his friend. 'All right, now let's go… and quickly!'

Usher kicked the horse into a trot and they both spared a last look back. The warrior was still lying face down in the grass, but there were now Picts emerging from the forest on the far side of the meadow. Passing through the hedgerow, they were soon out of sight and trotting down a wide path, but the image of blue-painted faces running across the meadow was firmly imprinted on their minds.

Chapter 8

ROMANS

'Stop! Usher, I'm falling off. Slow down! Usherrr. For pity's sake!' Cal's grip finally slipped and with a drawn-out wail, he fell from the trotting horse, landing in a painful heap on the path.

They had been travelling at a trot for some time, aware that a party of Pict warriors, and a Saxon with murderous intentions was in pursuit, and it hadn't been easy. Right from the start the horse had let them know it didn't like two people bouncing about on its back. It continually tried to break into a gallop, twisting its head from side to side, as Usher heaved back, sawing on the reins trying to bring it under control. It had been a constant battle between horse and rider since they had set off, during which Cal had been bouncing about, holding on as best he could.

After rolling on the ground, moaning in pain for a while, Cal gradually realised he wasn't actually hurt and was happier where he was than on the back of the horse. He became aware of movements and crunching sounds and opened his eyes to see the horse pulling up tufts of grass close to his head; it glanced across at him and snorted happily. Its warm breath was blowing over him, tangy and fresh with the smell of chewed grass. Squinting up against the glare of the bright sky, he saw Usher sitting high in the saddle, scanning back the way they had come.

'I think we're all right at the moment, but we should get moving as soon as you can get up.' Usher glanced down at Cal, then back along the path where they had been heading. 'The smoke was coming from close to here.' He peered down again. 'Are you hurt?'

Cal thought about it for a moment and sighed. Lying here looking up through the leafy branches at the deep blue sky, he felt a whole lot less hurt than he had all day. 'No, I'm okay. I'm going to walk for a while. I'll get on again if we hear them coming.' He heaved himself up, groaning a little, as he realised that he hadn't escaped completely bruise-free. 'I don't like horses,' he moaned. 'As soon as we can, let's just leave the horse and go on by foot, all right?'

Usher remained silent.

The late afternoon air carried a chill, and the sky, visible between the branches overhead, was beginning to reflect the orange of an unseen sunset. After walking a little further, the trees gradually thinned out revealing a wide grassy expanse rolling down towards an impressive Roman villa, the smoke they had seen before was rising from one of its large chimneys. Outside, a throng of people busied themselves among a number of wagons and horses.

'They're Romans,' said Usher, shading his eyes as he peered down the hill.

'How do you know? You've never seen a Roman before, have you? Maybe it's just people taking stuff.'

'Never met a Roman, but I can see helmets and uniforms.' Usher nudged the horse and started down the hill.

'I thought the Romans had all gone. Do you think they're friendly?' called Cal, walking after him.

'Well, whoever they are, we can't go back, and one thing we can be pretty sure of is that if they're Romans, then they won't like Picts, and hopefully that will go for Saxons as well.' They made their way down towards the villa and were about halfway, when five Roman warriors broke out from the crowd and came marching up towards them. Usher reined in the horse and they waited for them to approach.

'Well, I suppose we now get to see if they're friendly,' he mumbled.

'Who are you? State your business,' called the leading Roman as soon as he got close enough to be heard. He was big and heavily muscled, with an accent as thick as his neck. Having never seen a real Roman before, they both spent a moment staring at the formidable force before them. Each warrior was armoured in polished bronze or chainmail over hard-baked leather, with red tunics and capes that flapped softly in the breeze. They each carried a short sword and a large red shield with a round brass centre. Two also held spears with red and gold pennants flapping from the top. One of the spearmen had the skin of a wolf draped over his helm, which held Cal's unwavering gaze, as he trembled slightly.

'There's a band of Picts back there... and a Saxon,' reported Usher, after a moment. He slapped Cal's hand down as it reached towards the wolf helm, then saw the lead Roman's eyes dart to the top of the hill, then back again. 'They attacked us but we got away.' The Roman raised a questioning eyebrow.

'On the Saxon's horse,' added Cal, dragging his attention from the wolf-head helm and pointing to the horse, which snorted and nodded in agreement.

'Come with us,' ordered the Roman, and the small group made their way back down to the villa where Usher had to repeat his story to another Roman, this one wearing an impressive red-crested helmet, which once again captured the boys' attention. The Roman ignored their interest in his helmet, and after hearing there were probably no more than five or six Picts and not an invading army, he dismissed them, telling them to put the horse in the stables and get some food.

The villa was busy. People were coming out with armloads of things that they handed up into the carts before dashing back inside for more. The warriors, with their shiny breastplates and plumed helms, seemed to be doing little beyond standing about talking, or marching up and down while the other people did all the running and lifting.

Usher found an empty stall and tied the horse up, and it immediately began pulling mouthfuls from a large pile of hay brought over by a smiling stable boy.

'Nice 'orse, where'd yer steal it from?' the boy asked happily.

'The biggest, nastiest Saxon you ever saw,' said Cal, attempting to remove the smile from the boy's face.

'Ain't never seen a Saxon before,' said the boy, 'but I like his 'orse. Don't worry, I'll take care of it for yer.' He produced a thick green leaf from the folds of his tunic and offered it to the horse. They all watched as it delicately plucked it from his hand with thick rubbery lips, crunched it, and then nuzzled him for more. Reaching up, he patted the sleek black neck then began brushing it down with a handful of straw, chattering softly to the horse as he did so.

'I think we should just leave the horrible beast here,' said Cal, after being directed towards somewhere called the *culina*. 'It seems much happier with him and I can't bear the thought of bruising my backside on a horse ever again.'

'It's not the horse's fault you had a bad ride,' said Usher, gazing around at the huge building. 'It's a good horse; it just didn't like two of us on its back, you can't blame it. This place is incredible, look around you!'

The culina, when they found it, turned out to be a large bustling room dedicated to the making and serving of food. As they walked in, a fat woman waved them towards a long table against the wall where two men were already busily eating. They sat down and stared round at the general bustle, amazed at the busy efficiency of the place. People were coming and going all the time: collecting food, eating food, delivering food, or simply walking through. Others fussed over racks of meat roasting on spits and several large bubbling pots suspended above a massive fireplace. The smells wafting throughout the room were wonderful.

The fat woman, who they soon realised was in charge of the cooking, came back and, with a smile, set trenchers cut from the bottom of stale loaves of bread in front of them, and then filled them with a thick porridge of boiled oats, vegetables and some sort of meat that they couldn't identify. They were both so hungry they didn't care what the meat was so long as there was plenty of it. While they were eating, they tried talking to some of the people dashing back and forth, but it wasn't easy. Most were too rushed, even the two others sitting at the table said nothing, merely finishing their food and leaving without a word.

When they did manage to get a response from someone, it was only that no one fitting the description of Meryn or Nineve had come to the villa in the last few days, which threw Cal back into a black mood for a while.

'Anyone that comes 'ere will visit my culina at some point, and I'm sorry but I've not seen them,' explained the cook, before dashing off to attend to some minor emergency with the bubbling pots. They did learn that the Roman Prefectus, as the servants called him, had moved out of the villa with his family several days before, and that all the servants were busy packing up everything to be taken back to Rome. He was, so they were told, one of the last Roman governors to leave Britain.

'And we'll be the last of the servants to leave here,' said the cook coming back to the table. She wiped sweat from her brow and sat down next to Cal. 'The Ala have been coming and going for days, guarding the families' possessions as they're taken away, but they'll all be gone soon as well… shame, I'll miss the Ala.' She went all dreamy for a moment. Wiping her hands on a cloth, she stood and began stacking the loaves of bread she had taken from the oven and packing them in flat wooden trays, a small smile still playing across her face.

'What's the Ala?' Cal asked, breaking the silence through a mouthful of meat and vegetables. He glanced at Usher who merely shrugged.

The cook turned and stared at him, mouth open with a look of shock. 'The Ala? Why, that's the Ala… Primae… Herculaea. At least that's how the Romans say it in their tongue. To you and me it would be something like… The first Herculean troop.' She saw the blank look shared by the boys. 'The centurions outside.' They still offered blank looks and she sighed. 'The *Romans*, that's their unit's name. They call themselves the Ala for short… oh, never mind, do you want any more to eat?' She ladled another helping of food onto the soggy trenchers, and then went off in search of more hungry mouths to feed.

* * *

A finger brushed Nineve's face and she gazed up through misty eyes, swollen and still tear-filled from so much crying. Someone was there… but then not there, it was just misty white. She shook her head and blinked, to clear her vision. When a hand rose up in front of her, she tried to turn away as cold soft fingers gently touched her eyes.

Floating. A feeling of calm and peace enveloping her, she smiled as the fear and tension drained away leaving her somehow more complete than before.

'It is almost time, Nineve, my lady. Almost time for you to awaken, and return.' Around her, she sensed the presence of many people, their thoughts an insistent clamour at the edge of her mind. The speaker was female, someone that she felt she knew and trusted. Someone she had shared a bond with that stretched beyond mere lifetimes. *'You may set your guardian free, Nineve. He struggles needlessly against his bonds. Tell him you will meet again. That this is your time, not his, his time will come soon. He should carry greetings to your brother, and explain that you will join with them again… when the time is right.'*

Her spirit body lifted free and within an instant, she was approaching a large circle of stones, at the centre of which burnt a fire, its many-coloured flames reaching up to an impossible height, snatching and clawing as if desperately trying to claim part of the starry sky above. The glowing presence in white guided her forward and they joined with others, linking arms to concentrate the earth's spirit that she could feel swollen and potent in the earth beneath her feet.

Gazing about, she studied the druids as they swayed gently from side to side lit by the dancing flames. There were both men and women, young and old. Some wore the colours of the tribes, while others were robed, their faces hidden within the shadowed depths of their hoods. The group were chanting, creating a deep melodic sound that filled her body and then her mind until she was caught up in the spirit of the ceremony and her own voice joined with those of the others. An elderly woman broke from the group and threw a handful of herbs and powders into the flames. As she withdrew and rejoined the circle, the colours within the fire changed. Flames of green and blue leapt up accompanied by a strong pungent odour that filled the air, the tempo of the chant increased.

As her fingers began to tingle, Nineve gazed up and watched as a tall column of blue-white light exploded upwards to pierce the heavens. In that moment, she experienced a rush of awakening and understanding, it was as if a veil had been removed from her mind and her spirit's tasks and destiny lay spread before her once more.

* * *

The meal had been wonderful and the bed of straw above the stables the most comfortable place either Usher or Cal could ever remember passing a night. The sun was already high over the horizon when Usher placed a hand over Cal's mouth to wake him. Cal jerked away from the hand, and then stretched, making a satisfied moan as he did so.

'Shhh,' cautioned Usher. Cal's eyes flew open. Usher touched a finger to his lips, and then indicated that Cal should join him at the small circular window overlooking the courtyard.

'What's the matter?' whispered Cal, as he moved alongside. Then he looked down to see where Usher was pointing. Directly below them was a Pict, standing with his back to them, turning slowly surveying the buildings. He held the stable boy by a handful of his scraggy hair, the boy whimpered and struggled weakly in his grasp. Their attention was drawn to the door of the culina as a group of the villa servants tumbled out in to the courtyard. More Picts followed out as they kicked and punched at the slower ones to hurry them on. Last out was the black-garbed Saxon, he looked angry. Usher pulled Cal back, his heart pounding, barely daring to draw breath.

91

'Where have all the Romans gone?' Cal asked. Usher shrugged, and they both crept up and chanced another peek.

The black Saxon strode out to the middle of the yard before turning to address the frightened servants. 'I am Horsa, brother to Hengist, leader of the peaceful Saxon settlers in this land.' The stable boy was flung aside by the Pict holding him and he scuttled across to stand with the other servants, rubbing at his head.

'I was attacked near here and my horse was stolen from me,' continued Horsa, his strongly accented voice echoing around the yard. 'That horse is now in this stable. I want to know where the two thieves are who rode it in here. I wish, very much, to find them.' There was a low murmur from the servants but thankfully, nobody spoke or pointed up to the loft where Usher and Cal lay. Only the stable boy knew where they were, and he was still busy rubbing his head. With a nod from Horsa, two Picts dragged an elderly male servant from the line and threw him down at Horsa's feet. The man began to wail and grovel, and several of the other servants cried out, pleading for him to be let go.

'I didn't steal no 'orse,' wailed the old man, beginning to sob.

Glancing down, Horsa placed a foot on the man's neck and forced him down, pinning him to the tiles. When the old man struggled, he stamped firmly down and the struggles reduced to mere whimpers.

'We have to get out of here,' Usher hissed, as he headed towards the ladder. He peeked down through the hatch to be sure there wasn't a Pict waiting underneath and was relieved to see that the horse was alone. It stared back at him; its ears twitching in surprise at seeing a head appear through the ceiling. As Usher dropped down, quickly followed by Cal, a muffled shriek came from the courtyard, followed by more cries, and then the sound of Horsa's voice echoing from the walls as he questioned the servants again.

'Pass me the harness,' commanded Usher, in an urgent whisper. He straightened the fur he had thrown over the horse's back and then slipped the proffered harness over its neck.

'You really want me to get on that horse again?' hissed Cal, eyeing the horse uncertainly. It returned the stare as if echoing his concerns.

Usher stopped tying the harness and glanced round. 'No, Cal. I expect you to stay here and get yourself killed. Of course I want you to get on the horse, stop being stupid! It's only a short way to the gate and then we're out and away.' Ignoring the fact that Cal still hadn't moved, he tied a short length of rope to the door then carefully unlatched it. A quick glance out confirmed that Horsa was still busy with the servants, and that the body of the old man lay silent and unmoving in the centre of the yard. Pushing down a feeling of fear and panic, Usher climbed onto the horse and patted its neck softly. 'Get on!' he commanded, and Cal reluctantly pulled himself up behind.

'Promise me we'll either get another horse for me to ride or go back to walking as soon as we can,' mumbled Cal, taking a good hold of Usher.

'Agreed,' said Usher, then he pulled hard on the rope, the door sprang back with a bang, and the horse, with its riders clinging on, shot out into the courtyard.

They exited the stable much faster than either of them had thought they would, and headed directly towards the black Saxon. Servants screamed, Picts yelled then ran in, and Horsa threw up his arms as the horse reared in front of him, tipping Cal to the ground.

'I knew the horse was a mistake,' cried Cal. Jumping up, he ducked under the grasp of a Pict warrior, ran past the servants, and disappeared into the villa. The horse reared again, striking out at its former master who fell to the ground with a cry, then Usher managed to gain some control. He tugged heavily on the reins and the horse wheeled round to the left, scattering the Picts. Two possible routes presented themselves; the open gate, which had three Picts close to it, or the doorway to the villa that Cal had just dashed through. With no time to decide, he gave the horse its head as they spun towards the villa. However, it ignored the door to the culina and ran up the steps, through a bigger door and into a large hallway.

Wrong move, thought Usher in dismay. Then shouted, 'Cal, where are you?' His cry echoed through the empty villa, now stripped of its furnishings, mixing with the sharp reports of the horse's hooves as they moved from the hallway, past a large room that held some kind of pond, then into an even larger room with the sound of the Picts close behind.

'Usher!' Cal came down some stairs in a rush and clambered up behind his friend. 'How are we going to...?' His question was cut short as the horse, sensing fresh air, trotted on and then burst out onto a terrace and on towards a low wall.

'Hold on!' cried Usher, as the horse jumped. It cleared the wall but there was a steep drop on the other side and it landed awkwardly, a shrill scream escaping it as it stumbled. Finding its feet, it snorted and tossed its head then managed to carry them a good distance away from the villa, eventually stopping at the top of the hill where Cal slipped thankfully to the ground. The horse was shivering violently, there was foam all around its mouth and it was wavering from side to side. Usher dropped down and looked back towards the villa where running figures were coming up towards them.

'We have to get out of here, Cal, they're coming!' he urged, but Cal stayed where he was.

'I think the horse is hurt.' Cal stroked the horse's nose and it snorted and trembled again, swaying slightly.

'We can't help it. We have to get out of here and you're right; the horse is hurt, it can't take us further.' Usher started to move off into the trees.

'Thank you, horse. I'm... I'm sorry,' whispered Cal. He stroked its nose and still shivering and swaying, it tossed its head. With a sigh, he turned and followed on after Usher.

Trees covered the top of the hill, but as they emerged on the other side, they ran downhill across meadow-grass, towards more thickets of trees. This late in the year, the grass was old and yellow, and lying flat to the ground where the summer sun had dried it out and more recently the rain had pounded it. It made going downhill more of a long slide than a run. As they topped each small rise, they glanced back only to confirm that the Picts were gaining on them.

'In there,' said Usher, his breath coming in ragged gasps, 'we have to lose them.' They entered a large thicket of trees, which slowed their progress further as they frantically searched for a place to hide, but the trees were too thinly spaced to offer much in the way of sanctuary.

'What are we going to do?' Cal asked as they gave up and came out on the other side. There was another thicket a short distance further down hill, Usher pointed towards it, not having the breath to explain more, then ran on.

They were half way down when the Picts came out of the trees behind them, sighted their prey, and began to shriek and call, bounding down the hill after them. There was no alternative, nowhere else to run. The boys turned and drew their weapons; Usher still had Horsa's black sword and Cal had a long knife. There were four Picts closing in with several others still only unseen voices amongst the trees behind them. Usher swung his sword as the first warrior reached them, but it rebounded on the Pict's outthrust shield. The blue-faced warrior let out a scream that chilled Usher's blood and swung his blade in a deadly arc. Usher just managed to jump back and avoid it and then moved back in, stabbing forward with his own blade as he did so. Beside him, Cal had been backing away, but as the next Pict arrived letting out a shrill battle cry, he leaped forward; knife outstretched, and stabbed him in the stomach, wrenching the knife to the side as he felt it grate against bone. The man let out a terrible shriek and collapsed, clutching at his guts that were already spilling from the wound. For a second, Cal simply stared at him transfixed, and then, without warning, the next Pict was on him. The warrior lifted his axe, the blue-painted face split into an ecstatic smile and he shrieked his war cry into Cal's terrified face, and then an arrow embedded itself in his chest and he stared down, the smile turning to a look of bewildered shock. At the sound of a deep growl, Cal pushed the dying man away and swung his attention towards Usher. As he did, a grey blur leapt at the Pict holding Usher by the hair, enveloped his whole head in its jaws and shook him to the sound of cracking bone. The Pict's screams were muffled as the huge war-hound continued its savage attack before changing its grip to the man's neck and ripping his throat out in one easy bite, silencing him forever. The remaining warriors turned and fled, with the hound in pursuit, while from the trees emerged a small group of Romans.

One of the small band ran over to finish the dying Pict warrior, while their leader lowered his bow and called the hound back with a shrill whistle.

'I had a dream we would meet at this place and have waited here three days for your arrival.' The man smiled as if the whole notion was somewhat foolish. 'I'm not normally given to following dreams, and my men have borne this fancy well, considering. However, I am glad to say, all this has happened as I saw it and that I have not gone completely mad.'

'I am Ambrosius, son of Clarens, who was once king of all the tribes. I have come to make my rightful claim as king of the Britons by succession.' He stared at Usher then placed a hand upon his shoulder. 'And you... All I can say is welcome, brother; I have not seen you since you were a babe in arms.'

* * *

Calvador Craen turned from where he had been staring into the fire, listening to his old friend reliving the story of their youth. He had known what would be coming. However, when the moment had arrived, the old storyteller had stopped with a jolt, almost in mid sentence, his mouth moving wordlessly as the implication of the memory became apparent.

'Do you remember meeting Ambrosius that day, Usher?' Cal watched and felt some small pity as his friend grappled with his emotions. At last, the old grey head nodded and Usher Vance took a long drink from his tankard.

'Until this moment no, but how could I forget? I don't understand how...' He fumbled for his tobacco pouch and filled his pipe with trembling hands, then smiled across at Cal before continuing on with his tale, as eager to hear more as anyone else in the room.

Chapter 9

Ambrosius

'How many are with you?' The blue-daubed face loomed so close to Meryn that the fetid smell of his breath almost overpowered the pungent smell coming from the rest of him. The Pict worked the gag loose and Meryn moved his jaw around, wincing at the pain.

'You will tell me now… or I cut the girl.' The Pict smiled horribly, showing black broken teeth, and then dragged Nineve over by her hair. Drawing a stained knife from the folds of his cloak, he pulled her head back and pressed the uneven blade to her thin white throat. He stared down at Meryn, waiting for an answer as the blade slowly pressed harder, quickly drawing a crimson bead of blood. With eyes squeezed shut, Nineve wept silently around her gag.

'There are two others,' blurted Meryn… just boys, they're… '

'How many years do they have?' growled the Pict. The knife relaxed against Nineve's throat but he didn't let go of her hair.

'They're lads, just lads,' continued Meryn. 'Fourteen, fifteen summers; they're no more than that.' He noticed the calculating look the Pict gave before he barked something at one of the others.

'We were to meet a force from the Trinovante.' Meryn's eyes flicked across to the path in an attempt to strengthen the lie, but when he looked back, he saw the Pict cared little for anyone that might be coming to their rescue. Throwing Nineve to the side, the Pict replaced Meryn's gag and stood up, then turned to his two companions. There was a short conversation, and then he disappeared into the trees with one of the others, leaving only one Pict as their reluctant guard.

Meryn studied the Pict warrior as he moved restlessly past him. The way he paced reminded Meryn of a dangerous dog tied to a post, desperate to be cut loose. Every now and then, he would stop and cast a malevolent glare at his two captives, and then growl something under his breath. Meryn did his best to ignore him.

Whenever he thought the Pict wasn't looking, Meryn struggled, straining against his bonds, but try as he might he still couldn't get loose. Despair threatened to overwhelm him as he realised how helpless their situation had become. They obviously wanted the boys and Nineve, he shuddered to think what for, but him, they would no doubt kill. He choked down the rising feeling of fear and determined for Nineve's sake, if nothing else, not to lose control. Drawing in a deep breath, he gathered his reserves and centred his energies one more time, seeking the calm he knew would be necessary if there was to be an opportunity for escape.

The misty morning had turned into a beautiful afternoon, yet until then Meryn had been unaware of little past his immediate surroundings. Once he felt his body let go of the fear, he closed his eyes and tried to direct his concentration onto the cool breeze that occasionally played across his face, and then moved to the flicker of warm sunlight filtering down through the canopy of leaves. As he allowed tense tired muscles to relax, he accepted the burning pain from his chaffed wrists, and set it aside into a corner of his mind where it could no longer distract him. Sitting up with a straight back, he pushed against the tree for support and breathed in deeply through his nose, and then slowly out through his mouth, forcing the breath around the gag. His awareness extended as he tried to locate the Picts, the last having sprinted off a few moments before, leaving them alone with just the horses for company. After a moment, he decided that they were indeed unguarded, and that he could sense no other presence than Nineve as she sat close beside him.

However, before he had a chance to do anything more, something brushed against his arm and moved behind him. He opened his eyes and squinted back, trying to see what was happening. Someone shoved him forward, and the rough rope binding his hands began to vibrate and, after a moment, parted. The momentary relief of freedom this brought was short-lived as his circulation returned and his hands exploded in a throbbing agony of pain. He let out an involuntary moan.

'Shhhh.' The warning came as he began massaging his wrists. Nineve moved in front of him and began sawing at the rope round his feet with a sharp stone. As she cut, she glanced about anxiously, obviously worried that the Picts would return before she was finished. 'I must go,' she whispered. 'Please tell Calvador not to worry about me. Tell him I'll see him soon.' The rope parted and for a moment, she gazed up into his eyes. 'Thank you, Meryn.'

'We're both going to get out of here, Nineve,' hissed Meryn once he had wrenched the gag down from his mouth. 'How did you get free?' There was no answer. 'Nineve... Nineve?' He glanced about, then drawing his legs up, rubbed at them, trying to bring back some feeling to the cramped muscles. He stopped and listened for movement, and cast about again, but she had gone. There was no sign or sound of the girl anywhere. 'Nineve?' Seeing the rope that had bound her lying beside him, he picked it up and frowned. His rope lay ragged and frayed, not like this one. The ends of this one were cut cleanly, as if by a sharp knife; but she couldn't have had a knife, could she? Surely the Picts would have found it if she had? Anyway, if she had, why then use a stone to cut his? Someone else had cut her free.

Behind him, the sound of running feet came from further down the path. Meryn drew back behind the tree as one of the Picts came into view, breathing hard. The Pict drew up short as he realised the two captives were no longer tied to the tree, and then Meryn stepped out and struck him a sharp blow to the back of the head.

Dropping the branch, Meryn stooped down and retrieved the fallen man's sword, and after a further search of the campsite, was rewarded with his own bow. He watched as the Picts had examined it before tossing it aside. It was longer than their short bows and needed more effort to draw, something for which the Picts obviously had little appreciation. Grabbing a water-skin and a food bag from one of the horses, Meryn set off through the trees, scouring the ground for some sign to indicate the direction Nineve had taken.

After circling the camp twice, and finding nothing, he turned south, cutting from left to right across the trail, looking for any small track or sign. The more he searched, the more he became frustrated, all he found were animal tracks, and that puzzled him.

Later, as the light in the forest began to fade, his thoughts turned to spending a night alone without his charges and, not for the first time, began regretting sending the two boys off. There was no telling how far they might have gone, and now that Nineve had vanished, he knew he had failed completely. In the dark cold of the forest, Meryn laid his head down close to the main forest path, and began to pray for help from the spirits.

In the early hours of the morning, he awoke with a sudden start from a deep but troubled sleep, and spent a few moments of confusion as his senses screamed that there was movement close by. Rolling over, he saw the light of a half moon shining between the trees, illuminating the path in its silvery light, and watched, fearing to draw breath, as a tall shadowy figure strode past, trailed by two Pict warriors. One of the Picts was cradling his arm as if wounded, while the other carried himself with an air of dejection. They gave the impression that they had narrowly survived some violent encounter. It was hard to make much of the man at the front. His attitude was confident, almost arrogant, and he was walking without regard for his two companions as they dogged his steps. Meryn tried to focus. The light was deceiving, casting the man as a shadow without features, as a creature of the night. He shivered and dismissed the imaginings of a tired mind as the figures passed from sight.

Laying back down, his thoughts returned to Nineve and the boys. The girl's disappearance was a mystery that troubled him greatly; and the spirits alone knew where Usher and Cal had gone. Sleep would be a long time returning now that he was awake, and tomorrow was set to be another long day.

* * *

The smell of blood filled his nostrils, tangy and sharp. Saliva flowed unbidden, running down his tongue as it lolled over sharp teeth, there was a strong feeling of contentment. Then his head came up and his jaws snapped shut, sounds, close by amongst the trees. Scanning the darkness, he watched a rabbit hop out from the shadows, then turn as soon as it saw him and scamper away in fear of its life. Relaxing once more, he sniffed at the air, enjoying the myriad of scents that it carried and the knowledge of the forest it imparted to him. With a full belly, he had little interest in chasing rabbits, better to simply move on and rejoin the pack. A howl drifted through the forest and a moment later, another answered its cry, this one even closer. Lifting his head, Cal echoed the call of his clan and howled into the night.

'Cal!' Something was shaking him, pulling him away.

'No! Let me stay!' Opening his eyes, Cal saw Usher leaning over him with a frown of concern. 'Oh, leave me alone, Usher,' he mumbled, 'I was sleeping.'

'No, you were howling, like a wolf!' Usher grinned down at him. 'Are you all right?' Cal nodded, as sleep began to reclaim him and his eyes closed once more.

'Is your friend well?' Usher stood and saw Ambrosius silhouetted in the doorway holding back the stiff goatskin that served as a door.

'Just an evil dream, I think,' said Usher, leaving Cal's side. Passing through the door, he rejoined Ambrosius and his two companions.

'It's no wonder his dreams are filled with evil, brother. You've both had your share of troubles lately. The Saxons have been searching for you everywhere. They've tried to kill *me* on two separate occasions, which is understandable, but you? You, we thought were well hidden. I still don't know how they knew where to look, but they searched for you and for some reason, a young girl. Every village across the lands of the Iceni has been either searched or destroyed by Saxon and Pict war parties trying to find you.' He clapped Usher on the shoulder. 'But you evaded them like a true brother of mine. We are our father's sons.'

Usher nodded at the man calling him brother; it still didn't seem right, but then something in him said that everything Ambrosius had told him was indeed true. It felt strange. The thought that the people he had known as his mother and father, the parents he had seen lying dead in the smoking embers of their hut, were not really his parents. He had loved them, and he knew they had loved him, he keenly felt the loss of them, but he instinctively knew, now it had been explained, that they had merely been kind enough to take him in when asked. He watched as Ambrosius returned to his two companions. They continued their discussion while he resumed his study of the three men, three very Roman-looking men, who claimed to be Britons. He supposed if the armour was gone, and they wore proper clothes, but why?

'Why are you dressed like Romans?'

Ambrosius broke his concentration on the map the three were studying, and smiled at Usher.

'I told you. I've lived with the Romans since our father was killed and I was taken into hiding.'

Usher shook his head, his face set in a frown. 'But if I am your brother, why didn't I go with you?'

Ambrosius sighed. 'I do not rightly know, Uther. Remember, I had only eight summers at the time and had little to say in the matter. I've asked that same question many times over the years, but no one could provide me with an answer. I came to believe it was done so that if I were found and killed by our enemies, then our people would still have a true king, you! For whatever the reason, when our father was killed, the druids took you away and hid you here amongst the Iceni, while I was taken into the Roman Empire where the Romans schooled me and taught me their ways. However, I always knew that one day I would return to take up my birthright in Britain and become king, and that we brothers would be reunited. It was something I grew up being sure of, and now, Uther, its happening.'

'That's the other thing; you keep calling me Uther, but my name is Usher.'

Ambrosius shrugged. 'Your name is Uther. Maybe the family that took you in changed your name to help hide you; I don't know what they were told. But your name is Uther, and you should try to get used to that.'

Looking up into the kindly face of his older brother, Usher... or Uther, didn't know what to think. *Oo-ther.* He repeated the name to himself a few times, rolling it over his tongue; it would take some getting used to, if that was what he had to do. 'So how would you have found me if...'

'If we hadn't camped out in a remote thicket of trees for days in the hope a druid's dream might prove true? I cannot honestly say.' Ambrosius shrugged and glanced across to his companions who were obviously entertained by the exchange.

'It was a druid's dream? I thought you said before that you had dreamt of meeting with me yourself.'

'Oh, it was I that dreamt it, but I was visiting a druid's well, which makes it a druid's dream. Uther, I think you should join your friend and sleep. There'll be plenty of time for questions and talk later. We have a long ride ahead of us tomorrow and will be setting off at first light. Tirius, Marcus and I still have much to discuss before we are able to rest. When we rejoin my men in a few days, we will begin our preparations to march on Vortigern, and we still have that battle to plan.'

Standing up, Uther nodded to the three men and retired to the sleeping area where he lay down and listened to the low murmur of voices, and occasional whimpers of Cal as he slept. There was so much to take in. As if life hadn't been hard enough before, now he had to contend with being someone completely different. I'm a stranger to myself, he thought as he lay listening to the sounds of the night. His mind was still full of questions seeking answers and it took some time, but slowly he drifted into a troubled sleep.

The next few days were to prove hard in many ways. The band Ambrosius travelled with, which was about forty strong, were seasoned warriors and used to long periods in the saddle. Uther, and especially Cal, were not used to the long hours, punishing pace, or brief overnight stops in cold wet camps. When the journey finally ended, all either wanted to do was sleep in a dry bed and never sit on a horse again.

'I told you horses were a terrible way to travel,' moaned Cal, as he rubbed foul smelling paste onto the muscles of his aching bottom. Uther, who had already applied the salve, couldn't help but snigger as Cal waddled to his sleeping furs and fell face down, moaning in agony.

'I thought you were starting to like that black horse back at the villa. After all your moaning, you didn't want to leave him. These horses are no different.'

Cal opened an eye and fixed his gaze upon Uther in a serious frown. 'He had heart, that horse. His leg was broken but he still took us away from that Saxon.'

'Horsa.'

'Yes, Horsa. I think the horse just wanted to be as far away from that evil bastard as he could, I don't blame him either, but he carried us with him and that took a huge heart. I felt bad at just leaving him.' Cal closed his eyes and winced as he tried to change position. 'Truth is, I still don't want to get back on a horse ever again, or at least not for a long, long time.

More warriors joined them over the following weeks as the winter weather changed for the worse. Days of rain with scarcely a break were followed by storms that drove snow and ice into the makeshift shelters of the camp. It delayed the confrontation with Vortigern, but it also allowed them to become an organised fighting force. The will of the tribes to reclaim their land and beat back the Saxon invaders now combined with the Roman training introduced by their king. Ambrosius and his men brought with them the knowledge and ability to house, train, and feed the groups that came in from the various tribes when they heard there was finally an alternative to the rule of Vortigern.

* * *

'Uther? The storyteller is now Uther of legend, but, how can that be?'

'Be still!' Cal rose to his feet and searched the faces surrounding his old friend. 'Allow this story to be told. That you're here is a privilege. You are witnessing your history being revealed, and will show some respect.' The sudden light in his eyes calmed as he gazed down at the ashen features of his friend, and then turned to the innkeeper. 'Do you have a hot broth? Our storyteller is in need of something to give him a little strength.' The innkeeper nodded and went to fetch it himself.

'I... I'm sorry fer the interruption, storyteller. I meant no harm.' The man was a ruddy-faced farmer and appeared to be regretting his outburst. Several of his neighbours muttered about how inappropriate it was, and that it was only a story, but a fine story at that. At least it was if only there were no more comments from the likes of him.

'The storyteller can be whoever he wishes to be,' said the farmer's wife, slapping her hand against his large stomach. He groaned and edged back. 'Please, storyteller, go on. There won't be no more interruptions from him.' She glowered at her husband, and then settled herself, smoothing her skirts.

'You're doing fine, old friend.' Cal sat back as the innkeeper set a broth beside the leather chair then passed a second to Cal who took it with a smile of thanks. 'It was a long time ago. Your memories have been hidden for so long that when they return...' he left the statement unfinished.

'My name is Uther. I remember it so well, but why had I forgotten for so long ... and how long has it been?' He sipped at the broth. 'This is so unsettling. I want to stop, but then don't feel I can.' He cast about the smoky room and fumbled for his pipe and tobacco. Taking in the rows of expectant faces, he shook his head then stopped and gazed questioningly at his pipe. 'And how then...'

'Do you remember what happened to Meryn? He told us about escaping from the Picts and how he searched for Nineve,' broke in Cal. 'Do you remember what he had to go through before we eventually met again?'

Uther nodded. 'I remember. He was carrying a huge burden of guilt through the Weald with him. He thought we were all dead and was blaming himself for everything. There was something strange about their escape...'

Chapter 10

A Rusty Sword

For three days, Meryn meandered in a southerly direction, doggedly crossing the main forest path from east to west then back again. There were plenty of tracks to follow, but so far, none of them leading away from the main path had been made by man... or little girl. There was an abundance of deer, boar and rabbits, and it was these animals' paths that he walked, all the while seeking some sign to show where Nineve had gone.

Late in the third day, he was following a series of deer trails, still trying to head south, when he noticed a lighter area ahead amongst the trees. As he got closer, he could see there was a break in the forest canopy, a large patch of grey sky hanging above what appeared to be a massive patch of brambles. It would have been far simpler to go around, and he almost did, but a strong urge to seek what he was sure would be an open centre suddenly consumed him and he began forcing his way in.

The brambles were old and dense, crowding each other as they reached up towards the light. As he hacked with his sword and forced his way through, they tore at his clothing and scratched at any exposed skin. He spent as much time untangling himself as he did cutting through the heavy, thick stalks; yet the desire to continue only became stronger. Digging deep into his last reserves of both energy and curiosity, he pushed on.

This was, in many ways, his final push. His determination to track Nineve was fast losing a battle of wills with his stomach, having eaten little of any real substance in days. If he didn't find anything after all this effort, he would stop his search, return to the main path, and head south; his stomach rumbled as if in agreement with his thoughts.

'Quiet down there,' he muttered, then seeing a few old blackberries still clinging to the brambles, he snatched them from their thorny stem and crammed them into his mouth. They were hard and shrivelled this late in the season and tasted bad, but he swallowed them anyway, hoped they wouldn't sour his stomach, and continued towards the clearing.

The sight that presented itself when he did eventually burst through, carefully picking the last clinging stem away from his cloak, caused Meryn to hesitate, and then think very seriously about turning round and fighting his way back out. It almost did... but he didn't. There was indeed a clearing inside. It was roughly circular, completely surrounded by the thick wall of brambles, and overshadowed by some of the tallest trees in the forest. However, it was what lay within that had unsettled him, lush green grass growing through a circle of standing stones.

'Druid stones,' muttered Meryn in awe, as he cast about the clearing. He quickly scanned the shadows, seeking the druids who must surely call this place home, then finally exhaled the breath he had been holding when he realised that he was alone. He wavered for a moment, his half-starved brain unsure of what to do. It was dangerous to mix in the way of druids, but if they knew something of Nineve's disappearance, then he needed to explore the circle. With a sigh, he set off, skirting the perimeter while being careful not to cross into the circle itself.

The stones stood upright, were just over waist height, and looked as if in some ancient time they had erupted from the bowels of the earth, pushed by some immense force to point accusingly at the sky. He took his time to study each one as he walked past, listening to the silence, allowing his senses to explore the strange aura of the glade. What it was used for he had no idea, but he knew as a certainty that it was some kind of doorway between this world and the world of spirit, that was the way with druids.

Calm down, Meryn, he counselled, dragging his attention back to the stones. They reminded him of huge jagged, rotten teeth. Still slick with the previous night's rain, there was a stark contrast between the dark grey of the stone and the moss that grew on each in a variety of colours and textures. As he slowly passed each one, he noticed a tingling sensation. It was as if the stones were vibrating slightly and transferring their energy across to him. He reached out, stopping his fingers just short of the rough surface of the closest stone, and then thought better of it and quickly walked on.

Within the circle stood a larger stone, roughly shaped with a flat top, dominating the centre of the glade with its presence. The moment he saw it, Meryn felt his concentration drawn forwards as all fear left him, and a feeling that it was safe to enter within the circle overwhelmed him. He stepped confidently past the stones onto the soft grass.

While his mind confirmed he was safe, he was vaguely aware of his ears telling him the birds had stopped their singing and the wind was no longer moving the leaves in the trees overhead, he was walking the soft grass of the circle in almost complete silence. The only sound appeared to be coming from the stones with their soft vibrating hum, and the loud beating of his heart as it echoed in his ears. He approached the central stone and noticed for the first time that an object lay upon it, a sword, old and tarnished, its leather sheath rotting and decayed by the elements. He watched absently as his arm reach out unbidden, and then saw his fingers wrap around the hilt and slide the sword free of the crumbling leather.

Excalibur, the name echoed in his mind, as if attached to a thousand tiny bells, and there came a momentary spark of connection between him and the rusty blade. Trembling slightly, he laid the sword down and then, without really knowing why, removed his sleeping fur and rolled it round the ancient weapon before securely tying it with a bowstring.

Now, with the old sword slung across his back, Meryn felt exposed at the centre of the circle, and a shiver travelled through him. It was almost as if the stones had finished with him and were now trying to expel him. Fear once again fluttered in his chest as he glanced anxiously about the glade trying to see a way out. This was the strangest place he could ever remember being in and he was ready to leave. It wasn't that anything was specifically threatening, but it wasn't particularly welcoming either, it was all just so unsettling.

Running across the grass, he stepped outside the stones and found himself at a small open area cut from the brambles on the opposite side of the circle from where he had entered. The sounds of the forest filled the air again and the memory of how things had happened in the circle had already started to fade. He glanced around the little clearing, eager for distraction. Obviously, it was where the druids made camp when they were here. In the centre, a fire area still had wet grey ash and a few charred branches remaining in a black depression burnt into the earth. Six sleeping places were set about the fire, and in three, freshly cut grass and bracken formed comfortable-looking pallets. He bent down and felt one. It was damp from the previous night's rain. Scattered at the head end were herbs, their fragrant smell wafting up as his hand disturbed them.

A burning light of hope filled his heart as he crouched and studied the ground. Footprints were everywhere, but they were hard to read. At last, after some searching, he found what he thought was the footprint of a child. He traced his finger around the edge to define it further and crouched staring at it from various angles. It might well be Nineve's, but he couldn't be sure. What was apparent, however, was that several druids had been here recently, and a child may possibly have been amongst them, but why?

Completing a full circuit of the stones confirmed there really was no easy way out of the glade. How the druids came and went was uncertain, but it wasn't by any forest path that Meryn could see. He didn't like the idea of searching further, and certainly didn't relish the thought of spending the night in their glade, you never knew where you were with druids, and after him taking their rusty old sword there was no telling how they would react. Checking his direction by way of the sun, he forced his way back through the brambles and into the forest to find somewhere to camp.

The rain fell incessantly above the trees for three days as Meryn wandered utterly lost. It reached the forest floor in a misery of constant drips from the dense layers of leaves and branches above him, it felt like it had been raining forever. He was wet to the bone, tired, and almost delirious with hunger. It wasn't that catching food was a problem. Several rabbits had fallen to his bow, but finding wood dry enough to light a fire so he could cook them was impossible. Worse still, he was beginning to think his sense of direction was faulty. He couldn't find the main path and the trees of the Weald appeared to have no end. His optimism, which had flared at the druids' circle after finding sign of Nineve, was now ebbing, yet there was no alternative but to keep plodding. He was forever expecting to emerge into open fields, always believing them to be just beyond the next bit of forest. However, when he got there, all that ever greeted him were trees, ferns, moss and more trees. Stumbling forever forwards, he was soaked through, shivering and becoming convinced that the old druid had cursed him back at the well. That he was doomed to remain wandering the forest forever; or at least for several years until he staggered out in the mountains of Cymru in the west, or to the sea in the east as an older broken man.

Muttering to himself without realising he was doing it, Meryn was tripping along a narrow deer-path, slapping wet branches away as they reached out to taunt him in passing, when a long drawn-out wail echoed through the forest. It stopped him where he stood, one foot raised ready to set down… listening. He gently placed his foot and waited, unmoving for another sound to follow the first, and didn't have to wait long before it came. It sounded like a woman, screaming in pain and anguish. With fresh purpose, he picked up his pace and set off towards where he judged the sounds were coming from, glad now for the rain as it covered his approach. Scanning the trees ahead, he felt the threat of danger quicken his pulse and his mind became sharper than it had been in days. Checking his sword at his belt, he hoped the spirits of the forest had allowed his string to remain dry in its oiled pouch so he could use his bow, and then another scream rent the air and he realised he was close. He slowed his progress, calmly stringing the bow, as he crept forward, and glanced over a low rise.

At first he was puzzled by what he saw, a small group of people gathered at the base of a large oak tree. He judged four in the group to be men, and he could just make out the skirts of at least one woman standing with her back to him.

Another scream set the group in motion. The woman pushed one of the attackers roughly aside, and a young boy broke from the group, ran some way off and sat hugging his knees. Meryn could see the boy's eyes darting from side to side in obvious alarm and agitation, and when yet another scream filled the forest, he covered his ears, shut his eyes tight and began rocking back and forth. Meryn had heard enough. Whoever that poor woman was he couldn't just pass by and do nothing, not while she was being tortured. With a fluid motion, he placed an arrow on the bow, drew back, and released, the arrow flew across the distance and struck the tree, narrowly missing one of the men.

'Damp string,' he mumbled, then pulled his sword free and ran out at the group, shrieking his battle cry in an attempt to appear as ferocious as possible, but as he ran up the cry died on his lips and came to a stop, sword held high, it was blatantly obvious they were all ignoring him.

'Wait, Elen my love. Please try and wait.' It was one of the men, appealing in a whining voice to someone Meryn couldn't see. The speaker was crouched down, desperately gripping the hand of whoever was lying against the tree. Meryn lowered his sword and tried to comprehend what was happening; still puzzled that none of the group was acknowledging him standing there with a drawn blade.

'They've gone to fetch the old woman,' the man continued, 'she'll be here soon, really. You just have to wait a bit longer and...' Elen, whom Meryn figured to be the woman against the tree with her knees up, didn't wait for the man to finish but screamed again, the shriek an inhuman sound that shattered the stillness of the dripping forest. Screaming yet again, she reached out with both hands and pulled the man and the other woman towards her with a savage show of strength. They both struggled to get free, but she held on, continued heaving herself forward, as she dragged them down, her face echoing the pain of her cry. Everyone, including Meryn, gazed at the heavily pregnant woman and wondered anxiously what they should do.

'Breathe Elen, just breathe and everything will be all right,' crooned the woman standing at poor Elen's side. As she spoke, Meryn noticed she was desperately trying to pry Elen's clenched fingers from her arm. 'Jared has gone for the old woman, they'll be here soon and everything will be fine.'

'Fine, Tilly?' spat Elen. 'Do I look... like everything is... fine?' Her face contorted as another wave of pain took her. 'Aaaahhh, help me... or a curse on you all!'

'What do we do, Tilly?' whined the crouching man, thrusting his panicked face out towards her. 'You're a woman, you should know!' The two other men standing over them shared worried expressions and one even shook his head in resignation. The boy who had fled earlier still had his hands over his ears and was rocking back and forth even faster. He was now humming loudly, trying, to block out the sound of Elen's screams.

'I don't know... I... I...' Tilly glanced about, her eyes finally resting on Meryn. 'Do something, please. She's come early... we was gathering firewood, her waters broke and... please, the old woman's coming but we don't know what to do.'

Elen screamed again.

'Me, I don't know much, girl... hardly anything at all,' said Meryn, once the scream cut off. He instantly realised that it might not have been the wisest thing to say. Everyone who wasn't screaming was staring at the man who had just professed some small knowledge of childbirth, each displaying similar expressions of abject relief. The young father glanced back down to his wife.

'It's going to be all right, Elen. There's a fellow here who can help you!' Elen answered with another scream and Meryn backed away.

'Listen, I said I don't know much, and I meant it.' Wiping a hand across his face, he tried to think back to the time that he had indeed witnessed a child being born. Back then, he had merely been an observer, more as support for the expectant father than help for the mother. By the time the village woman had handed the father the screaming infant, they had both been slightly worse for the effects of the ale they had been consuming all evening to 'wet the baby's head.' Meryn cast about the soggy glade and decided that, while there was nobody else present with a jot of sense, he might as well try to do something.

'Very well, I'll do what little I can, but I warn you, it won't be much.' Eager hands drew him forward as he hurriedly dropped his pack and the rolled-up rusty sword.

He glanced across at the contorted face of Elen and tried to offer her a reassuring smile. She was squeezing her husband's hand, the man's face reflecting the pain of her grip along with the feeling of total inadequacy felt by every father at the birth of his child. Of course, reflected Meryn, these poor souls are going through all this in the middle of a forest on a rainy day with Meryn Link as their only hope of salvation. How did I get in the middle of this? He looked up at Elen, and then around at the others.

'Get something to put on the ground... for the baby when it comes.' He clawed at his thoughts. What else had they done? 'How long has she been like this?'

'Some time now, but the old lady should be here soon, she'll know what to do.' The husband smiled up at him then whipped his head round as Elen screamed again. Her legs drew up, her face went bright red, and she looked set to explode.

'I don't think your *young* lady can wait for the *old* lady,' observed Meryn. 'This baby may well be here soon.' He crouched down and tentatively lifted Elen's skirts.

'Hey! What are you doing?' The husband appeared shocked that Meryn should do such a thing.

'He... has to... you...' Elen's face grimaced in pain as she spat out the last word, '... fool... aaahh!'

Meryn glanced up from his quick surveillance of the situation. 'The baby's head is showing. It'll be here soon.'

'Well get it! Help her,' the husband implored.

'I can't just get it! The baby will come when it's ready.' Meryn stared into Elen's pain-filled eyes. 'Are you ready to give a big push?' She nodded, and bore down, squeezing hard on both her husband's and Tilly's hands in the process, all three screamed.

'And again,' instructed Meryn.

Elen pushed, her face contorting with the effort, and the three screamed out into the forest once more.

'You're doing really well, Elen, I'm so proud of you.' Tears were tumbling down the husband's face, but his words of comfort were answered with a look of scorn and yet another scream.

'Push!' cried Meryn.

Another four monumental attempts and the efforts of Elen and the others were rewarded with the howling cry of a newborn infant as it spilt with a rush between Elen's legs. Meryn scooped the little blue bundle up, wrapped him in a shawl that Tilly handed over, and then placed the baby boy on Elen's chest. Stepping back, he gazed down at the group that was crowded round, cooing happily at the wrinkled little face.

He was just realising that it was over, his presence no longer required, when a bustling black shape shoved him roughly aside with a bony hand.

'Elen! Elen girl, don't you fret. I'm here now and ready to care for you!' The little old woman crouched down, lifted Elen's skirt and then glanced up at the baby. Without further comment, she began tying off the rubbery umbilical cord that still attached mother to child.

Meryn picked up his things and, with a last glance back at the baby, walked off in the direction the old woman had come from, more eager than ever to find the village.

A cold wet drizzle was blowing in from the east as he emerged from the trees. Above him, dark grey clouds tore past while even darker thunderheads built up in the distance, threatening that an even greater drenching was to come. Yet despite the threat of another storm, little could dampen Meryn's relief at finally escaping the clutches of the Weald.

A short walk later past a few outlying roundhouses, and he was standing on the edge of the village of Rudge, a larger community of maybe twenty dwellings gathered loosely together. He waited patiently as a small flock of sheep were encouraged along the narrow central lane towards a stockade, ready to be sold. Moving in further amongst the buildings, he saw that a number of people were doing their best to set up benches in the mud alongside the road. Some had even thatched rain covers to shelter their owners while they peddled their wares to the small crowd filtering by. As Meryn took it all in, relieved to be amongst his fellow man once more, two small children dashed past him laughing happily, and a moment later, an older girl appeared, calling out after them.

'Thea, Brom, come back, you little good-for-nothings!' As she pushed past, she bumped into Meryn, who was forced to step back, almost tripping over his own feet. She came to a halt.

'Sorry 'bout that... you all right?' She glanced after the fleeing youngsters then, shaking her head, turned back to regard Meryn, taking in the sword and bow.

'I'll be fine. At least, I will be, if I can find somewhere to dry out and get something to eat,' said Meryn, offering the girl a weak smile.

'The warriors are gathering through there.' She waved a hand past the market. 'Shouldn't wonder you'll find what you need with them.' The sound of stifled giggling drew the girl's attention back to the children and she sped off calling after them once more. Hoisting the sword and pack onto his shoulder, Meryn walked on towards the bustling market.

A heavy traffic of sheep, cattle and people had churned the street into thick mud and there was little escape from it even at the sides where the stalls stood; Meryn quickly became coated to the knees.

'New knife, my friend? Needles, or some pins for your good lady?' Meryn shook his head at the trader and pushed on, passing others making similar offers, from benches laden with a variety of items. There were tools, some of which he noted were poorly made, some items of clothing offered by two young girls who gazed at him open mouthed as he passed, and a number of stalls heavy under the weight of vegetables, pies, and pots. He stopped and watched with interest as an older man bartered some sheep for three Roman coins, a sack of grain and a short sword, and then moved on in search of the warriors' lodgings. Thunder rumbled closer now and the rain began to fall in earnest. Around him, people scurried for cover and Meryn picked up his pace, eager to get warm and dry. At last, he saw three chariots outside a large barn and guessed he was at the right place. A boy was leading two horses away from the closest chariot, and he could hear raised voices coming from within.

Dragging open the door in anticipation of a warm fire, he was about to walk inside, when a huge warrior came storming out towards him, forcing him to jump back out of the way. It took a moment to realise the warrior wasn't simply pushing past, but had been forcibly ejected by the small knot of fury and muscle that followed him out.

'Don't yer ever take the name of the Iceni 'n' blacken it with yer foul tongue,' spat the little man as he stood over his far larger opponent. He reached up and straightened the band of polished bronze he wore round his brow to keep in check a tangle of red hair, hair matched in its fiery colour by a long flowing beard. His eyes, behind a myriad of wrinkles, flashed light blue as he began menacingly shifting a large axe from one hand to the other, obviously waiting for the right moment to plant it in the other man's head.

The aggressive little man was dressed in the manner of the eastern Iceni tribe. Leather leggings, a heavy linen tunic and a coarse woollen cloak, pinned with a decorated brooch. The torque at his throat was thick and heavy, and looked to be made of some precious metal. The cloak, in comparison, appeared to have been made for a man of larger stature, as much of it was trailing behind him in the mud. Meryn decided that if the slurring of his words was any way to judge a man, then he was heavily into his cups.

'I meant no disrespect, Samel,' the fallen man stammered, as he got to his feet to tower over the bristling Samel. 'I's only said ...' but the big man had no time to finish as Samel noticed Meryn for the first time and promptly forgot his present troubles.

'Meryn, Meryn Link!' He pushed the big warrior out of his way with the edge of his axe and the man wandered back into the barn, muttering incoherently.

'As I live and breathe,' continued Samel, beaming up at Meryn. 'Meryn Link, and here ready to join with his oldest friend in battle.' He held out his arm and Meryn gripped it. They stood like this for several moments, forearm to forearm, happily slapping each other on the back in the pouring rain.

'Well met, Samel,' said Meryn, clearly delighted to have found the little man. 'It's been a long time.'

'It has indeed. Come. Drink with me,' said Samel, as they broke apart. 'You'll know a few of the others inside and you're sorely needed if we're to hold our heads high in battle over the coming weeks. Some among us still believe hulking size is the only requirement of a great warrior.' His face creased into a grin as he gazed up at Meryn, and tapped the side of his nose while lowering his voice to a loud whisper. 'Sometimes I need to cut a few of those big oafs down a bit, just to let them know who the real warriors are! Remind them that we're all the same size when lying in the mud, eh?'

He turned for the door as thunder crashed overhead and the rain tipped down in torrents, seemingly doing its best to remove the little hair left on Meryn's head before they got inside.

Meryn had known Samel since they were young and foolhardy enough to be part of a small raiding party that had regularly attacked Roman supply columns. They had hunted and been hunted up and down the land for years, until Meryn had judged he was too old to keep going, tried his hand at farming. To be back in the little man's company was like revisiting the past, and the two friends spent until late into darkness, drinking, talking and laughing together.

Meryn learned that Samel and his band were heading towards the growing army of someone called Ambrosius, and that they were sorely disappointed not to have found him already.

'It's confusing, to say the least,' moaned Samel. 'We'd set out to join with Vortigern, when we heard tell of this Ambrosius, and that he has returned as our true king, eldest son to old King Clarens, so they say. Anyway, now that you're with us it'll be like old times again.' Samel beamed at Meryn, before tipping up his leather tankard and then gazing about for something palatable with which to refill it.

'I have to find my young friends before I do anything else. 'Tis a thing of honour, a pledge of safety that I made and need to be able to keep, I have to find them.' Meryn pushed a flagon of mead towards Samel. 'It's a strange thing, but the spirits drew us together, and ever since then, there have been little things to remind me that there's something special about these young people.'

'Like your meeting with the druid? Or perhaps the birthing in the forest?' said Samel, grinning happily.

Meryn cringed. He had only just finished telling how he had finally found his way out of the forest. 'Well, maybe not delivering the child, but meeting the druid, yes, and then also finding that old sword. I mean, what would I want with a rusty old sword?' He took a long drink then belched softly as he lowered the tankard. 'Then there are those Picts that were taking such an interest in them. It may have been coincidence the first time with the raid on their village, but the same group catching up with them a second time?'

'They're rounding up children all over, or so we've heard. Looking for someone special.' Samel drew a dagger and stabbed it down into the table and his face took on a darker look. 'If my boys and me catch any, we'll put paid to them; you can count on that.' He pulled the dagger free and returned it to his belt.

'So where do you think these kids of yours have got to?'

Meryn's face creased in a frown. 'I wish I knew. The druid sent us south, said we'd meet a man and know him if we saw him.'

'That's just the sort of vague advice to be expected from a druid.' Samel spat out the word 'druid' with obvious distaste. 'Maybe it's me yer meant to find!' he continued happily, but Meryn shook his head.

'It's a pleasure to find you, Samel, but I think the druid was talking to the boys. Apparently, my task is to save a king, but I think I was meant to stick with them to do that.'

The little man's bushy red eyebrows rose in surprise. 'Saving a king is a worthy task if ever there was one, and another reason for you to join with us. We aim to join the army of a king, King Ambrosius. Maybe it's him you'll be saving?'

Meryn shook his head. 'No, I've made too many mistakes. First sending those poor boys away, and then losing the girl, they may all be dead for all I know. I'll get no chance to save any king as the druid foretold, and who knows… Britain may fall to the Saxons because of it.' He hung his head in his hands and Samel looked on in pity, shaking his head.

'You poor ol' fool, but then, maybe the spirits have just nudged you back on track, by pushing you into me? In my experience, that's just the sort of thing spirits will do. Don't explain nothing clearly, but push and pull a man till he's all messed up trying to figure them out, best to just let it all happen, I say. Tomorrow, we'll ride to join Ambrosius and find yer that king to save, eh? Now stop yer whining and find us another flagon of mead.'

It was late in the morning when the three chariots rode out of Rudge. The rain was still falling without let and it didn't appear as if it was going to stop any time soon. The chariots were heavy, uncomfortable contraptions that the horses slipped and struggled to pull through the thick mud of the village. As they left, they found slightly firmer ground, but it was still all Meryn could do to hang on to the side of the bouncing frame, trying to control the contents of his stomach. When they made it onto the main path beyond the village, the ride smoothed out and they picked up speed, however, it remained a discomfort with three men in a chariot designed to carry only two.

Samel appeared little affected by the previous night's drinking as his chariot led the small group towards the Roman road and regularly cracked his whip over the backs of the two dark brown mares; the powerful little horses drawing them along at a smart pace. As the morning wore on, Meryn became accustomed to the ride, his stomach settled down and he began to enjoy the experience a little more. Even his worries were beginning to fade a little. He was still heading south, and at this pace, his hopes began to rise that he might still catch up with the boys before they got into any harm. He consoled himself with the knowledge that he had seen the black Saxon and two of the Picts return to the forest camp without captives, and that maybe the boys had actually won through. The fate of Nineve, however, was still causing him concern. If she was with the druids, as he suspected, then she would at least be safe from the Picts. However, if she had somehow become lost in the forest... Meryn elected not to think like that, it didn't do him any good and instead concentrated on the road ahead.

The rain set in and fell without let for three full days of travel. Thankfully, the Roman road proved to be free of mud, unlike the local roads, and although the journey was somewhat miserable, it at least allowed the chariots to continue at a good pace. Towards the end of the third day, as the light was beginning to fade from the slate-grey sky, they left the hard surface of the Roman road, crested a rise, and saw the collection of huts and shelters that housed the hopes of the Britons. They had finally found Ambrosius and the collected might of the tribes.

* * *

Uther glanced up at the small group of chariots that had topped the rise behind where he and Cal were practising weapon skills with Ambrosius and some of the others. Groups of warriors from the various tribes had been drifting in for days now so it was only a momentary distraction. Sometimes a large group came in, but more often, it was smaller groups of two or three at a time, and then chariots and cavalry like those he had just seen, coming from one of the larger tribes or bands that had been part of the Roman army before it departed.

'Come on, Uther, concentrate!'

Uther snapped back in time to see the wooden sword flash towards him. He stepped to the side at the last moment and deflected the blow as Ambrosius had taught him, but his arms and shoulders were tiring. His guard dropped long enough for Ambrosius to jab him in the ribs and he fell to his knees, waiting for the pain to subside. As he crouched there, he wished he could go back into the warm roundhouse and dry out, but the practice would continue as it did every day while the army waited to do battle.

'You're doing better, little brother, but in battle, that sword would be real and it would have killed you.' Uther nodded, stood up, and launched himself at Ambrosius with a flurry of blows that drove the startled king stumbling back. When he had recovered himself, Ambrosius smiled, acknowledging a good combination of moves and some definite improvement from Uther.

Chapter 11

Nightmares, Dreams, and Reality

Cal jolted awake. In a distant corner of his mind, the howl of a wolf was slowly fading while the rich earthy scents of the forest continued to linger in his nostrils and the memory of a chill wind blowing through the trees still swam before his eyes. He was cold, but his body was slick with sweat.

Wiping the back of his hand across his forehead, he exhaled the breath burning his lungs and stared up into the darkness of the communal roundhouse. A lasting vision still played across his mind, of a new moon peeking from behind the clouds to reveal a company of wolves. He tried to dismiss it, but the vision stubbornly remained.

Uther's voice came as a whisper through the gloom. 'You had another dream, didn't you?'

Cal turned his head. He couldn't actually see Uther's face, but he heard the concern in his voice, and could imagine the worried frown on his friend's face.

'It's so real. As real as… as anything else is that's happened to us lately, Usher… sorry… Uther.' There was silence for a moment before he continued. 'That's another thing I can't get used to either.' He gave a great sigh. 'When did our lives suddenly become so complicated?

You're Usher from the village, not...' He left the sentence unfinished as tears began to sting his eyes.

Around them, Ambrosius and the six others continued to sleep, the sounds of snoring and coughing coming from more than one of them. Chill, rainy weather had brought its share of coughs and colds, and any warrior without a runny nose or touch of fever was the rare exception.

'When I dream, it's *real*,' continued Cal, lowering his voice. 'It's not like a normal dream; I'm actually there. The wolves are in the woods, near where we were riding today. They were watching us as we rode past, I know they were.'

'What are they waiting for?' Uther asked. Then throwing back his furs, he scuttled across to the embers of the fire, dropped on a few sticks, and bent down to blow life into them, coaxing the damp wood into producing a flame. It flared, lighting up his face and sending shadows dancing about the cold roundhouse. After feeding it some larger pieces, he crept back to his bed, still waiting for Cal to respond.

'I've tried to keep them out of my dreams, but it's getting harder and harder,' said Cal. He sat up, leaning upon one elbow, and stared into Uther's eyes, seeking some sign that his friend either understood him, or was about to dismiss the whole notion as another nightmare. 'I can run with them in my dreams, Uther. They're waiting for me to lead them, to take them on the hunt.'

'Then lead them, Cal.' Uther reached over and placed a hand upon his friend's arm. 'This whole experience is beyond anything we could ever call normal. I think we have to follow wherever fate and the spirits lead us. We have little choice at the moment.' The fire suddenly crackled and spat as someone dropped a log onto it. The man, still half-asleep, didn't look over at them, but Cal lay back down and tried to find a more peace-filled sleep, his mind still unsure where the divide really lay between dreams and reality.

* * *

Meryn had been in the camp of the Britons for five days, living alongside Samel and his men and spending much of his time brooding over the misfortunes that had befallen him since leaving the druid's well.

When they first arrived, there had been rumours around camp that the younger brother of Ambrosius had recently ridden in. However, it hadn't once dawned upon Meryn that this young prince, the boy, who, so the rumours claimed, had escaped capture as several hundred Saxon and Pict warriors scoured the country trying to find him, was one of the two boys he had also been searching for. With nearly three thousand men, women and children in the camp, and the number growing daily, there was little wonder the two hadn't crossed paths yet, but of course, it was only a matter of time.

The day began the same as the others since arriving. Meryn was training alongside Samel, the pair passing on their skills to some of the younger warriors who had arrived with ample bluster, yet little in the way of experience or training.

'Go on, hit him!' shouted Meryn. 'He's only a little runt of a fellow. Surely, a great hulking brute of a lad like you can beat a little red-haired mouse like him?'

Each time Meryn goaded the boy on, Samel glared across at him. Meryn knew that Samel hated any attention drawn to his size, and that he was dangerously close to being the target of the Iceni warrior's axe. However, the taunts were pushing the loud-mouthed youth into making several mistakes, which of course was good for Samel, and, he reasoned, for the lad's training. Better to learn here than the battlefield. He wasn't much more than a boy, and had twice suffered the consequences of a botched attack. With the first, he had received a kick to his stomach, and now the flat of Samel's axe to his backside had just sent him sprawling in the mud. The young warrior rose on this second occasion, humiliated, angry, and caked in mud. Meryn watched as the boy began circling, sweeping his sword from left to right, cutting the air with a blur of cold steel, biding his time rather than rushing in for once.

'Don't listen to him, boy;' growled Samel, 'all he can ever do is pluck that bow and flap his lips about facing an enemy. Archers are a cowardly bunch, hiding behind the real fighting warriors like you and me as we face our enemies blade to blade.' The boy was learning, but, between them, the training bout had progressed to something far more serious, and the lad looked to have murder on his mind.

'Remember, boy, we're only training. Don't do anything foolish. Nobody wants to get seriously hurt here, let's save that for the Saxons and stand down, eh?' But the young warrior wasn't listening. With shouts, and cheers of encouragement from his watching friends, he leapt forward and delivered a hefty strike toward Samel that would have taken the head from a lesser man. As he ducked beneath the whistling blade, Samel decided he was through with the lesson. Leaping forward, he drove his axe in a sweeping arc that sliced into the boy's leg, dropping him to the mud with a howl of agony.

When Samel stepped back, ready to defend himself lest the boy's friends jumped him, Meryn dashed forward, reaching the fallen fighter before anyone else. A quick examination proved Samel's aim to be true, it was merely a flesh wound, just enough to stop the boy and, hopefully, to bring him to his senses.

''Tis a tiny scratch and nothing more,' commented Samel, as he pushed past the circle of onlookers. He held out his hand and the young warrior hesitated, just for a moment before taking it, and they clasped forearms as warrior brothers.

'You're a fine fighting man, my young friend,' growled Samel, as the youth struggled to his feet. 'We'll knock a few more of those rough edges from you, and then I'll be happy to have you at my side when we meet the Saxons.' With that, he strode away, a giant of a man, even if he was only chest height to most.

Meryn bid the injured boy sit again and then, selecting several herbs from his pouch, prepared a mixture with a little water and rubbed the paste into the wound, his patient stifling a cry as he did so. That done, he pinched the two sides together and placed a large green leaf around it then bound it tightly with a strip of twisted bark.

Once he had finished, he helped the fallen warrior back to his feet as the cry of; 'Ambrosius!' was taken up by several around him. Men, women and several groups of children all surged forward pushing him along with them. Meryn tried to see where they were heading and glimpsed the tall figure of their king making his way through the ranks of training warriors, a huge grey battle-hound not far from his side.

This was the first time Meryn had seen Ambrosius so close and he was impressed. The young king was a striking figure; a strong, tanned face framed by long, unkempt hair, he was wearing armour that shone above the gloom of the day. He was talking to a band of warriors dressed in the clan colours of the southern Dumnonii, greeting them as old friends. After a few moments, he walked on, stopping to talk to others, before encouraging them to continue in their practice and offering advice.

It was then that Meryn noticed that two of the group following in the trail of Ambrosius appeared somewhat familiar. He began pushing his way closer through the crowd of warriors; his stride lengthening as he realised it really was them.

'Usher... Cal?' There was a lot of noise from the crowding warriors around them and it took Meryn several attempts before Cal heard his name being called and glanced over his way. Meryn saw Cal grin in recognition then he turned to tug on Usher's arm, pulling him round until he too saw Meryn. They hurried across, shouting greetings as they came, and hugged him, clearly delighted to see him after being parted for so many days. Unfortunately, the first question from Cal's lips immediately sobered Meryn, bringing him back to the truth of his inadequacy as a guide and protector.

'Meryn, thank the spirits you're safe. Where's Nineve?'

Meryn stared into Cal's eyes then glanced across at Usher. He saw the smiles slide from their faces, and felt his heart drop with them.

'Meryn? Where is she? Where's Nineve? She was with you, wasn't she?' Cal reached out and grabbed the old archer's arm, desperately searching his face for answers.

'She's with the druids, boy,' said Meryn, his voice little more than a whisper. 'She helped me escape from the Picts, I don't quite know how she got free, but she did, and then cut my bonds, but then she was gone.'

'Gone? What do you mean gone? She's eight years old, she's not allowed to just go!'

'Steady, Cal. Let's give Meryn a chance to tell us what happened, shall we?' Uther drew the trembling Cal away and Meryn followed as they strode in silence along the muddy walkways of the camp to the roundhouse, ignoring everything else around them.

Pushing through the door-flap, Cal dropped down in the darkness by the central fire, and stared up at Meryn, waiting for some kind of explanation. Uther sat down next to him and began feeding wood into the flames while Meryn gathered himself, ready to try and explain what he had gone through. When he did start speaking, it all came out in a rush as he confessed everything that had happened and all the mistakes he had made since they parted. He told how the Picts had captured them as they fled through the fog, and of how Nineve had managed to cut the rope binding his hands, only to have completely disappeared when he finally freed his legs moments later.

'Last thing she said was that she was all right, and I was to tell you she'd see you soon. Then, after I'd gotten my feet free, I glanced up, and she was gone... vanished. I spent days combing through the forest, searching for some sign of her, but found nothing more than a single footprint, and that might not have been hers.' He went on to tell them of the birthing and as Ambrosius stepped into the roundhouse, he had just finished telling of his meeting with Samel and the others. Meryn fell to his knees before his king, only to be drawn to his feet a moment later by a smiling Ambrosius.

'I thank you for your support,' said Ambrosius, 'and if you are the archer my brother has told me so much about, then you are most welcome at my hearth.' Meryn nodded and told how he had met Uther and Cal, and then of his recent journey in the Weald. Once he had done, he lapsed into a sullen silence as Uther took his turn to tell Meryn of their escape from the Saxons and of their fortuitous meeting with Ambrosius.

Ambrosius had arrived with four others, and as they became comfortable about the fire, Uther soon had them all captivated with his description of the Roman Villa and their narrow escape from Horsa. As the tale unfolded, Meryn felt his grim expression, turn to one of surprise when he heard how Usher had discovered he was actually named Uther, was the brother to Ambrosius, and how they had been parted as children to secure the line.

The talk continued long after daylight had faded into night. They cooked a meal of venison and barley porridge and the conversation turned to war, plans for the future and the parts each would play in the coming days.

Ambrosius spoke of the tribes that were still sending in their warriors and how they continued to be frustrated by the lack of any real information about Vortigern and the Saxons.

'I have some of my most trusted people visiting the tribes, spreading the news that we're building a united fighting force to meet the Saxon threat, and as you know, our ranks continue to grow. Others are out trying to find something of what Vortigern and the Saxons are planning. However, so far anyway, none have returned with any real information beyond that Saxon boats continue to land. We suspect that our enemies are gathered at Dinas Emrys. It's Vortigern's stronghold in the mountains of Cymru, about ten days' march from here. Until we know more, we can only stay here and continue to gather strength.'

'Well, my path is clear at least,' said Meryn. 'I spent many days on Nineve's trail and I aim to continue until I find her.' He placed a hand on Cal's shoulder. 'You two are in good company here. You found the man the druid sent us searching for, and now you have to stay and support him. I believe that Nineve is with the druids, so I mean to find her and try to discover what interest they have in her. I shall go to Glastenning, to the druid council, they must know where she is, but then of course, whether they'll talk to me when I get there is another thing, and even if they do, there's little chance it will make any sense, but I have to try, and so I'll start there.' He glanced over to Ambrosius.

'I would surely hate to miss fighting for my king. There was a full moon two nights ago. If I were to return before the coming of the next full moon, would I be in time to march with you?'

Ambrosius shrugged, and then nodded. 'I doubt we'll be ready before then, so you may well be in time to join us, but hurry, we need trained archers.'

Meryn stood up. 'Then I shall leave at first light.' He turned back to Cal. 'Don't worry, I will find your sister. Would you boys walk with me back to my camp? I have something there that I think is meant for Uther.'

A few moments later, as they stepped from the comfort of the round-house, the cold and darkness of the night covered them in its damp, chill cloak and a cold wind quickly robbed them of the fire's lingering warmth. Thankfully, it had stopped raining, but clouds still covered the moon and they had to wait until their eyes adjusted to what little light there was.

Uther glanced about, trying to see something of the camp as Cal and Meryn came out behind him. The sound of singing and the beating of drums floated through the darkness, and then a few muted conversations and laughter coming from a little further away. He stared into the darkness trying to make out the path, but other than a few stars, the only light was coming from the sentry fires on the perimeters of the camp and a few isolated fires within, to help people move about.

'It's freezing out here,' muttered Cal, as he came alongside. 'Is that you, Uther?' His breath emerged as a plume of white in the cold air before the wind quickly snatched it away.

'Yes, it's me. Do you think it's going to snow?'

'It'll be another few weeks before it snows,' said Meryn, joining them, 'although, it certainly feels cold enough.' He held up the burning branch taken from the roundhouse fire, and his face shone bright in its guttering flame. 'Ready?'

Keeping close together, they slowly picked their way through the sleeping camp, passing more sounds of conversation, snoring and the angry tones of an argument as they searched for Meryn's camp. When they finally made it, they were heartened to see a warm fire awaiting them with Samel and the others gathered around sharing a pot of stew. Samel glanced over as they entered and welcomed them with a cry of relief.

'Meryn! Oh, thank the spirits you're back. My head's pounding fit to burst. I'm in need of one of your infusions.'

Meryn nodded. 'Sit with Samel for a moment, boys. I'll fetch willow bark and feverfew for him and the... well, the thing I have for you, Uther. Although right now I feel a bit silly giving the rusty old thing to you,' he muttered, as he moved away.

He was back a few moments later, and after handing the fur-wrapped bundle to Uther, he sat down and began to sort through his herb pouch. Finding what he was looking for, he put several pinches of dried leaves and some powder into a small wooden cup then ladled in some hot water from a pot hanging above the fire.

'I wish I had some honey to offer, but I don't.' He offered the steaming cup across to Samel.

The smell of the infusion filled the hut with a delicate flowery scent and Samel took the cup with a smile of gratitude.

'It smells wonderful, thank you.'

Meryn glanced round at the sound of Uther's voice, and saw him lift the sword from its wrapping. As it came free, he felt a tremor of disbelief run through him. Gone was the rusty tarnished relic that he had taken from the druid's circle. The sword that Uther held up gleamed in the firelight, its blade polished to a brilliant silvery sheen. Its bronze crosspiece intricately engraved with the body and scales of a dragon, and the pommel, as it rose above the black leather grip, emerged as the roaring head of the mythical beast.

'This is the sword, Excalibur,' murmured Uther in awe. 'I have no idea why I know it has a name, but it does, and I know it to be my blade. Where did you get it, Meryn? And how did you know it was meant for me?'

Meryn remained silent, staring at the sword, his mind trying to understand the change in the weapon, or at least the illusion of change, had it really been a rusty relic?

'The spirits and the druids are playing some great game here, boy. We're merely stones, caught in the flow of their plans. I discovered that sword within a druid's circle and also heard the name "Excalibur" when I touched it, but I can't say how I knew it to be yours. It's just one more question I shall put to the druids when I find them.'

Uther tied the sword at his hip and thrilled at the feeling of power it gave him. He glanced across at the old bowman. 'Thank you for bringing it to me, Meryn.'

'You are most welcome, Uther. May it protect and never fail you.'

Life returned to its normal routine within the camp until, just two days later, with a chariot borrowed from Samel, Meryn headed out to the Roman road. It was early as he drew away, a cold grey sky floating past reflecting the bleak landscape that lay beneath. Winter had placed its first frosty grip upon the land, painting the camp and surrounding countryside with a dusting of white that covered the mud of the fields, bringing with it a temporary icy beauty. The heavy chariot wheels rumbled and jarred as they carried him over the frozen ground, crunching through the ice-capped puddles. When he reached the stone surface of their road, he mumbled a silent prayer. It was a prayer that carried thanks to the spirits of the land for allowing the Romans to build the road, yet also an apology that the stone would cut him off from their guidance. It would take him in speed and relative comfort almost all the way to Holy Glastenning, and at its heart, the Isle of Avalon, spiritual home of the druids.

His mind still whirled in a turmoil of emotions as he tried to piece everything together. The druids had a strong influence in what was happening in the land, and nothing could be taken at face value, that much was becoming more and more apparent. The decision to go to

Glastenning had been made, but he was unsure if it was because he had chosen to seek word of Nineve, or that they had designed for him to come to them. Whichever it was, there would be no turning back. He would arrive at the sacred Isle of Avalon before sunset the following day.

* * *

As the lone chariot headed out, the practice fields were already ringing with the sounds of training. Close to the road, a small group had gathered, watching intently as two combatants pushed each other in an entertaining show of their abilities.

Ambrosius stepped back, his face creasing in a frown of concentration as he became aware of the silence around them; all other practice in the area having long since ceased to witness, what was becoming, a most unusual bout.

He had been sparring for some time, but what had started out as just another lesson had quickly escalated into a battle of wits, plunging him into a situation that found him reaching deep into his reserves of ability and stamina.

He sensed, rather than saw, the blur of shimmering steel and moved swiftly, blocking the strike as it came into his left side. A fraction of a moment later, he just managed to retrieve his blade in time to defend against the next sweeping cut as it flew down at him from an unthinkable angle. It seemed that whatever he did, he was still being forced back. Stumbling under an unexpected blur of cuts and thrusts, at last he finally managed to check his opponent, and put his superior strength and Roman training behind a combination of his own in an attempt to regain the advantage over his far smaller companion. He realised he was becoming desperate to take back some control of the fight. However, try as he might, it soon became apparent that no advantage was going to be found and he was forced back to a more defensive strategy. It wasn't enough. With a sharp intake of breath, he threw himself backwards, narrowly avoiding the bright blade as it thrust towards him, the point missing him by a hair's-breadth and he slipped in the mud, to land in an undignified heap.

He gazed up and stared along the length of steel at the opponent who had bested him. Drawing ragged breaths into his lungs, he waited for the moment when he would be able to speak again.

'That sword... has changed you...' He gasped, then coughed and accepted the help of two of his men to regain his feet. 'I'm glad you're on our side, brother. You were showing promise before this Excalibur was gifted to you, but now...' He shook his head in wonder. 'The spirits favour you, that much is clear.'

Uther studied the blade and replaced it in its sheath before answering. 'I don't know what to say,' he said softly. 'When I grasp Excalibur, it's almost as if we become one. Time runs slower and it feels as if energy is pouring into me, almost to the point of bursting. It's as if I have all the time in the world to dance with the blade.' He gave a grin and looked about him at the gathered warriors. 'Who will be next to test me?' There were some takers, but as the day drew on it was apparent that none could hope to best him.

* * *

The wolves gathered around, tails wagging with excitement as they licked his muzzle, welcoming him back into the pack. Then they ran, and a feeling of exhilaration filled Cal as he felt the cold wet earth beneath his paws and finally gave himself over fully to being a wolf.

The trees were soon behind them, giving way to rolling, open meadow and a star-filled night that stretched overhead to light their way. The smell of wood-smoke from the humans' camp gradually faded, replaced with the rich aroma of damp earth and grassland. Cal rejoiced in the feeling of freedom and knew it was a love that the other wolves shared as they ran beside him.

Rabbits fled in front of them and he experienced a great delight when he saw their heads pop up, eyes shining in the starlight, and ears twitching as they waited for them to pass, only to disappear again when one of the other wolves got too close. They smelt good.

Back into the forest again, the pack stopped and waited while those that had lagged behind to feed caught up. Cal raised his head and howled into the darkness, calling the rest of the pack towards him, and then as they began to arrive, he set off through the trees once more, eager to be moving.

Later, as the sky in the east began to lighten with the first blush of a promised sunrise, the wolves found a place to rest amongst the caves of a rocky escarpment, and the pack settled down to sleep away the daylight hours. When the sun set once more, they would be rested, ready to hunt, and then to run once more.

* * *

'You spin a fine tale, storyteller, wolf creatures, ancient curses, magical swords and the like, but you're not still trying to tell us all this is true, are you?' The red-faced farmer ignored the elbow he was receiving in his stomach from his wife, accompanied by the cold stares and mumbled comments from his friends and neighbours.

Uther tried to focus on the man, dragging his attention back to the present. He glanced across at Calvador Craen, but his old friend gave no indication that he had heard the question, or was even aware that the tale had been interrupted.

Uther sighed. 'Well, I couldn't honestly say if it's true or not. However, I am telling my story as I remember it to be true, warts and all. If it makes you more comfortable to believe it to be a tale of fantasy, then I shall take no offence.' He drew on his pipe and gathered his thoughts while the farmer smiled as if he had just won some kind of contest.

'Where was I?' Uther's brow creased in thought. 'I think I should tell you more of Meryn and his determination to find Nineve. Now some of you may have heard tell of the Isle of Avalon, lying as it does at the centre of Holy Glastenning. It was so named because it rises at the centre of a sea of marshes. When Meryn reached the end of the road and finally arrived at the Isle it was sunset, the light was filtering through the clouds and into the mists of the marsh, painting the air with a strange orange light that Meryn found decidedly unsettling, to say the least. It made him cautious and he was wise enough to approach the druids' Tor quietly, leading the horses by hand over the last part of the narrow path before stepping up and onto the Isle itself. The air was filled, as he later told it, with the beating of drums and the mournful droning of horns. Meryn claimed that the steady chanting of the druids only joined in as he set his first foot on the Isle itself, and that when the voices began, they vibrated through him to the very roots of his soul.

Chapter 12

AVALON

'Steady, girl... *whooo there*, steady now.' The younger of the two mares was jumping and shuffling nervously, making the chariot creak and shake as Meryn tried to calm her. 'Hush now. Don't you go listening to those ol' noises, that's just those druids playing their games.'

As he held the harness, stroking and patting the horse's neck, its eyes rolled and it snorted, and then with a sudden flick of its head, it pulled away hard and he struggled to keep hold. Beside it, the older more experienced mare held her back, trembling but still trusting in Meryn to guide her. The archer drew a deep breath, unable to blame the horses for their discomfort and gazed about, trying to calm his own beating heart.

It was late, the sun was setting, and a thin mist was beginning to rise over the marsh rushes. In the fading orange light, it was getting harder to see where the track ended and the marsh began. It was becoming dangerous. Meryn wondered, and not for the first time, about going back and making camp some distance away until morning rather than continuing, but then gathering his courage, urged the younger mare on with a tug on her harness towards a large standing stone which marked the end of the path and the start of the Isle. This, he decided, was where he would leave them and seek the druids.

The beating of drums continued to build, floating along with the deep melancholy wail of the horns that were rising and falling in great waves of sound, rolling down the Tor over him, then out across the reeds. The chanting was also getting louder, and didn't seem to be coming from any one direction. The eerie sounds were helping unnerve both Meryn and the horses.

'Calm down, my lovelies… there's nothing here to hurt you.' He cast about, trying to see where the voices were coming from. They sounded close, but only reeds, trees and the Tor stared back at him.

Tying the horses to a convenient branch, he continued to mutter assurances as they danced from side to side, the younger one still seeking an opportunity to bolt. Using lengths of cloth to cover their eyes and ears to lessen the distractions, he secured grain bags round the horses' necks. The younger mare shied at first, but then as she smelled the grain she quietened down and began to eat, ears still twitching at each change in the sounds as Meryn unhitched the chariot ready to push it a safe distance away.

Meryn gazed up the hill towards the Tor, and began to walk. The top remained hidden from the base of the hill because apple trees, planted to either side of a narrow path that wound its way upward, obscured his view. The trees had lost their leaves this late in the year, and the only evidence that they were actually apple trees was the few rotting black remains scattered amongst sodden brown leaves beneath.

A figure stepped out, stopping Meryn with a jolt.

'Be welcome here at Avalon,' intoned the druid. 'You may pass and walk the path to enter the first world of spirit.' The druid's face was gaunt. He was bearded and smeared with ash and mud. His eyes held a vacant, distant expression. A long grey piece of cloth cinched at the waist with a belt of twisted bark was his only article of clothing. It was dirty and torn, and appeared to offer minimal protection from the cold, yet the druid showed little concern. The chanting became louder, joining the drums and horns in a crescendo, and then stopped abruptly, dropping silence like a weight upon the Tor. Before Meryn had opportunity to speak, the druid waved him past, and then placed a hand upon his arm as he drew level.

'There is no place for edged steel upon the path of Avalon.' His eyes slowly dropped to the sword at Meryn's waist. He stood unmoving as Meryn untied the sword and placed it, together with a long knife, into his outstretched arms. 'Walk in peace upon this sacred Isle, Brother.' The druid bowed his head and walked backward, fading from sight amongst the copper-toned mist that wove through the apple trees.

A cool breeze caressed Meryn's face and his fears rose threatening to overwhelm him. Digging deep to gather his resolve, he walked on.

The path continued to lead upwards, the drums, horns and chanting accompanying him with every step. Twice he passed druids standing silently amongst the trees, each time he expected them to approach but they ignored him, their minds apparently otherwise engaged. Then, as he rounded the second turn of the path, a young woman stepped from between the trees and held her palm out towards him, firmly blocking his progress.

'There is no room upon the path of Avalon for material beliefs, nor delusions of self. Shed them now and walk on, healer of the flesh, guardian of the dragon line. Pass now into the second world of spirit.' Reaching up, she gently touched his forehead, and then her arm dropped and she stepped to the side, casting her eyes to the ground as she backed into the mist.

Meryn waited a moment, unsure of what her words could mean, and then walked past, studying what he could still see of her as he did so. She appeared young, but maybe not as young as he had first thought. Long golden hair tied in heavy braids framed a pretty face with a thumbprint of blue woad set in the middle of her ash-smeared forehead. The last thing he did as he passed was to look down and notice that her feet were bare, muddy and wet.

By now, the last remnants of daylight had all but disappeared. The sunset was no more than a bruise on the distant horizon. Gazing ahead through the gloom, he could just make out figures setting burning torches, drifting through the trees, parting the mist like spirit wraiths. When he glanced behind him, the girl had gone.

He trudged on, moving higher, and as he did, the chanting rose and fell, before dropping to little more than a whisper that seemed to dance amongst the trees, born on the freshening wind. The drums and horns also became fainter, and he was more aware of his own laboured breathing as he strode ever upwards. As he reached the first of the flickering torches, another druid stepped out in front of him. It was an old man this time, bearded, wearing a wrap of dirty linen with a hood of the same material covering his head. His eyes gazed past Meryn, out into the gloom, staring at something that only he could see. He was leaning upon a heavy staff, with shells, leaves and polished amber hanging from the top. By now, Meryn was feeling light-headed and was actually glad for the rest. He stood swaying slightly, regaining his breath as he waited for the druid to speak.

'You awaken into the third world of spirit.' The druid passed the staff to Meryn who took it gratefully and leaned his weight upon it. Beneath his fingers, the smooth wood felt familiar and comfortable in his grip, he began to feel a little stronger. 'Time occurs within an instant,' continued the druid. 'Past, present and future, within time, we are all as one, split amid experience, forever striving to return home.' The druid bowed his head. 'Walk on, Brother.'

'Gibberish,' muttered Meryn, and then pushed on.

The path was becoming even narrower, each shadow the spluttering torches cast seemed to rise up and writhe about him, dancing to the sounds on the Tor like creatures born of nightmare, taunting him and distracting his progress, challenging his belief in the reality of his surroundings.

At three further points on the path, druids stopped him, welcoming him to different levels of the spirit world. He had long since abandoned any attempt at trying to understand what was happening. It had all become a dream from which he could not awake. So far, he had been given, a crude clay cup filled with cool refreshing water to 'cleanse his mind of barriers and borders' a linen wrap to 'shelter him from fear and prejudice' and lastly, a crown of thorns to 'remember every lesson humanity has learned, and then suffer the pain of man as we continue on in ignorance.'

Meryn had winced and almost stumbled as the druid placed the crown on his head, but he had leaned on the staff and allowed the druid to push it firmly into place. Now, as he struggled on, blood running down his face and his breath laboured in his ears, he felt waves of emotion building deep within him. It was all becoming too much, too confusing. The drums, horns and chanting were battering his senses and despite the chill wind, he felt his flesh was burning up; it was all he could do to place one foot in front of the other and stagger onwards.

Using the wrap to wipe blood from his eyes, he squinted around, trying to see how far he had come. It was dark. Little was visible beyond the path. A star-filled sky stretched overhead and the moon was rising in the distance, its light reflecting upon a distant lake far away towards the horizon. Then he noticed a halo of colours surrounding the flames from the torches, and as his eyes sought further, he saw a similar aura of light flickering around the apple trees. Gazing about, the phenomenon was repeated around every object within sight. He stared at his staff as it pulsed with a purple and blue light, then down at his hands, which reflected the same colours but the edges were tinged with orange and yellow. The chanting rose once more and, drawing a breath deep into his lungs, he forced himself on, the cold wind blowing even harder, compelling him to lean forward as he struggled to place every step.

Towards the top, where the path began to level, a smaller figure appeared. She stood, waiting for him to approach, arms crossed in front of her and a blue and purple aura of flickering light surrounding her. Meryn wiped at his eyes again, and then blinked to clear his vision, his mind struggling to settle.

'Nineve?' Quickening his step, he called to her again. 'Nineve! Nineve, is that really you?' He knew the wind was robbing his voice of any power even as he shouted out to her, but to see her after fearing her lost for so long, he couldn't stop himself trying.

As he drew closer, she put a finger to her lips and stepped forward.

'Welcome back to Avalon and the seventh world of spirit, Merlyn.'

He gazed down at her, trying to understand. It was Nineve, but he also recognised that the small girl before him was now far more than the eight-year-old child he had so recently come to know.

'Are you well, Nineve? Have they... hurt you? Nineve, why... ?' The girl rose up on her toes and pressed a finger to his lips to silence him.

'All is well, Merlyn. You have travelled the world of earthly illusions for many long years and now, you have walked the path into spirit in search of me, just as you promised long ago that you would. Past, present and future, all are as one, do you remember? It is here, upon Avalon, long ago, that you chose you would awaken... let go, Merlyn. Your mind still struggles to hold onto earthly beliefs. Let... go...' her voice seemed to echo through his head. 'Remember your spirit, Merlyn... remember.' Reaching up, she lifted the woven thorn-branch from his brow, and then smeared ash down his cheeks and across his forehead. 'You are the druid Merlyn, and now is the time for your spirit to reclaim its memories... for the circle shall soon be complete.' She drew him along the path to the top of the hill, and then towards an altar of large forbidding stones.

He stumbled forward in confusion, peering round through bleary eyes as he allowed her to lead him, his mind frantically grappling to make some sense of everything that was happening. Surrounding the central stones, slowly closing towards them, were some thirty druids. The air was filled with chanting, the beating of drums and blowing horns of every description. They reached the altar; Nineve took his hand and placed it gently against the largest stone. He felt the cold rough surface beneath his fingers and memory hit him like a thunderclap.

Several moments went by. He didn't remember falling to his knees, but there he was with the cool stone upon his forehead, the only sound was the whispering of the wind. Hauling himself up with the help of his staff, he turned to regard the circle of now silent druids.

'I am, once again, the druid Merlyn. I thank you for the awakening of my spirit. It has all been an… interesting experience. The circle will soon be complete.'

Nineve walked towards him, a smile lighting her face. 'Welcome back, Merlyn. We find ourselves, once again, amid interesting times, you and I.'

Merlyn drew in a deep breath and gazed about him. He felt the wind upon his face, saw the stars in the sky, felt the weight upon his bones, and recalled now how all this had been so necessary, *would* be so necessary. The rebirth of souls was a serious business, and as Nineve had rightly pointed out, these were indeed interesting times. 'I thank you, my Lady of the Lake. It is good to know you once more, and to know also that the spirits have brought us together at the appointed time; for soon the dragon shall arise.'

* * *

Dinas Emrys, Vortigern's stronghold, was hewn from the same dull grey stone as the ragged mountains that surrounded it. In summer, it stood cold, damp and drafty, a bleak colourless monument that rose in testament to the fears of its owner. Now, with winter setting in, it had become positively inhospitable. The occupants, gathered in the large hall, were wearing their thickest furs as protection from the cold wind that whistled freely through the numerous gaps in the stonework, howling like spirits possessed as it wrapped around them, chilling them despite all efforts to keep warm. The fireplace was huge, but then so was the room. Twelve people sat watching from the heavy oak table as Vortigern, flanked by two dark robed mages, raged and vented his disappointment at his guests. Eight of the twelve present were Saxons.

'What good are you to me? Constantine's brat, Ambrosius, gathers his army and the tribes rally to him, it sickens me. His brother and the girl have still to be found and, for all we know, they may already be with him.' Vortigern, his face contorting in barely controlled anger, paced beside the large open fireplace, his voice echoing around the stone chamber. 'Did I really ask so much?'

The man who claimed the right to rule the Britons wasn't a big man. In fact, he had a thin frame and carried himself with a slight stoop. What he did possess, however, was a temper that once unleashed could break a man twice his size. He felt no fear for the giant Saxon and his men. Deep-set eyes, grey and as cold as his fortress, stared out at the Saxons over a cruelly hooked nose and a short black beard.

'Sit down,' growled Hengist; throwing the bone he had been gnawing over his shoulder. Two large dogs that had been waiting patiently, drooling with anticipation, pounced on it, growling and fighting over the offering. Sucking the meat juices from his fingers, the Saxon leader stared up at the glaring Vortigern, clearly unimpressed by the King of the Britons. 'Sit down. You are blocking whatever heat the fire offers.' He wiped his hand down his heavy tunic, adding to the variety of stains already upon it. 'We will keep looking for the children, although I still fail to see why. I place little store in the visions of these mages.' His eyes flickered to the two hooded figures. 'We should just meet with this Ambrosius and drive him into the sea. My men are warriors, while most of his rabble have never even held a sword!'

'You gather the children because I wish it so!' stormed Vortigern. 'When we kill Ambrosius and you leave, I do not want any other members of his line remaining to threaten my rule. We shall find the brat and end the line of Constantine for good. As for the girl, I have it on good authority that she is important to my enemies, she must also die. Do not question me, just do what I have paid you for, and find them. Also, be aware that my intention is to march upon Ambrosius within one cycle of the moon. Be sure that you and your men are ready!' He turned and strode from the hall with the four other Britons hurrying after him.

'We should kill them all now and take this land for ourselves. Enough of this searching for children and making happy with blustering fools.'

'Hush, brother.' Hengist scowled at Horsa across the table. 'We shall claim this land but only when the time is right. For now, we shall accept their gold, eat their meat,' he picked up a rabbit's leg and waved it at his brother, 'and bide our time. Let us use them for a while. Allow them to kill each other before we grind what remains of their warriors into submission.' He pushed the platter of meats to his brother then lifted his tankard of ale and tipped it back. The little that didn't dribble onto his chest made it down his throat and he belched loudly before slamming the tankard back down onto the table. 'Nothing has stopped us so far. We control nearly all land between these gods-cursed mountains and the eastern coast. The tribes of the Britons are pathetic; any backbone they may once have possessed has been bred out of them by the Romans. This Ambrosius will fold as all the rest have.'

'So why pander to this fool Vortigern?' Horsa slammed his fist onto the table and rose unsteadily to his feet. 'Why, dear brother, do we remain in this rat hole of a fortress freezing our arses off? Why haven't we stretched his miserable carcass across a rock, cut the living heart from his chest and fed it to the crows?'

Hengist glanced up at his brother and then picked over the plates for another piece of meat. Satisfied with his choice he gestured for his brother to sit down and then reached across and patted his arm when he did. 'We do what we do because I say so. I lead and I say it is better to unite with Vortigern against the rest of the Britons and then, when our boats arrive with the spring thaw, we can play a different game. For now, eat and drink! Our hosts would expect nothing less. Later, we get to hunt. Our host complains of wolves in the area scaring away the game and I have promised we will rid him of this inconvenience.'

'More likely his foul moods and sour expression have scared all the game away.' A rare smile split Horsa's face. 'That or it's more probable that these cursed mountains hold little of any nourishment for game. Beyond the forest there is nothing more than rocks, wind and rain. We are the only things skulking up here. I doubt there are wolves here at all; he's simply running from shadows again. However, if there are wolves, they will at least prove a diversion until we get to kill...' The sentence was left unfinished as three servants entered and hurriedly dropped more food onto the table. They were obviously frightened of the Saxon guests, which pleased Hengist and his men. They backed out as quickly as they could, followed by a string of threats and laughter. As the heavy door slammed shut, the dogs resumed their squabbling and the Saxons returned to their feast.

* * *

'They were hard times for all, what with the Romans leaving. It left our Britain open to all sorts, but then I have Saxon blood in my veins, as do many here, so I can't complain about that.' There were murmurs of agreement in the room and Uther glanced up, only just realising he had been interrupted again.

'Sorry?'

'Your story, I remember my grandfather talking about it when I was a child. Course it were long before his time as well, but I like the way you tell it as if you were really there.' There was silence around the fire as Uther blinked across, trying to make out the old woman's face. It was the farmer's wife this time, her husband smiling quietly, beside her.

'I was there.' Uther looked across at Calvador Craen who had turned around to observe the exchange.

'I'm sorry, storyteller, but the times of which you speak were...'

'Please allow my old friend to continue with his tale,' interrupted Calvador. He stood up and placed a hand protectively on Uther's shoulder. 'I promise you won't be disappointed.' Thunder boomed outside and the sound of a loose shutter banging came from another part of the inn. The storm was getting closer.

'Don't you worry none, sir, I'm happy to listen to the tale; I was only pointing out where it just couldn't be right, but don't you mind me.' She settled back down and her husband whispered something in her ear that made her smile.

Ignoring them, Calvador Craen addressed his friend. 'The Saxons led a fine wolf hunt, eh, Uther? Tell us about that. I for one would like to hear more about the wolves.'

Chapter 13

CRY OF A WOLF

Cal lifted his nose and sniffed at the damp air. People smell; an odour thick with stale sweat, cooked meat, ale, mead and smoke. It was drifting faintly through the trees, mixing unpleasantly with the fresh and earthy aromas of the forest. He turned his head and sniffed again, seeing several of the other wolves do the same before whining and glancing his way. Fear of man was a deep primal instinct for the wolves and they wanted to leave.

Padding forward to the edge of the trees, Cal gazed up at the stone fortress. It was ugly, a small mountain of piled rocks set starkly apart from the surrounding land and forest. It put a bad taste in his mouth just to look at it. He licked his chops. A breeze rustled the trees bringing more bad odours. Glancing to either side, he searched for the source of the offending smell. There, moving close to the edge of the trees, a small group of men, blind to the darkness of the night beyond what the light from their burning torches revealed. They were hurrying along, trying hard to keep up with two large dogs that were pulling hard against the ropes that held them. The dogs had their noses pressed to the ground, their tails wagging furiously as they followed the scent of the wolf pack.

Hunters again. Three times over the last eight nights that the wolves had kept their vigil, the doors to the fortress had swung open and Saxons and Picts had come out seeking to hunt and kill them. So far,

Cal had managed to keep the wolves one step ahead, combining his instincts as a wolf with his memory of being human; once again, he knew it was time to leave. Giving a short bark, he turned and led the pack on a steady run south through the dark forest, crossing and re-crossing their path to confuse the dogs and finally following a small stream for a stretch. As the sound of barking faded into the distance, they slowed to a steady lope having enjoyed the exertion of the run, their tongues lolling happily from the side of their mouths, their breath steaming in the cold night air. They continued towards what had become their regular daytime lair, a series of small caves, high up amongst a rocky outcrop that offered a good viewpoint should the hunters ever manage to get this close.

Dawn was lending a rosy glow to the eastern sky by the time they arrived. After a last check to see that the pack was together and safe, Cal lay down in the entrance of a small cave; the sound of the pack howling, calling the few stragglers to catch up, fading as he fell into a contented sleep.

The following night, the wolves returned to the fortress and Cal immediately noticed a difference as he reached the edge of the trees. A lot more people had arrived, with more wagons, and there was much more activity than on any of the previous nights. Behind him, the wolves were nervous, making small whining sounds as they milled about, unable to settle. Turning round, he wagged his tail, and then stood, walked out of the tree line to show he had no fear of the humans' camp, and sat down to observe what was happening.

There were thousands of men now camped in front of the fortress, an area that just a few days before had been clear desolate hillside. As he tried to take it all in, he saw more arriving, Saxons, some Picts, and a few others he didn't recognise, lighting their way with burning torches. This new group was directed to an area close to the forest, and he watched with interest as they made camp before retreating into the trees to wait.

Around him, the wolves grew more restless, clearly unhappy as the sounds of men throwing up shelters and calling to each other drifted back to them. When three men entered the trees to find firewood, the wolves slunk back into the shadows to watch silently. They also watched Cal, waiting for him to signal them to leave, but he didn't. Instead, as the men left with their wood, he trotted forward, snarling when one of the wolves made to follow him, giving a clear message that they were to stay where they were.

Knowing the humans had limited night-vision, the silver grey wolf that carried the consciousness of Calvador moved silently into the Saxon camp. The humans' scent was heavy in the cold night air and was thick in odours most unpleasant. It mixed with the slightly more acrid smoke that drifted from the camp's numerous fires to aggravate his highly sensitive nose. Moving from shadow to shadow, he padded amongst the hastily constructed huts and roundhouses, avoiding several stumbling figures, and listening to the few whispering voices that he came across; but any conversation he managed to overhear was in a language he couldn't understand. Feeling slightly frustrated, he began to make his way back to the security of the forest. He set off, but then noticed a large fire crackling and spluttering close to one of the largest huts with several people gathered around it. More logs were tossed on and glowing embers burst up to float away into the dark star-filled sky, the sight enticing him closer as the flames forced the darkness to retreat and dance as shadows, eager to rush back in should the flames begin to falter. Six men stood about the fire, warming themselves as they passed a flagon of mead between them, talking loudly and laughing at some shared joke.

Keeping low, Cal crept forward.

The language was the same foreign tongue he had been hearing elsewhere in the camp, which again meant he couldn't understand anything. However, something made him wait a little longer, maybe it was merely the comforting lure of the fire. He contented himself in studying the men.

They were big, bearded and wrapped against the night's chill in cloaks of coarse wool. The flames from the fire reflected upon conical helmets, pulled down over cloth hoods to keep the cold wind from their ears and necks. A nose guard hung from the front of each helmet, which, as the light from the fire threw shadows across their faces, made the warriors appear as frightening apparitions to the young wolf as he skulked nervously in the shadows. Stilling his nerves, Cal tried to concentrate on their conversation. It sounded as if they were complaining and moaning, probably about their march here, or the cold and the necessity of being at Vortigern's bleak fortress, but they seemed to be enjoying the mead. Twice he heard the name Ambrosius and was just about to move away, believing he could learn no more, when a figure strode from the darkness making him shrink back with an involuntary whine when he saw who it was, a Saxon dressed from head to foot in black.

'Horsa!' The six warriors jumped to their feet. The one who had hissed the warning to his fellows stepped forward to greet the newcomer.

Cal realised he had been gradually edging back and stopped moving, forcing himself to stay and see what would happen. Horsa had clapped the warrior on the shoulder and accepted the proffered flagon of mead. He was drinking greedily, heedless of the pained looks of the others as they saw their mead flowing so freely down his neck. Another man appeared from one of the shelters, this one dressed in normal clothes and a felt hat, tied under his chin. He made to walk past, but then changed his mind and turned to address Horsa in a crisp arrogant voice that Cal had no trouble understanding.

'I will repeat to you what I have just told your brother. We march on Ambrosius at first light. King Vortigern has decided to end their threat before the weather worsens rather than wait the season out through to the thaw. Have your men ready, we have a three-day march ahead of us.' He spun on his heels and strode off, disappearing into the darkness without waiting for any reply. The black warrior shook his head, appearing weary as he addressed the others. There was an angry dialogue of Saxon curses when he had finished, and then without warning, all eyes turned to the shadows where Cal was lying and he heard a word he understood, *'Wolf!'*

A chill fear struck him. Springing to his feet, he ran, heedless of any caution, relying now solely upon his speed to put distance between him and the Saxons and it wasn't long before the angry cries faded behind him. When he reached the forest, the other wolves ran out to him, tails wagging, licking his muzzle, and lying down in front of him, relieved and happy that he had returned. After dispensing with the minimum of greeting rituals, he led them on a run through the forest, taking them as directly as possible back to the caves where he could safely leave the pack and awake in his human form.

'Uther!' Cal lurched upright, his eyes wide and staring, reflecting the light from the hut's flickering fire. Drawing in a series of ragged breaths, he allowed his sleeping fur to fall to the side as he rubbed at his face and tried to slow his beating heart, momentarily overwhelmed with the shock of returning to his body. 'Uther!' Glancing to the side, he cursed the inability of his human eyes to see in the dark. He could just make out the sleeping form of his friend, the furs drawn tightly up around his face keeping the chill draughts at bay. 'Uther, wake up!' Leaning across, Cal shook him roughly by the shoulder until his friend's eyes flashed open. 'They're coming, Uther... the Saxons are coming!'

* * *

A wet and rainy morning found the camp in a state of frenzy. Word had spread quickly that the Saxons were marching and they would soon meet them in battle.

With nerves on edge, and a belly feeling as if it were alive with bees and butterflies, Uther stood close to Cal and gazed about, as each tribal chieftain barked their commands, organising their men. The two friends had become accustomed to the comfort and routine of the camp over the last few weeks, and to see it in uproar like this was unsettling to say the least. All about them people were loading chariots and wagons, dismantling shelters or feverishly sharpening weapons.

Many were hurriedly preparing food, passing it out as soon as it became ready, with warriors eating as they worked.

'Hey!'

They glanced round and saw the familiar figure of Samel striding towards them. The little Iceni was crunching on the remnants of an apple, turning the core over to see if there was a bite left that he had somehow missed. With a momentary look of disappointment, he tossed it aside and approached, cleaning his fingers through his beard.

'We get to fight, I hear.' He clasped each in turn by the forearm by way of greeting. 'About bloody time if you ask me!' A broad grin split his face. 'Meryn's gonna be sore if he misses all the fun.'

'He's not come back then?' Uther asked, and his shoulders dropped as Samel shook his head. 'I had hoped he would be here.'

'He asked for one full cycle of the moon,' said Samel. 'It's been scarcely half that since he went off, but don't you worry about old Meryn, he'll hear all the noise and come running soon enough, you mark my words. Anyhow, I didn't come to talk of him. I came to ask if you'd like to join with me. I have two of my boys sick with fevers, so we have a chariot free. I thought you might want the use of it?'

'That sounds like a fine idea,' came a voice, and they turned to see Ambrosius and three of his men walking towards them. 'We travel today to Mount Badon,' continued Ambrosius, 'the site that has been chosen to meet with Vortigern.' He placed a hand on Uther's shoulder and addressed them all. 'I would be pleased if you and your band would ride alongside me.' Samel offered a nod in agreement and drew himself up as Ambrosius lowered his voice and addressed him directly. 'You may need to give my brother here a lesson or two on the finer points of a chariot's use, Master Samel, and I would ask you to look over them both when the time comes for battle. However, I think it best if you stay to the rear of the battle. We cannot both expose ourselves to our enemies - our people must not be left without a leader if we both should fall.'

'We need no milk-mother,' spluttered Uther, his face reddening. 'Cal and I will be just fine and we won't be left behind. We will, however, be looking out for you, brother. If you need our help, just call, we'll not be too far away.' Ambrosius grinned and Samel failed to contain a burst of laughter.

'I thank you for that, Uther. We shall all look out for each other on the battlefield, and I for one will be riding with more confidence knowing that you are both close.' As Ambrose strode away, Samel pushed Uther and Cal towards the waiting chariots.

'Come on lads. A chariot isn't so hard to handle, I'll soon show you how.'

However, the chariot was hard to handle, at least for Cal it was. After a brief attempt with the reins, he gave up and passed control over to Uther, who, with some practice and shouted instruction from Samel, did fare just a little better, and sort of managed to get the horses to do what he wanted. Much of the problem was the mud within the camp. Branches, laid as paths, made it easier for people to get about on foot, but the horses and chariots were having trouble, moving sideways as often as they were going in a straight line. That was, until they became caught in icy ground and one of the many deep ruts making it impossible to do anything but go in a straight line. The horses seemed happy enough, obviously more used to the conditions than their passengers were.

'I feel sick,' shouted Cal, tapping Uther on the shoulder.

Uther glanced at him, and then quickly snapped his attention back as the chariot slid to the left and one of the horses lost its footing. 'You feel sick or you're going to be sick?' asked Usher, raising his voice over the rumble of the chariot.' His answer came as Cal hung over the side of the bouncing wooden frame and noisily expelled the contents of his stomach into the mud, much to the delight of the onlookers.

'Hey! Mind the chariot, boy,' shouted Samel, from his seat on a fallen tree as Cal glared at him, wiping his mouth on his sleeve. Samel clapped his hands and let out a shriek, and then a below of laughter. There were four of them watching the spectacle of Uther and Cal's efforts as charioteers. Sometimes offering advice, but mostly, like then, just laughing.

'You must have eaten something bad this morning, eh? Well, don't you worry, lad. There's nothing like a good chariot ride to set you straight. Take her down to the wood and back. Let them really stretch their legs.' He ran over and slapped the closest horse on its rear. Jumping with shock, it gave a loud whinny and set off with Cal holding on as best he could and Uther pulling them round towards the distant tree line. They had almost made it to the trees before Uther managed to bring the horses back under control and they came to a stop. Cal slid from the back and lay in the wet grass panting and lifeless while Uther looped the horses' reins to the closest tree.

'Are you all right?'

Cal didn't move. He lay with his arm covering his eyes and his chest heaving as he drew in deep, ragged breaths. 'I knew I didn't like riding horses, and now I know I don't like riding in chariots, either.' He lifted his arm and glanced over towards the trees. 'Uther... don't move.'

Uther glanced up to see what had startled Cal and stared into the wood. His jaw began moving up and down slightly, as if some part of him wanted to say something but couldn't find the words.

Cal's voice softly broke the silence. 'They won't hurt us... at least I don't think they will. I've never been this close to wolves without being part of a wolf myself.' Uther continued to stare into the shadows between the trees where three pairs of yellow eyes regarded him silently. Behind him, the horses suddenly pulled against their reins, jumping in the traces as they caught the wolves' scent.

'Are they... your wolves? The ones you were with, I mean?' Uther began, edging back towards the chariot.

'No... they're not. I think we had better leave... let's get out of here.' Moving slowly, Uther untied the panicking horses and just managed to jump on beside Cal as the pair turned and fled, dragging the chariot behind them.

They arrived back to find Samel sitting alone on the tree trunk, grinning.

'Look at the pair of you now, bred to the chariot you are, the way you handled it coming back here. Now go gather your gear, we're leaving just as soon as you two are ready.'

The clouds parted late in the morning and the sun made its first real appearance in days. Even Cal cheered up. The rest of the day went by in quiet contemplation with thoughts left pondering the coming battle as the great column of men, horses and chariots filed out of the camp and headed north. By late afternoon, they had their first sight of Mount Badon. From a distance, the peak appeared like a giant anthill as people worked feverishly on fortifications and the construction of a triangular fort, the bare bones of which were silhouetted against the pale pink sky of the setting sun.

They rode in and were directed to an area on the southern slope, close to the shelter that had already been erected for Ambrosius. Samel and his men immediately began to unload the poles they had dragged from their previous camp and started to assemble their own large shelter. Cal and Uther joined in. Darkness came early as clouds brought back the rain, but the shelter was complete and the sounds in the camp changed from the shouting and cursing of construction, to the softer noises of warriors settling in for the night. Three young children brought bowls of greasy porridge laced with boar and some kind of root vegetable and Uther sat staring absently into the dancing flames of the fire, struggling to keep sleep at bay even while he ate. It had been a long exhausting day. Combined with the rising tension as thoughts turned to the coming battle, he was ready to rest. Lying down in their warm furs, it wasn't long before both he and Cal were asleep.

It was a strange experience to fall asleep as a weary boy and then awake just a moment later as a well-rested wolf, but Cal was getting used to it and took only a few moments of peering round, sniffing the air to clear his thoughts. He raised his head from between his paws and gazed about absently. Several of the other wolves were close, still sleeping, lying in the mouth of the cave with the cold rays of the half-moon painting them in its silvery light. Getting up, he shook himself, and then bowed down, stretching his forelegs before standing and shaking out each back leg in turn. A breeze ruffled his fur as he stared down into the near darkness of the forest below and sniffed at the cool evening air.

Thirsty, he trotted down to the small spring at the edge of the forest and lapped happily at the sweet water. When his thirst had been sated, he continued looking, watching as the ripples on the water settled to a smooth mirror-finish, allowing him to stare, transfixed at his reflection in the moonlit surface as a silver wolf gazed back at him. Moving his head from side to side, he marvelled at the face that copied him, and then with a jolt of shock, realised the acrid smell encroaching upon his senses was smoke.

Raising his head, he sniffed at the breeze, trying not to give in to the feeling of panic that tugged at him, smoke and people. He tensed; his worst fears realised, and glanced around. Before he could decide upon a course of action, a high-pitched yelp came from the rocks above him, followed by the angry snarling and barking of dogs and wolves, the exchange ended abruptly after a series of terrified squealing yelps. Cal ran back up the path, his human consciousness at last urging caution as he neared the top.

The hunters had found them. They must have approached from down-wind so the wolves wouldn't smell them. Crawling through a clump of bushes, he stared out at two wolves lying dead on the path, their eyes staring sightlessly past him. Cal's world spun and he fought the urge to vomit. He looked up as a Saxon warrior approached and tried to pull his spear free from the closest wolf. With his foot placed on its lifeless chest, the warrior heaved on the shaft and cursed when it didn't immediately come free. Next to him, a large black dog was savaging the dead wolf at the throat, growling and shaking it from side to side. At last, the warrior's spear broke past the wolf's ribcage, making a wet sucking sound that made the warrior laugh. With a parting kick to the lifeless carcass, he cleaned the spear on its fur and moved away with the dog following, tail wagging. Cal crept after them.

Closer to the caves, three other wolves were trapped, snarling and struggling under a heavy rope net. Cal stifled a whine, and then offered thanks to the spirits that it was only three and that the others must have gotten away. He could smell the wolves' fear, but there was nothing he could do for his three trapped pack mates so he turned away, intending to get into the forest and find the remaining members of the pack. But instead, another wave of panic hit him as he faced Horsa climbing up towards him with a spear in one hand and a burning branch in the other that he was sweeping from side to side.

Horsa saw him and screamed. 'Wolf!' then took a mighty leap and stabbed his spear down in a vicious arc.

Baring his teeth in a snarl, Cal sprang to the side, dodging the spear-tip as he tried to get past and down into the forest. Horsa corrected his thrust and quickly stabbed again, narrowly missing Cal, who spun just in time. A bush blocked his way and Cal had to turn to the side giving Horsa the opportunity to strike again. The metal head of the spear caught him, grazing his back leg as it passed making him yelp.

'Yaaahhh!' Horsa screamed, and thrust the burning branch into Cal's face, singeing his fur in a noxious cloud of smoke, but fear only gave him more energy and he managed to push past. Another series of high-pitched yelps from higher up the hill signalled the end of the wolves in the net, and Cal dashed on, panic now overwhelming him. Turning at the last moment, he narrowly avoided another Saxon waving flames, and then a blue-faced Pict loomed up from behind a bush and loosed an arrow. The arrow missed, but Cal realised he was fast running out of options; they were boxing him in. Another wolf ran past; ignoring him in its frantic bid for freedom, providing a distraction that Cal took advantage of. With a mighty leap, he soared over the head of the Pict, and landed below the killing ground. A rush of relief ran through him as he sped for the tree line, but then a shock of confusion ran through him as his back legs collapsed beneath him and his energy seemed to melt away. He rolled to a stop, barely conscious, stunned to find himself down and unable to move.

A blinding wave of pain finally caught up and flared through him and for some moments, his vision became lost within a blistering white light. Gradually, it receded into a calm release as he exhaled his last breath and gazed in despair at the moonlit trees. The smell of damp grass was rich in his nostrils and he could feel his tongue hanging from the side of his mouth, he suddenly felt thirsty again. With his vision slowly dissolving into a red mist, he watched absently as Horsa bent down to stroke his fur.

He was floating above the body of a poor dead wolf… and then… he wasn't.

* * *

'Well, if he died, how come he's sitting there blocking the heat from the fire?' The farmer laughed and his wife joined him with a shrill cackle. Several others stood up to leave and there was a muttering about proper stories and how the storyteller had ruined what could have been a nice tale; they were meant to have happy endings. It wasn't right, especially for the children.

Calvador Craen shot to his feet and rounded on the noisemakers. His hand shot out towards the door that someone had already un-bolted, and it banged shut, each bolt slamming home with a crack that reverberated around the room. 'Silence!' His eyes flashed yellow in the firelight as people hastily found their seats again. 'Open your minds and cease your foolish prattle… peasants, lest I show you how much of the wolf remains.' He bared his teeth and a low animal growl filled the room. Seeing everyone was returning to their seats, he took a deep breath and forced himself to relax. 'Continue, Uther. Tell these fools about my death, but do not ask them to pity, nor mourn me, reality is something larger than their small minds could ever hope to grasp.'

Chapter 14

Mount Badon

Uther gazed up at the lifeless body of his friend and tried to summon the emotion to deal with what he was seeing.

Samel came up beside him and placed a hand on his shoulder. 'What happened?'

Uther shifted uncomfortably. He felt sick, unable to gather his thoughts or emotions properly. It was hard for him to comprehend, but trying to explain it to someone who was unaware of Cal's nocturnal life in the body of a wolf was close to impossible. Uther shrugged. 'I don't know; I wish I did. He was asleep, he… he must have simply died in his sleep.' His mind felt numb and he just wished Samel would leave him alone, but the little man continued.

'No, lad, there was a spear wound… I saw a spear wound in his side and his sleeping furs were awash with blood. You must have heard… have seen something. Did he go out last night?' Samel stared down at the body laid out on furs, arms crossed on his chest, eyes closed as if asleep. 'Those keeping watch say that none passed, and I believe them.' He suddenly dragged Uther around by his cloak, forcing him to look him in the eye before lowering his voice. 'My men say none passed to do this, Uther. The spirits have had a hand in this.' He let go of Uther and stared back at Cal's body as it lay upon the piled branches. 'This was not a natural death and I don't mind telling you it scares me.'

'There's nothing natural about any of this, Samel. It's been one long bad dream since Picts raided our village and our families were murdered. Cal was my best friend and I ...' Uther choked back a wave of grief that threatened to overwhelm him. 'I really don't know what I'm going to do without him.' He thrust the flaming torch into the funeral pyre and stepped back as the flames took hold, crackling and spitting in their haste to consume Cal's body.

'Goodbye, Calvador, I will sorely miss you,' whispered Uther. 'Run free until we meet again, somewhere across the shadowland.' He stood staring at the fire, watching as the heat drew flakes of ash high up into the grey sky and fancied he could see his friend escaping with them, running with the breeze. He continued to keep his vigil until long after the others had left to prepare for battle and the fire had consumed Cal's body, dying down to hot glowing coals. It was nearing sunset when Samel came and led him away.

'You must rest, Uther. Tomorrow we fight. Calvador's spirit will be with you, but you need your strength. You must eat something, and then, please, you have to sleep.' Uther nodded; unable to argue, and then felt his legs buckle under him as a huge wave of grief finally overcame him.

* * *

The weak light of dawn brought more rain to further dampen the spirits as the warriors they waited, sheltering under their large oval shields, the feathers tied into their hair moving gently in the breeze. While some gathered in close groups to stave off the chill, those blessed with a prize battle hound kept the animal close, sharing its warmth and courage.

The Iceni were a mass of blue and green cloaks on one side, the white and yellow of the Trinovante covered the slope to the centre, while the darker blue of the Brigante and Catuvellauni stood further to the right, with a myriad of other tribal colours that Uther couldn't immediately identify making up the ground in between. Each warrior wore their spirit signs, the dreaming they personally identified with, daubed upon their shields as a talisman and as another means to identify friend from foe in the fever pitch of the coming battle.

The tribesmen had very little real armour shared amongst them. Some wore tribal helms, while others had adapted Roman armour, now painted and decorated so the spirits would recognise the wearer as a warrior of the tribes rather than Roman and so aid his battle or ease his passing into the shadowland should they fall to an enemy spear or blade. Uther noticed many warriors sitting naked, daubed only in swirling spirit-patterns of blue woad as protection, the feathers of crows and eagles hanging in their hair, their expressions vacant as they gazed down into the misty valley before them.

Almost all had been awake since before first light, either unable to sleep in the knowledge of what the new day would bring, or because they had been labouring through the night to secure the hill fort, the last refuge should the battle go badly. Earthen embankments had been thrown up against the log sides, leaving a deep ditch to cross that any Saxon, Pict, or rogue Briton would need to overcome before reaching the walls and those awaiting them inside. Below the fort, other ditches protected the approach slopes to further frustrate the attempts of any would-be attackers. Uther considered the approach and decided that anybody expecting to get as far as the fort would require the stamina of a horse.

Shifting his weight in the chariot, he cast about the rain soaked valley. Mist was drifting amongst the shrubs and bushes, lower down where it was still untouched by sunlight, hidden, but rising amid the clouds. To either side, the forest stood in shadow, clinging stubbornly to its share of the night; it seemed in little hurry to join the misery of the day. His attention came back to the warriors on the hillside, separated into their individual tribes, even while they waited to fight together as Britons. The majority were waiting, half way up, seated on the wet grass while the horsemen and chariots remained out of sight to either side of Mount Badon. It was a grim day in many respects, thought Uther, and it promised to become even grimmer. A trickle of rainwater ran from his helmet, down his neck and under the mail and leather of his armour sending a shiver through him.

The rain lessened and the quiet tension of the morning began to give way to surges of pent-up adrenaline. As he watched, the tribesmen started rousing each other into some order of battle readiness. There were a few practice charges down the slope, several fights, and plenty of yelling, shouting and cursing, which was gradually building up into a constant dull roar.

He saw a number of female warriors in the ranks, and then noticed they were actually among the more vocal in their attempts to bring on the fighting spirit. They were baiting the men and calling challenges to the women of other tribes, much to the approval of their male companions.

'Is it always this way?' Uther asked.

Samel glanced over to where a woman swinging a battle-axe was screeching abusive challenges across the empty battlefield in front of her. 'Pretty much, the waiting is the hardest part. Our scouts have been coming back since well before sunrise with reports that the Saxons are approaching. They're well aware that many of them will die today, but they also know that there are only two ways to enter a battle. You can either attack consumed with the fear of what might happen to you, or you can attack as a warrior, bringing a terrible fear down upon your enemy. The first of the Saxons will probably be in the forest already, watching us right now as they wait for the rest to catch up. They'll show themselves soon enough.'

The horses tried to pull forward, jerking the chariot as they did so, but with a snap of the reins, Uther held them back.

'Steady, lad, they feel it as well. Keep them from breaking away for a little longer, it won't be long now.'

'I have them,' said Uther, and then after a moment, he added. 'Do you have no fear, Samel?'

Samel looked up at Uther, studying him for a moment. 'Of course I have fear, lad, but it's fear that makes me the most terrifying warrior on the battlefield. More importantly, it's fear that will keep me alive.

My love of life is too great to die here today. The secret is not to *deny* your fear. Everyone on this hill holds fear in his belly. The mark of a warrior is how he deals with it. Hold it in and pretend it's not there, and it will kill you. It'll creep up your spine, climbing with icy fingers to whisper in your ear until you turn and flee screaming from the battlefield with piss running down your legs. However, if you take it and understand it, then you can use it and turn it loose upon your enemy!' He gripped Uther's shoulder. 'Come, lad, this battle will still be some time in beginning; let's go and find your brother.'

Uther hauled the chariot round and manoeuvred the horses up towards the top of the hill, with horses, men and chariots parting to let them through. They found Ambrosius easily enough; he was standing close to the hill fort with a group of chieftains gazing out across the valley, waiting for the first sign of the enemy forces to show themselves.

Mount Badon had been chosen as the battle site for several reasons, or so Ambrosius had explained to Uther. Vortigern would have to pass this way if he intended to march his forces south, and when he did, he would be all too aware that they waited for him here. The pretender couldn't simply pass by and leave the threat of them behind him, he would be forced to meet them and deal with them while the opportunity was presented, there would be a battle.

The site also held significance to the druids. They had urged Ambrosius that if he sought victory, then this was the correct place for this battle. They had spoken to the spirits and counselled the ancestors and all their signs and visions pointed to this being the site of a great victory for the tribes. When Ambrosius had first visited, several weeks before, and seen that from the vantage point at the top of Mount Badon he could look down into the valley, he had finally agreed. From the top of the hill, the whole battleground lay before them. Below was the undulating expanse of the open valley, with the dense, dark vastness of the forest crowding in to either side. While at the far end stood the smaller hill, around which Vortigern would most certainly gather his troops.

As Uther and Samel dropped from their chariot to join the group surrounding Ambrosius, the first of Vortigern's forces began to emerge from the trees across the valley. Uther gazed across as a group of about a hundred Picts broke from the tree line and filed quickly across to the left of the field. The tribesmen on Mount Badon stood and roared their challenge as the Picts formed up. The loud moaning of horns filled the air. Then the tribesmen began hammering on their shields with swords and axes, shouting, yelling and howling to unnerve their hated northern enemy.

No sooner had the Picts settled when the Saxons emerged, rank after rank of them, filing out of the forest paths. Uther soon lost count, guessing the number to be near ten thousand as they formed up in a wall of shields around the opposite hill, and they were still coming. He glanced down at their own forces and realised how heavily outnumbered they were.

'Do you see Vortigern?' Uther asked, and Ambrosius, who was studying the assembling Saxons with a frown on his face, pointed to the trees on the right of the far clearing.

'My guess would be that he's in that group moving towards the hill. From what I've heard of him, he won't want to get too close to the actual battle today. He has always preferred his killing to be done for him by others,' Ambrosius sighed. 'The druids told me years ago it was Vortigern who sent a Pict to kill our father. We must make him pay for that, Uther, and, spirits willing, he will pay for it today.'

He pointed to the largest group still gathering in the centre of the lowland. 'These men here will be the first to attack. They're some of his best troops, seasoned Saxon warriors all. When we fought for Rome, we faced men such as these when they tried to cross the great Rhine River into Gaul. They will try to force a breach in our lines and attempt to split our forces.' He indicated the trees to either side. 'There'll be more in there waiting to sweep in if they manage to do it.'

Uther gazed up at his brother, amazed at his understanding of their enemy and the cool detached way he could see how the battle would be fought. He glanced down the hill again. 'How will we stop them? We're so few.' Fear rose from his stomach, draining his mouth of moisture. Reaching back for his water skin, he drank greedily.

Ambrosius looked at him and smiled. 'We are Britons, Uther. The people of this land.' He gestured to the writhing, eager ranks of tribesmen in front of them. 'We are the Iceni, the Catuvellauni, the Trinovante, Atrebates and Parisi to name but a few of the clans gathered here. What chance, you might ask, do these Saxon invaders have against us?'

Before Uther could reply, the Saxon war drums began to beat and the solid mass of men in the centre surged forward, hefting swords, spears and axes high. The shield wall remained solid, each shield overlapping that of its neighbour as they strode onward. Behind the wall the warriors screamed their own challenges back to the waiting Britons as ale and mead were passed along the line. On Mount Badon the tribesmen replied, the deep moaning call of the horns almost lost amongst the rising battle cries and clamour as each warrior drummed their spear against shield and stamped their feet while the chieftains tried to hold them back. The noise rose to form a roar that echoed around the small valley, until it was filling the air, mixing with the fear, excitement and blood lust.

'Hold fast!' cried Ambrosius above the clamour, as he saw the ranks of tribesmen begin to sway and move down the hill. The order was passed forward, and each chieftain repeated the call, reinforcing it with savage kicks and abuse to keep the line for which they had been trained. The Saxon horde was now halfway across the valley.

Raising his hand, Ambrosius signalled to the wooded area on his left, and several hundred archers ran forward to form ranks on the lower slopes. He repeated the signal to his right and more archers emerged on that side. As the Saxons reached the base of Mount Badon, they slowed, bunching almost to a standstill while the ones at the front began their climb. At a signal, the archers loosed their first volley of arrows and death rained down upon the massed Saxons, the sound of the arrows hitting the shields and howling screams of the injured becoming one with the roar of battle. The archers continued firing into the surging ranks, forcing the Saxons to bunch together, until all their arrows were spent, and then they ran forward, swords and axes raised, as they formed their own shield wall, eager to be amongst the first to meet with the enemy.

'Return to your chariot, Uther,' cried Ambrosius, as he struggled to hold the rope restraining his huge war hound as it strained to get free. Its angered barking almost lost now amongst the terrible noise all around them.

'Take your group and come in from the right. I will attack from the left and we'll strike and scatter them as the tribes join the battle.' He raised his free arm, and then abruptly dropped it, signalling the chieftains to let loose the main ranks of warriors. With a roar, the tribes attacked, screaming down the hill hurling their spears before crashing into the wall of Saxons with a terrible clash as weapons and shields met and the screaming began.

Dragging himself away from the terrifying spectacle of battle, Uther forced his way back through the confusion of men as they hurried to mount horses and chariots, and leapt up next to Samel. As they came free of the crowd and brought the chariot down from the hill, he saw Samel's men watching, glancing up towards them, anxious for Samel and Uther to return so they could be away. They drew alongside and skidded round as Uther turned the horses towards the battleground, and Samel called to his men.

'Come lads... what are ye waiting fer!' The little Iceni clung on as the chariot lunged forward and set off towards the terrible sounds of battle waiting for their first sight of the Saxon wall. The chariot lurched dangerously, tipping up on one wheel before coming down with a thump and sliding round the base of the hill then they continued on, bouncing over the rough ground, the screaming, bellowing and noise of battle becoming louder and louder the closer they came. Uther glanced back to see the sixteen chariots under his command following steadily, the bouncing chariots bristling with spears and savage looking warriors.

The chariot bumped again, tipping abruptly up before crashing down again. 'Steady lad!' shouted Samel, over the uproar. 'Don't turn us over before we get there.' Rain returned as a steady drizzle, and he risked releasing a hand from its steadying grip on the side of the chariot to wipe a sleeve across his face, quickly slapping it back on the rail as the chariot jolted once more.

As they covered the ground towards the tangled mass of men, a larger group of Saxons appeared from the forest and ran screaming out towards them. Uther glanced back at Samel to see if he had noticed.

'Ignore them,' growled Samel, glaring across at the running men. 'Bring us round to the back of the main battle, lad, that's it... at 'em, lads!'

The bouncing chariot closed on the main group of writhing, fighting men, and as they did, the nearest Saxons turned to see them bearing down, their fear evident when they realised they were directly in the chariot's path. Drawing Excalibur with his right hand, Uther gripped the reins against the edge of the chariot with his left, and they ploughed into the solid mass of the battle, the impact registering with a series of sickening thumps and jolts. The horses charged on as they had been trained to do, trampling the first group of terrified men, and then rearing up and kicking out and biting at others who were trying desperately to escape being crushed or maimed. Now in the thick of the fighting, but still moving, Uther drew in the stink of battle, a heavy mixture of blood, urine and fear.

They slowed as the battle closed about them. The chariot jumped and fell as the horses struggled to pull it up and over fallen bodies, while in front of them, Saxons and Picts panicked to get clear of the raised hooves and evil yellow teeth that tore lumps of cloth and flesh from any warrior that came close enough. In these first terrifying moments, it was all Uther could do to crouch and hold on, as faces, swords, and axes flashed past him, the screams and defiant battle cries a constant and terrifying roar in his ears. With a jolting thud, an axe embedded itself in the edge of the chariot close to where he held on. Snatching his hand back, he saw Samel stab down with his spear, retrieving it a moment later dripping in blood. The chariot continued, bouncing from side to side.

'Get up, boy! Fight!' roared Samel.

Uther rose to see that the chariots were all still moving cutting a swathe through the surging ranks of Saxon warriors. The closest tribesmen were battling towards them about thirty paces away. Lashing out with Excalibur, he felt the weapon dance in his hands, meeting the resistance of flesh and bone, and the first Saxons fell back in a spray of blood, wounded or dying. He tried to blank his mind to the agonised looks and terrible screams, reasoning that these were the invaders and had to be turned back. Still, as he fought, the small part of him that remained a boy locked itself into a corner of his mind and wept.

The rain fell with renewed intensity and the ground beneath the fighting warriors and was soon churned into a thick mud, slick and stained rich with the blood of the dead and dying.

By midday, the battle still raged and the rain still fell.

Keeping the chariot moving, Uther entered the most intense part of the battle once more. On the far side, he caught a glimpse of Ambrosius with the other chariots, the King standing tall above the battling warriors as they fought their way through the enemy's flank. Slapping the reins down on his horses' backs, Uther felt them lurch forward once more, dragging the chariot back onto the Saxon shield wall.

'Yaaahh!'

Then, as the clouds parted briefly spilling a ray of sunlight down onto the bloodshed below, the two groups of chariots met and the battle turned in favour of the tribes. With the Saxon forces, now divided, the ferocious tide of tribesmen and the incredible power of the chariots began to turn the battle. The Saxons may have had more men, but Ambrosius had trained his forces well, and this battle that had been long in its planning, was becoming a massacre.

As his chariot broke into open ground once more, Uther wheeled about, trying to come back onto their flank. Smaller groups of Picts and Saxons saw they had slowed to make the turn and so tried to stop them, but Samel's axe, alongside Uther wielding Excalibur, dealt death to all that came within range. Then as the chariot began to pick up speed once more, a bearded axeman ran in and, with a shrill cry, brought his blade down, catching Uther a heavy blow to the shoulder. Uther cried in pain, then thrust out with Excalibur, and the Saxon fell away screaming. With his shoulder pulsing in fiery agony, he brought the chariot away from the battle and passed the reins to Samel, then glanced down at his numb arm hanging useless at his side.

'T'aint cut, boy. He missed you with the blade, just caught you with the shaft.' Samel turned the chariot round again and headed back towards the knot of fighting men. 'Here we go again, boy. Strap yourself on and let's prepare a feast for them crows.' He cracked the reins down on the horses' backs. 'Yaaahh!'

Uther just had time to strap his useless arm to the chariot rail with a length of hemp rope, and they were back in amongst the boiling cauldron of the main battlefield with bloody conflict stretching far out to either side.

Time seemed to slow. The chaos of battle floating from one moment to the next, moving before him in a blur of blood and anger, and then came a moment that would live with him long after the battle had faded into nightmare. A Pict, his blue-daubed face drawn in a scream of anger, emerged from the crushing mob of fighting warriors and just as quickly, slid from Uther's sword spitting a foam of crimson bubbles. As he fell away, the Pict reached out, caught him, and clung to him, using the last of his strength in an attempt to drag Uther with him to the ground. Trapped within the grip of the dying man's gaze, Uther felt himself being drawn over the side rail of the chariot before the rope securing his arm stopped him with a jolt. His consciousness snapped back, with the noise and pain of the moment almost overwhelming him. Then, the strong grip of Samel caught him as he struggled at the edge of panic, and managed to pull him back onboard.

'Come, boy. The horses need to rest.' The chariot came round and, once clear of the fighting, they headed slowly back to the sanctuary behind Mount Badon. Uther felt weary to the depths of his soul. He rubbed sweat and rain from his eyes, and stared out at the small isolated groups of ferocious fighting that remained amongst the droves of fleeing Saxons. Hundreds lay dead or dying upon the field and he wondered at the madness that had brought them to this day. Tentatively unstrapping his arm, he experienced a moment of relief when he realised that, through the pain, he could still feel his fingers and could just about move his arm again. They made it to the sanctuary of their own lines where a group of children met them bearing fresh water, food, spare blades, and spears.

'Drink.' Samel handed him a water-skin and shook his head as Uther gulped greedily. 'Slow down, lad, you'll make yourself sick.' He was grinning as Uther pulled the water skin from his mouth coughing and spluttering. 'There, told you so... now, are you ready?'

'Ready? Ready for what?' Uther glanced out to where the fighting could still be heard, knowing what Samel was going to say but unsure if he could summon the energy to return to the fight. Samel merely nodded and pulled Uther back up.

They rounded the hill, the chariot rumbling and jumping beneath them, and saw a group of the Saxons were attempting to rally and come back, driving Pict warriors before them. It was only a moment later that the chariot slammed into them.

Twice more, Uther and Samel led the other chariots back into the fight, helping to collapse any sense of order the Saxons managed to muster. The horses were nearing exhaustion now; the sharp, almost sweet smell of their sweat was heavy in the air. When the chariot slowed, the horses' heads dropped and their nostrils flared drawing great gulps of air into their lungs. Although foam streamed from their mouths and their sides were heaving, they weren't staggering so Samel judged they could keep running. They wheeled about for a third time, and then saw Ambrosius, with two other chariots, break out of the battle and head at a gallop towards where Vortigern and the Saxon chieftains stood on the far rise, the long loping run of Ambrosius' war hound leading the way. With Uther once again taking the reins, they followed, veering to the right to attack a small group of fleeing Picts as they went.

Ahead of them, Ambrosius and his chariots neared Vortigern. Several warriors ran forward to intercept them, but as they clashed, the chariots scattered them and kept on going. Others closer to Vortigern formed to stand as a group extending their spears, ready to defend their king as he studied the chariots' approach.

Uther and Samel were some way behind but could clearly see Vortigern now. He was the thin, bearded man, surrounded by several other Britons and two large Saxons. Uther felt a shock of recognition when he saw the one that had chased them at the Roman villa; the one Cal had named Horsa. He gripped Excalibur, longing for the chance to face his personal enemy, and then his attention returned to Vortigern, whose gaze of surprise at seeing Ambrosius approach changed to one of alarm as the chariots broke through the final line of defenders with an audible crash, scattering warriors as it came.

Using the momentum of his chariot, Ambrosius neared his rival and launched his long Roman javelin. It seemed for some moments that everyone present was watching, following the path of the javelin as it turned almost lazily in the air, before seeing it drop down to strike Vortigern in the chest. The metallic clash and meaty sound of its impact as it pierced first the man's armour, and then entered his body, carried clearly back to where Uther approached, watching as if in a dream as the pretender collapsed back into the arms of a cowled druid.

Ambrosius wheeled his chariot at the last moment, lifted his fist in triumph, and retreated having finally avenged their father. Uther slowed and made ready to turn his own chariot around, and then cried out, as a Saxon spear seemed to appear out of Ambrosius' chest, a crimson stain quickly spreading across his tunic. He continued to watch, disbelieving, seeing Ambrosius gaze down at the spear in shock, and then the chariot swayed precariously, as the King of the Britons collapsed to hang over the edge. The chariot's other occupant managed to keep them moving while he hauled the slumped body back inside, struggling to keep control of the horses as he did. The stricken chariot passed and Uther turned and followed, unable to accept that his brother had fallen, then glanced back to see Horsa, having run down the slope to throw the spear, punching the air, mocking the gesture of triumph made by Ambrosius only moments before. Uther felt his eyes fill with tears of fury. Too far away for Horsa to hear anything that he might shout, he pointed Excalibur at him, marking him for the next time that they should meet, but either Horsa failed to notice, or he merely chose to ignore him.

They rode back through the battlefield where the fighting had all but ended. Warriors from both sides were limping away, many helping injured companions. Women were running out from behind the lines to search the dead for their men folk, competing with the crows that had already started their feast, squabbling amongst themselves to pluck the eyes from the dead and dying.

They arrived back at the shelters behind Mount Badon to see a knot of men converge on Ambrosius' chariot as it came to a stop. Uther jumped down and ran towards them, desperately concerned for his brother. As he neared they turned, and then one after another, dropped to one knee in front of him.

'I cannot be king!' Uther rounded upon the tall druid and rubbed at the tears that continued to come unbidden to his eyes. 'I don't understand any of this. My village burns, my best friend dies, I discover I have a brother and then he dies, and now you... Merlyn show up, but then of course you used to be called Meryn, back when the world was just a slightly saner place.' He shook his head.' It's not happening, none of it is!' Slumping down, he held his head, it hurt, and all he wanted to do was wake up and have someone tell him everything had been a bad dream.

Another voice joined in. 'But you are King, Uther, the start of a new line of kings and a new beginning for this land. It will be you and your line that unites the tribes and makes this one kingdom.'

Uther glared across at the girl in the light blue robe. 'And don't think I've forgotten about you, Nineve. Your brother died, why do you not mourn him? Don't you wonder what caused his death?'

Nineve rose from her place at the fire, walked softly towards him and laid a hand on his arm. 'Calvador has left this life, Uther, but his spirit lives and knows we shall all meet again. Come.' She drew him up and before he knew where she was leading him, they were outside with the chill night air misting his breath. 'Look above you, Uther, a sign, written across the night sky. It heralds the start of your reign and confirms your right to be king. The druids foretold of this Omen, many hundreds of years ago and we have waited, planning patiently ever since.' They gazed up for a few moments, marvelling at the large comet, frozen in its flight amongst the stars. The tail, a hand-span long, was frosted at its edges, giving it the appearance of some strange mythical creature flying overhead.

Behind them, the skin of the roundhouse door was pushed aside and Merlyn emerged, spilling light from within as he came. He walked up beside them and placed a hand upon Uther's shoulder. 'It is the dragon comet, Uther, and you are to take its name. The bloodline that you shared with your brother can be traced back to the warrior queen, Boudicca of the Iceni, she who first expelled invaders from these shores, and from her, even further back through the years to those who ruled with the ancestors. Ambrosius was a good man, but through no fault of his own, he had become more Roman than Briton. He had taken a Roman name, even if he had a Briton's heart. Your brother helped bring you to this point, but Ambrosius was never destined to be king; it was always going to be you. You are Uther Pendragon, King of all the Britons.

* * *

Uther stopped speaking and gazed into the crackling fire. He remembered it all now, remembered ruling a kingdom, remembered his wife, Igraine, and his son, Arthur... and then, with a start, he remembered...

He glanced up at Calvador. 'Am I...?'

'Complete your story, Uther,' murmured Calvador Craen, as he smiled down. 'We shall leave soon.' He turned and addressed the rows of silent listeners. Some were white with fear, while others, such as the farmer and his wife, still looked set to cause trouble. Cal held up his hand before any of them could say anything. 'My friend here has nearly finished his tale. You are witnessing the end of a legend. Uther Pendragon shall soon leave you to return to your history books, and then you may debate what has happened here tonight for as long as your memories allow.' He turned back to his friend. 'Go on, Uther, please.'

After a moment, the old storyteller nodded and continued. 'My brother had killed Vortigern, but the Saxons weren't in any hurry to go back to their boats and leave. Throughout that terribly cold winter we gathered to the north where construction began on Pendragon castle.' He stopped to light his pipe before continuing. 'Of course the castle would take years to finally complete, but it was that winter that we started with the timber construction.

'I sent out riders to all the tribes again, asking for more men to help drive the invaders from our shores and they came in their hundreds, which in turn caused more problems as we struggled and learned to feed, train and house that number of warriors. It was Beltane when we finally met the Saxons in battle again, blossom was on the trees and the fields were alive with flowers.' He smiled, his face creasing into a thousand lines as he remembered. 'Of course, Hengist and Horsa had also been busy through the winter...'

Chapter 15

PENDRAGON

Uther stared out from the crest of the hill and wondered again, how has my life come to this? Below him, at the foot of what was now commonly known as Pendragon Hill, a town of sturdy dwellings continued to grow daily, with merchants greeting traders as they brought in livestock and supplies to accommodate the ever-expanding populace. Warriors from all the tribes continued to arrive, answering their new king's call to fight for their land against the Saxon invaders and become a nation of Britons. Uther gazed at the construction going on that covered the three smaller hills before him. The main group of buildings were in the valley beside the banks of the small river and the busy road that ran alongside it.

There were several training areas, with warriors practising their weapons of choice, improving their skills under the supervision of the Roman-trained fighters that had arrived with Ambrosius. It was those trainers, with their knowledge of battle tactics, who had helped win the battle at Mount Badon. The memory of that awful day filled Uther's mind, as it did all too often. For a few moments, he returned to the battle, hearing the awful screams and cries of pain as if he were there once more, riding upon the chariot in the midst of a sea of screaming humanity. The awful ugly emotions of hatred, anguish and fear, surrounding him, carrying him away...

'Sire... we are ready for your inspection.'

Startled from his reverie Uther shuddered and turned to see Berin clutching a roll of parchment to his chest, smiling at him nervously. Berin was a thin, haggard little man, his eyes pinched and underlined with dark smudges from reading and writing reports by candlelight for too many years. He claimed that Christian monks raised him, and that he had spent his first twenty years in their service. However, after an introduction from Merlyn, he had now firmly attached himself to the service of Uther and become his much-welcomed shadow, organising the camp and the construction of the fortress, which was growing slowly behind him.

'Yes, Berin, I'm sorry for keeping you waiting.' Uther noticed Berin blush and glance over at Merlyn. The old druid was standing not far away, in the shade of a tall oak, quietly observing the exchange, smiling at their obvious discomfort. A king never apologises, the memory of Merlyn's words came to Uther unbidden, and he had to stop himself from apologising again. Instead, he walked to the edge of the large hole being excavated from the top of the hill, and peered down at the men below toiling in the dirt and mud. He watched as a worker dropped down a ladder into a deeper section in the corner; the diggers of this part were out of sight, using ropes that led down into darkness to bring up full leather buckets that slopped their slimy contents back on those working underneath.

'As you can see, the well progresses, and with your approval we can begin construction of the walls.' Berin, who had come up beside him, pointed to where a group of men were trimming heavy tree trunks a short way off. Uther took it all in while Berin fidgeted, moving from one foot to the other as he awaited some sign from Uther that he was happy with how things were progressing with the basic layout of the building.

'Everything looks fine, Berin. You and your men are working faster than we expected. When do you think it will all be completed?' He glanced across at Merlyn to see if he had said the right things and the druid offered a slight nod as Berin beamed.

'Thank you, Sire. We will be ready before the solstice.' He bowed and moved off towards the group of workers trimming branches from the tree trunks and started talking and pointing towards the hole.

Berin departed allowing Merlyn to stride over and join Uther. 'Come, we have a battle to plan.' Leading Uther by the arm, he guided the young king away.

They made their way down the hill, passing more workers digging huge ditches, while others piled the excavated earth into defensive mounds that would further hinder any would-be attackers to Uther's fortress. Picking their way through the confusion, they headed towards the largest of the roundhouses, known as the great hall, where the chiefs and reeves had gathered. Uther began to feel the familiar fluttering of fear in his stomach as he thought about addressing the assembled council. Reaching to his side, he gripped the twisted wire hilt of Excalibur, the cool touch beneath his fingers lending him strength as he ducked down and pushed through the skins hanging across the low doorway.

He stood behind the looming shadows of large warriors, all facing away from him towards the centre of the great hall. It took a few moments for his eyes to adjust to the dim smoky atmosphere, with its heady aroma of burning pine resin, and was thankful that he wasn't immediately recognised. Through the gloom above his head, he could just make out the intricate carvings on the huge oak beams; deer, bear, boar, and of course wolf, surrounded by twisting, beautifully rendered branches and leaves. His gaze dropped once more to the occupants of the hall. It was noisy and several heated exchanges were already underway as rival chiefs took the opportunity to air old grievances. However, as the more easily identifiable figure of Merlyn entered and stood beside him, the druid's presence seemed to spread and the noise in the hall slowly died down as faces turned towards him.

Lowering his hood, Merlyn strode through the crowd towards the centre where a large fire burned fiercely beside a raised platform. He clambered up, and stood alongside the heavy oak chair, gazing out over the restless crowd. He made a striking figure, in every part; he was now the epitome of a druid, instantly commanding the respect of every warrior in the room. Grey robes cinched about a thin waist, long grey hair falling about a strongly featured face, now blessed with a fine white beard and whiskers that flowed onto his chest. The hand that clutched his druids' staff was almost skeletal.

After a few moments, to be sure all eyes had turned in his direction; he struck his staff down three times, the incredible booming sound silencing any who had yet to take notice of his presence.

'Quiet, all, hush now… for I will have you bid welcome… to Uther Pendragon, war leader of all the tribes and King of you Britons.' Merlyn hung his head and, with a rumble, all those assembled dropped to one knee as Uther slowly made his way to the platform.

A step was pushed forward and he climbed up, walked the two paces to the throne, and sat down. As he gazed out at the grim faces revealed by the light from the fire and flickering torches, he was glad he was able to sit because his legs felt like they had been crafted from un-baked bread. He jumped as Merlyn brought his staff down again, the resounding boom filling the roundhouse, dislodging motes of dust and straw from the thatched roof, letting in rays of sunlight to pierce the darkness. As one, the warriors stood and bellowed, 'Pendragon!'

Silence returned, and then one man pushed through to the front and stared up at Uther, barely suppressed emotion forcing his face into a snarl. Stabbing out a finger towards the seated king, he swung back to address the gathering.

'I challenge the right of this… impostor to rule. I, Pascent, son of the murdered Vortigern, am your rightful leader.' The room erupted into angry cries and a flurry of heated exchanges that subsided as Uther leapt to his feet and approached the edge of the platform. A hush descended in anticipation of how their king might react.

'Welcome, Pascent, son of Vortigern,' said Uther, his voice sounding calmer than he felt. 'I deeply regret the death of your father, as do I regret and mourn the loss of my brother, Ambrosius, who also fell at Mount Badon. The time of Briton fighting Briton has to end. We have a common enemy in the Saxons and must unite to drive them from our shores… join us.' Uther held out his hand towards the angry man. However, when he saw the look that Pascent threw him, he realised sadly that the situation was not going to be reconciled peacefully.

Spurning the offered hand, Pascent made to turn away, but then spun back, drew his sword, and brought it down in a silvery arc intending to sever Uther's unprotected arm. Uther managed to draw back as the blade slid past, feeling the soft breeze of its passing before it bit deeply into the newly built platform. The new, green wood trapped it soundly, the attacker's face turned an even deeper shade of crimson as anger and embarrassment overtook him. The warriors in the roundhouse became silent, watching in awed fascination as Pascent tugged pathetically in a futile attempt at releasing his blade.

He stopped, chest heaving, weeping uncontrollably as rage and grief ran free.

'I hate you,' he spat, his voice trembling and barely controlled. He renewed his struggle with the sword. 'Without you and your bastard brother, you… you… just give me my throne, you… Aaahhh!' the sword finally came free and he staggered back several paces, forcing several onlookers to complain loudly as they moved to avoid him, and then he ran back in to attack Uther once more. Two chieftains moved to stop him, but before either they or Merlyn could do anything, Uther had stepped forward, jumped the flashing blade, and swung a kick at his attacker's jaw. It struck with all of Uther's pent-up frustration, and connected with a solid crack that sent Pascent back into the arms of the closest chiefs.

'Do not harm him further,' commanded Uther, as Pascent's body was lost to sight amid the angry crowd. 'He's suffered enough. We have to direct our efforts to ridding these lands of Saxons, not Britons.' The unconscious Pascent was carried away as Merlyn came up beside Uther.

'Well done, King Uther.' He patted Uther's shoulder, his blue eyes sparkling as he smiled. 'That was very well done indeed and it will no doubt grow in the telling. Their respect for you increases.'

With the excitement over, the debating returned and Uther sat slumped on the uncomfortable chair, trying to take an interest in the arguments that went on for the rest of the day. On several occasions, he was called upon to settle disputes between both tribes and individual warriors, asked his opinion on the tactics to be employed in the coming battle, and even questioned on his knowledge of the Saxon leaders. Having now fought several times with Horsa, he was able to give a good account of their enemy. The council became silent and attentive as his story was told, growing and expanding as he recounted it. He felt better having something to offer this gathering of seasoned warriors as he described their encounters in the Weald, the Roman villa, and at Mount Badon, but when it was all told, he returned to being little more than an observer, leaving much of the debate, once again, to more seasoned minds. It would clearly be some time before Merlyn's lessons would really make him a king.

At the start of every day, and then later, continuing into each evening, Merlyn would speak of the history of the tribes and the line that had ruled to make him the king among kings. He learnt of the tribes across the sea, the Saxons, Jutes, Angles and Gauls, and of the fierce northern tribes of Britain, the Brigantes, Lugi, Albini and Picts, all of whom coveted the fertile lands of the south that the Romans had so recently deserted.

'It is our sacred duty to preserve this land, Uther. Yours shall be the line that safeguards this fragile alliance for the next thousand years, we must turn back these Saxons before they become stronger, and attack them as soon as we have the men to do so.'

After several weeks, it was Samel who finally presented a plan that all could agree upon, a plan to strike at the heart of the Saxon invasion without having to lure them onto some pre-designated battlefield.

'There!'

Uther gazed down at Samel's finger where it pressed between two lines on the vellum map. He had already been told that the map was a drawing of their land and that the lines, apparently, signified the eastern coast of Britain and the north-south road into the old Roman City of Londinium. It wasn't easy to see how those few lines could be anything other than lines, and as he glanced about, he was relieved to see most of the others appeared equally bemused.

'And where are we?' asked a heavily bearded warrior, whom Uther seemed to recall was chief of one of the southern tribes.

'We... are here,' Samel's finger stabbed down, 'and we want to go to Aeglesthorp... there... on the East coast below the big river.' The little warrior glanced up, cast about the room of intent faces and was dismayed to see little sign of understanding. 'Oh, come on, it's simple! We make our way through the cover of the Weald and surprise them... here, can't you see it?' He jabbed his finger down on the map again in obvious frustration, the force bunching the velum to one side. Merlyn gently smoothed the map out again and nodded at Samel.

'It's a fine piece of deduction, Master Samel, but why Aeglesthorp? It appears to lie upon a smaller river, does it not? Is there any reason...'

'I've seen 'em. The Saxons... they're bringing their supplies in here and it's now their main settlement.' Samel leaned closer and traced his finger along the line of the river towards open sea. 'If we cut the belly from the snake, then it stands to reason that the head and fangs will have less bite!' At last there were murmurs of understanding and agreement, and the serious business of planning the details began in earnest.

As the days moved into summer, Uther began to wear the mantle of kingship a little easier. He still didn't feel born to the role, but at least now he didn't have the feeling he was wearing another man's crown.

A typical day would commence with lessons with Merlyn, followed by a meeting with the tribal chiefs and elders, reeves, and minor kings, where Uther would deal with the constant bickering and disputes and listen to the reports brought in by scouting parties. Skirmishes with the Saxons were becoming more commonplace, allowing the warriors to test themselves while gauging the extent of the Saxon expansion. It was a favourite tactic of Uther's tribesmen to travel in the fast-moving chariots or as small bands on horseback attacking Saxon settlements in fast raids, harrying the enemy then moving on before any resistance could be organised. It was a similar tactic to the one the Saxons themselves had used when first arriving in Britain. On the whole, the better-trained Britons accounted well for themselves; but it was after one of these encounters where they had suffered some severe losses that Uther discovered a Roman practice that he could not approve of.

'Sire, there is a reason the Roman troops are disciplined like this,' explained Tactus, one of the Roman trained men that had been in Ambrosius' original group. He was looming over the kneeling figure of an Iceni warrior who had barely finished making his report. The warrior had been leading a band to test the southern limits of the Weald, when they were surprised by a larger Saxon war party. As the Iceni told it, the Saxons had fallen on them without warning and several of his younger warriors, un-blooded and still fresh from the training field, had turned and fled, leaving the remains of the party to fend for themselves. They had suffered heavy losses.

'You believe that killing one man in every ten from the survivors of this Iceni group will send a strong message to the rest of our warriors. This I can understand, it would send a very strong message,' said Uther, in a low voice, his anger barely held in check. 'However, it is not the message I wish to send. I do not want our people to fear us... to fear me. The burden of guilt lays upon our shoulders for not training these men better before sending them out. This Roman practice of decimation, as you call it, has no place in this land.'

With a nod, Tactus allowed the Iceni to rise, but the warrior immediately fell at Uther's feet.

'You are truly my King, Uther Pendragon; I thank you for my life and will repay this debt many times over.'

'There is no debt.' Uther sent the man on his way and even Tactus appeared to approve of the decision.

Every evening, when the burdens of leadership could be set aside, Uther practised with sword, bow and spear. He was also becoming more proficient upon the chariot, tying off the reins and shooting the bow or throwing a spear into a moving target. The moving target was usually Samel carrying a straw bale, and far from fearing the weapons aimed at him, the little Iceni taunted Uther, especially when he managed to avoid being hit, and thumped the side of the chariot with his sword as it sped past.

However, a great sorrow still weighed heavily on the new king's shoulders, the death of Cal. He continued to mourn his family and friends back in the village and the more recent death of Ambrosius, but those losses were slowly healing, while the death of Cal continued to remain an open wound in his soul, outweighing all else. Scarcely a day went by without his thoughts drifting to the shock of finding Cal dying in a pool of blood, his friend's eyes open, staring about the darkness of the roundhouse without seeing him, still more wolf than boy. In Uther's mind, the blame sat squarely upon the dark shoulders of Horsa, whose face still haunted his dreams. In the dead of night, it was always the black Saxon who approached, parting the mists of his dreams with a spear dripping blood, mocking him and laughing in his face. In the battle on Mount Badon, he had seen that same spear taking the life of Ambrosius and it wasn't a tremendous leap to believe that it had taken the life of Cal as well. The future of Uther Pendragon, King of all the tribes, was uncertain in many respects except one, he knew for a certainty, that he would face Horsa in battle.

It was early summer when the reeves, chiefs, kings, and finally the druids, pronounced the omens all correct and the combined forces of the Britons were ready for war. The Saxon invaders had spent the winter months spreading out across eastern Cient, the land of the Cantiaci tribe and northwards through Trinovantes territory, taking control of the largest Trinovante settlement of Camulod. Merlyn had explained that it was at Camulod where the warrior queen Boudicca had fought one of her most famous battles, defeating the Roman legions with a far smaller force. Ultimately, of course, the Romans had returned and had ruled the settlement as Camulodunum, constructing impressive fortifications for its defence, but now, the Saxons had taken Camulod, and were pushing north into the land of the Iceni.

Once again, in the gloom of the great roundhouse, Uther addressed the largest gathering so far, as he readied his people for war. The nerves that had plagued him months before, whenever called upon to address the chiefs had faded, as he finally become familiar with his role as king.

'We are about to take the battle to the Saxons at Aeglesthorp, and then, once we have beaten them there and cut off their means of retreat, will strike north and take Camulod.' Uther paused to scan the many faces in the roundhouse before raising his voice. 'You know as well as I that we face no easy raid. This will be a battle far greater than we fought at Badon, for our enemy has grown. Yet we are now so much more than we were upon Mount Badon that day. We are no longer just individual tribes, we are Britons!' An enormous roar erupted around him and he held his hands up in an appeal for quiet. After a few moments, he was able to continue. 'As our main force travels through the Weald, the chariots will take the old Roman road through the lands of the Ciantiani. Spirits willing, we shall meet upon the battlefield in eight days.'

He stood and drew Excalibur, the sword ringing with a shrill cry as it came free from its sheath. Holding the blade aloft, Uther gazed out across the crowd of fierce, excited warriors, the energy within the roundhouse so palpable that he could feel it flowing through his body, raising the hairs on his arms and the back of his neck, before surging out to join the room once more.

'This is our time... let us take back what is ours. Let us finally claim this land as our own!'

* * *

'What witchcraft is this? You speak of times long since dead; of times we call history, yet you speak of these things as if they have only just happened and that it was you who lived them. You mock us poor folk an t'aint right.' The farmer's wife stood, eyes blazing, and glanced about for support. 'I do not fear you, storyteller, nor do I fear your strange friend there, neither.'

Uther held a finger to his lips, stopping the speaker short. 'Shhh.' His reaction brought smiles and some laughter from the audience, the children giggled and even the farmer was smiling at his wife's discomfort. 'Last year, you listened when I told you of rescuing a princess from a tower as tall as a mountain, and the year before I fought sea monsters in the depths of the sea. I even remember a story a few years back, when I told you of flying to the moon in a boat made of petticoats and kisses. Why, pray tell, do you get so upset now? Sit, and please humour two old men a little longer, and maybe I can tell you something of when your ancestors reclaimed their land.'

'Yes, but I know of this time you speak of. My grandfather used to tell us about when one of my ancestors fought at Badon Hill, but that was twelve hundred years ago. You silly old fool, this is the year sixteen hundred and eighty-three. Not four hundred eighty-three. All these people you speak of are dead... long dead.'

For a moment, the storyteller seemed to fade a little. It was as if a pulse of life lifted him away and then set him back again, something within changed. He ignored the irate old woman and leaned forward to place an arm on the stooped shoulder of Calvador Craen.

'Something went wrong... is that right, Cal? What happened?'

Calvador Craen glanced over his shoulder at the old woman and then back to Uther. 'The hour is late, Uther. We still have more of your story to tell, and then we can finally go home. We owe these good people an ending, an ending that has been so long in coming. Don't you agree?'

Uther nodded. 'I think I know how this ends.'

Still complaining, the farmer's wife was persuaded back to her seat by her husband and friends, and the story allowed to go on.

Chapter 16

The Tribes

'I cannot pass…' Cal's voice sounded hollow in his ears, without strength or substance. Feathery fingers of mist swirled around him as he stared up at a large bleak gateway. It was a tall structure obviously of immense age, crudely constructed from rough, axe-cut timber and overgrown with ivy and moss. It stood as an impassable barrier before him.

Awareness was slowly descending upon him. It felt as if he had been wandering in a dream for ages, possibly days, he wasn't sure. It was all so confusing. First there had been pain, then fear and regret, and finally here, this place. He knew he should be able to move on, that there was somewhere drawing him towards it, but when he pushed on the gate, it didn't so much as sway.

A feeble whine sounded from by his side and he glanced down at the big, silver-grey wolf. It gazed back and pushed closer to his leg, obviously as lost and confused as he was. Reaching down, he stroked a hand through its soft fur, and then glanced back up as the wolf looked past him into the mist and began to growl.

A voice, speaking slowly, dry and old as if contrived from all the many incarnations of man came as a breath through the mist. 'Calvador, your patience has been requested before you are allowed to pass these gates, and once more enter the realm of spirit.' The speaker, a tall form, hidden beneath a dark, ragged cloak, emerged from the shadows, a cold white hand clutching a staff in a tight grip the only clue as to what lay beneath the folds of cloth. As the figure moved slowly towards them, it became evident that time itself couldn't number his years.

'There is one who has requested your presence,' continued the gatekeeper, 'One who has asked that you may be allowed to journey once more from the shadowland, to once more walk amongst the host of man.' The gatekeeper lifted his staff and pointed, inviting Cal to turn and look behind him. Moving through the mist was someone he was at once familiar with and he felt a surge of emotion as his mind fought between spirit and the memory of flesh.

Cal's head snapped back around as the gatekeeper's staff struck the ground, the sound reverberating as a low roll of thunder between dimensions. The spectral figure raised its head and the void within the hood gazed past Cal at the approaching druid.

'Merlyn. You have interceded in the passing of this spirit. Take him, but know you that his spirit beast shall remain. He has but one night of your choosing before he must return to these shadowlands and pass this gate.'

Merlyn nodded. 'As shall it be.' They watched as the gatekeeper faded back into the mist, then the old druid turned to Cal. The wolf gazed up at both of them, still pressing close to Cal's leg.

'Cal... I have a little problem with Uther.'

* * *

'Alric!'

Alric opened his eyes and stared up through a fluttering green canopy of leaves. He was comfortable and had been dozing, quite content to spend a few hours of their patrol lazing about and resting. It was, after all, a beautiful day, one of only a few that this wet and windy land had yet to offer and for once, for just a short space of time, he had been feeling content.

'Alric,' hissed the voice again, 'riders coming.'

Stirring from his reverie, Alric rolled over and lifted up onto one elbow. Taking a deep breath, he focused his attention, listening, his mind unconsciously sifting through the sounds of the breeze in the trees and the furtive movements of his men around him, and then his eyes flashed open as the rattle of a harness and a distant murmur of voices reached him. Cramming his helmet onto his head, he searched down the wooded slope to the old Roman road. 'Where?' he murmured softly, glancing across to where his second, Osric, was pointing west with the blade of his seax.

Osric turned and grinned, his mouth scarred and twisted, exposing the stumps of shattered teeth, a wound earned from a skirmish with the Jutes some years before. 'Local tribesmen... probably another small war party.'

'Be ready!' Alric stood, drew his sword, picked up his shield, and leaned against the closest tree, waiting for his first glimpse of the enemy. To either side, word passed up and down the line of waiting Saxon warriors. They were a large party of twenty-eight, more than a match for a bunch of roving locals. The Britons tended to travel in smaller mixed groups of between ten and fifteen male and female warriors, half of which, would hopefully be slain in the first moments of their attack.

Movement between the trees and he eagerly sought for detail to see what would emerge. It looked like a wagon, maybe two, then came the crunching grind of heavy wheels to confirm it, followed by the whinny of a horse. He smiled. Wagons would mean richer pickings than just a raiding party. With a wave, he sent Osric down the line to command the flank, bows were drawn and he signalled his men on. They crept forward silently, seeking cover from tree to tree, impatient now to fall upon the enemy.

However, as they began to run and the first arrows were loosed, Alric realised there must be more than two wagons. Then, as they emerged from the trees, he became aware of just how many more there were... and that they weren't wagons.

It had been a long day and the steady rumble of the chariots' wheels had cast a soporific effect upon Uther. The ride was too bumpy to actually fall asleep, but the warmth of the sun and the chance for his mind to relax and wander after so many months caught up in the stress of duty was somewhat, sublime.

In the last two days, they had passed several settlements, mostly small Catuvellauni villages, but now closer to the coast, the last few communities had been mixed with Saxons, the two groups struggling together for a peaceful coexistence. Soon they would be entering the more hostile territory claimed by the main Saxon invaders and word had been passed to be vigilant, but it wasn't easy on a day such as this.

Uther's chariot was in the middle of the line with sixty chariots in front, a similar number behind, and over a hundred mounted warriors positioned to the rear. Sharing his chariot was Samel, who since setting out had chattered incessantly about the land, the weather, chariot tactics and 'the bastard Saxons,' but even he had lapsed into silence as the day had worn on.

An indistinct cry from the lead chariots was the first thing to shatter the peace of the afternoon, quickly followed by a scream from one of the horses. Then, from the shadows of the trees, came a flight of arrows, one of which embedded itself in the side of Uther's chariot with a heavy thunk, and the line of chariots exploded into action.

'Where are they?' cried Uther, as he craned to see around the confusion of jumping horses and moving chariots. The clash of metal from the front of the line answered him before Samel could and he felt the chariot lurch beneath him as Samel pulled the horses round. Shouting at others to move aside, Samel guided them at a trot down the line towards the sounds of battle. As he did, several of the horsemen galloped past.

A roar of Saxon battle cries erupted from the forest and several Saxons came running from the tree line. The sight of them coming towards them, big bearded men wearing the familiar Saxon helmets, each brandishing a sword or axe and screaming out their challenges, brought back the horrific memories of Mount Badon to Uther. Drawing

Excalibur, he immediately felt fear turn to resolve. However, before he could do anything, he realised that there couldn't be more than about thirty of them. He lowered his sword and searched the darkness between the trees to either side, but no hidden troops came screaming to the aid of their fellows. The Saxons were ridiculously outnumbered, and sure enough, the attack faltered before it had really started. A few continued to run on, but most, seeing the number of warriors they were attacking, had already turned and were fleeing, desperate to reach the safety of the trees, for most it was too late, the chariots and horsemen were already upon them. A flurry of arrows took down several and then the lead chariots wheeled round and, picking up speed, charged back on them and any of the Saxons still standing were caught in a killing ground.

The chariot horses had been battle-trained to keep moving forward when they clashed with a man, so the first run of five chariots broke into the small group of Saxons, trampled many and chased the few survivors back into the trees. Uther felt a wave of nausea as he watched the slaughter, but it was over quickly, too late to be brought to a halt.

As several survivors ran past, Samel thrust the reins into Uther's hands and leapt from the moving chariot before Uther could cry out and stop him. Bellowing his battle cry, the little Iceni brought his axe down into the back of the closest Saxon as he scrambled, panic-stricken in retreat up the slope to the trees. Quickly, heaving his blade clear, Samel was up and disappearing into the forest after another.

Uther returned Excalibur to its scabbard and gripped the side of the chariot to support himself as the horses moved, then glanced back up the line. Most of the chariots and horses had remained unmolested on the path; their riders unable to do any more than shout their support. The chariots could not manoeuvre on the road, it was too confining. He felt lucky there weren't more of them. Samel soon reappeared from the trees and jumped back up beside Uther, a grin spreading under his red whiskers. 'We got most of them, but you can be sure a few will have escaped to spread news of our coming.'

'Why would such a small group attack us?' Uther asked, handing back the reins. 'I don't understand. They came with no chance other than being slaughtered.'

Samel shook his head. 'Don't know why, lad, maybe because they're stupid and deserve to be butchered and thrown back into the sea? Who can tell how the mind of a Saxon works?' He shrugged. 'Actually, I'm guessing they didn't count on there being so many of us. Did you see the looks of surprise when they saw us? They were expecting someone else.'

The chariots reformed, and this time, at Uther's order, they did so two-abreast and moved on, a little more vigilant of the trees and bushes that crowded the road. Several times during the day, they came across parties of Saxons, but they were small groups that turned and scattered rather than encounter the larger force.

The day ended, with light to spare, in an easily defendable area where the horses could graze. Sentries were set at the perimeters, and the camp tried to rest in the knowledge that the following dawn would bring them very quickly to Aeglesthorp and the main Saxon camp.

* * *

Alric cursed as an unseen branch whipped across his face. It wasn't the first; his face and arms were already sore from the punishment inflicted by the forest. As the light faded, they had been forced to slow their flight, six riders, all that remained of his patrol, limping home. Although tempted to stop and tend the wounds carried by several of his men, he was unwilling to rest for the night. He had to get back to warn Hengist that a massive force, with hundreds of chariots and mounted warriors, was closing on them. The horses were beginning to tire, if they started dropping it would end the matter, but it couldn't be much further. The sting of the branches hurt as they reached out to scratch at him, but what really burnt was the voice in his head constantly asking how he could have been so stupid? How could he have been so undisciplined? He had come out of the trees, expecting to see a couple of wagons and a few guards, only to be presented with a line of chariots stretching as far as he could see. At that awful moment, he had believed he'd attacked the whole of the tribal nations with only twenty-eight men… fool! He could vividly recall the moment his bladder had almost emptied and that instant of certain knowledge that he had condemned his men to death. For the thousandth time, he cursed his stupidity and wondered how he could present it to Hengist and not have his throat cut.

When they finally emerged from the Weald and rode out towards the flickering sentry fires of Aeglesthorp, it was late. The stars were twinkling overhead and the smell of salt water from the estuary hung heavily in the air. Although they had been moving slowly for some time, the horses were exhausted and unsteady on their legs. The poor animals had been pushed beyond their normal levels of endurance and Alric had to coax his mount over the final distance. As he stopped and jumped from its back, it staggered, dropped its head, and gave a ragged snort. It stood, swaying slightly, refusing to move even when a handler came forward and tried leading it gently towards the stabling area. Alric patted its sweaty neck then strode across to Hengist's hut. Two torches burned outside the entrance, signifying that Hengist was still awake and willing to receive visitors. Alric thanked the gods for this one small mercy; waking Hengist would be a sure way to die, but he would have had to do it.

Chapter 17

THE COLD LIGHT OF DAWN

Uther Pendragon shivered in the early morning light and gazed about absently, willing his mind to wake and his body to warm. It was ominously quiet in the small copse of trees; there wasn't even any birdsong. Long shadows stretched towards him from the distant village of Aeglesthorp, laying uneven across the large grassy meadow glistening with morning dew. Behind the village, the eastern sky was promising another fine day, with the first blush of sunrise painting the scattered clouds with pastel shades of pink and orange. A cold breeze whispered across the field, blowing softly through the long grass, making the mist stir and dance, drawing Uther's attention for a moment. As Samel joined him, he gathered his cloak tighter about his shoulders and shivered again, watching his breath emerge as a cloud into the chill air.

'The river's on the far side,' said Samel, pointing towards the distant village.

Uther studied the village once more. He could just make out the dark shapes of clustered roundhouses rising above a low stockade. Behind the settlement, the high masts of several Saxon longboats, drawn up onto what Samel had described as 'a small shingle beach,' showed black against the soft light of early morning.

With a sigh, Uther waved a hand towards the darkness of the forest, and then quickly returned it to the warmth of his cloak. 'And our main force with Merlyn should be waiting in the trees there?' The forest appeared gloomy, empty, and home to little more than spirits, as far as Uther could see. 'Send two men to make contact. I want to be sure they're there to back us up before we attack.' Samel nodded and turned away.

Returning to his study of the village, Uther stood a little straighter as men started to emerge from behind the stockade and form into their defensive shield wall. His unease continued to grow as they carried out and divided long sharpened stakes amongst them. It didn't take a lot of working out to realise what these would be for, the Saxons were ready for them. When the first line of chariots attacked, the horses would be impaled as the stakes were raised, and the chariots quickly overcome. He continued watching as the numbers grew, until over a thousand Saxons were crowded along the field, silently staring across at the trees where Uther and his tribesmen waited. *We're hugely outnumbered again*, realised Uther with a growing feeling of alarm. More emerged, some moving left in front of the forest, while others turned to the right to spread further around the intended battlefield.

As they ran out they carried weapons, a shield, and firewood, the last item dumped in growing piles that could be torched when the battle commenced.

Well, they know we're here, thought Uther, and then he glanced about for Samel. He saw the little Iceni making his way back through the trees, sharing a joke with one of his men. How could he laugh at a time like this? Cupping his hands, he hissed a warning. 'Samel... they know we're here!'

Samel frowned and trotted over. 'Shhh, be strong for your men, King Uther. I'm well aware that they know we're here, I've seen 'em... couldn't really miss 'em, could I? Some of those Saxons from the attack yesterday must have gotten back and given the warning, but those men over there will be just as cold and scared as we are, more so, hopefully. They don't know how many we are and they don't know when we'll attack. The longer we can wait the better.'

Two bowls of porridge were passed forward and the two friends indulged themselves in silence for a while, savouring the taste and the glorious warmth that filled them. All too soon, Samel ran a finger around his empty bowl, and then sucked it noisily. He glanced back down to see if he'd missed any, frowned, and then reluctantly handed it to the waiting man and returned to his study of the Saxons.

The sun was now above the horizon and the shadows on the field were drawing back as the sun rose, the rays that lanced through the village lending an orange tint to the mist as it drifted over the field. Samel examined the effect with a critical eye.

'I hadn't noticed until now, King Uther, but do you see how the mist is lingering above certain parts of the meadow? It shows where the ground is holding water, where it's marshy.' He pointed to a spot not thirty paces into the field. 'Do you see there, where the mist clings to that darker patch? The grass is taller and it'll be soft under the chariots' wheels and will bog us down if we don't find firmer ground around it. We'll have to wait for a little more light and hope we can see a way through.'

Uther nodded, and then glanced behind him at the chariots and horsemen waiting patiently amongst the trees. There was a heavy tension hanging in the air as they each contemplated the morning ahead. Some were tightening harnesses and tending their horses, while others sharpened weapons, stones gliding slowly along blades already keenly sharp, the sound coming as a soft rasping whisper amongst the trees. A good number were still eating porridge or waiting patiently, doing what Uther was doing, staring out of the shadows across the field at the Saxons.

'How many are we?' Uther's question came out as a rush, momentarily betraying his fears. He stopped, drew a calming breath, and gripped Excalibur beneath his cloak. Feeling the fear crawl back down to his belly, where it seemed to lie, ready to rise again with a rush, he smiled. 'I'm sorry, Samel. What I meant to ask was how many are we now? Have the others caught up yet? And did we hear anything back from Merlyn?'

'We're still one hundred and twenty chariots, and over a hundred horsemen,' replied Samel, glancing across at the rising sun. 'There'll be another two hundred horsemen with us before the sun climbs much higher, we should at least wait until then before committing ourselves, and no, we haven't heard back from Merlyn yet.'

'But you sent those men into the forest ages ago?'

Samel shrugged. 'I did, but they wouldn't necessarily have found them straight away, would they? They'll be keeping out of sight, keeping their heads down. Don't worry, we'll hear from them soon enough.'

Realising there was little he could do, Uther went back to observing the Saxon side of the field and muttered a prayer to the spirits that ended in a plea for Merlyn to have been granted safe passage with his four thousand warriors. The forest still looked awfully dark and empty to him.

As the sun crested the village, they received word that the horsemen had been sighted and Uther felt some of his anxiety subside. One hundred and twenty chariots and three hundred horsemen wasn't a huge force, but it was certainly an effective one, especially against men on foot, which was all he could see in the Saxon lines.

The Saxons had few horses, since they arrived on the shores of Briton without them and could only round up so many from the local settlements or on the moors where the horses ran wild. He glanced about for Samel, finally spotting him sitting up in a tree with one of his men.

They were pointing at the field, working out where the softer marshy parts were and where there might be a firmer path through. He watched as they began their climb down, and then saw them halt their descent and begin pointing excitedly to the rear of their position. There was a muffled conversation, and then Samel clambered down a few branches and hurriedly dropped through the last, landing heavily.

'Mount up!' There was a flurry of movement amongst the closest riders and the order was passed along the line and back to those that waited in the trees.

'Our horsemen have just joined us,' said Samel, reaching Uther and grasping his tunic to steady himself. He stopped and drew in a deep breath, clutching at his stomach, the fall having winded him more than he had first let on. 'But as we watched them come in, we also saw Saxons. They're moving from the trees to the south, lots of them. We would have missed them but we saw them crossing an open patch of ground, they're surrounding us!' He dragged Uther towards their chariot. As they mounted, a Saxon drum began to pound out a deep steady beat that was quickly joined by more drums and then the deep mournful drone of horns. The morning became filled with a cacophony of noise as the Saxon warriors all around the field stood and joined in, roaring their challenges and rattling their weapons and shields together, the sound at once terrifying and deafening to the waiting tribesmen.

'They're coming at us,' cried Samel. He grabbed the chariot reins, all pretence at stealth now abandoned. 'They're going to try and scatter us out into the field and bog us down!' His face was flushed crimson with anger, and flecks of white spittle hung in his beard as he spat out his hatred for the conniving invaders who had out-foxed them. 'Well, they'll not catch us that easy. Out!' With a crack of his whip, the chariot lurched and rumbled forward as Samel led them out, searching for the firmer ground that he had spotted from his perch in the tree. 'The bastards surrounded us!'

Uther could do little more than grip the side of the chariot and force his mind to try and catch up. In what seemed an instant, all their plans had changed. He hung on as they creaked and bounced over the rough, uneven ground into the open field and away from the immediate threat emerging behind them. The low-lying sun was blinding when he glanced over towards the village, but Samel seemed to be taking them south, away from the waiting warriors. 'Where are we going? Do you have a plan?' Uther asked, raising his voice over the incredible clamour from the Saxons. The fires were now alight and smoke was already drifting across the field, adding to the confusion.

'You're the King,' cried Samel. 'I'm just taking us around the soft ground in the centre and away from those sneaky buggers behind us!'

Uther groped for the hilt of Excalibur and scanned the battlefield. Much to his frustration, the trees of the Weald continued to remain dark and silent, while all around, the Saxons surrounded them, cutting off any chance of escape. As an added danger, if they weren't careful, they would be forced into the boggy centre of the field where the chariots would be less manoeuvrable or possibly completely trapped. Things suddenly seemed very bleak indeed. He glanced back, his heart racing with indecision and uncertainty. The chariots had all left the trees now and the horsemen were following with the first Saxons screaming out after them, the whole procession of tribesmen, flushed out like so many deer on a day's hunt, and still the trees of the Weald remained dark and empty of any help or inspiration.

Bringing his hand down hard upon the chariot's edge, Uther cursed. 'Damn you, Merlyn, where are you? We have to reverse this situation before it gets out of hand.' He attempted to calm himself as he scanned the Saxon ranks.

'Get out of hand? I would say this is already out of hand,' shouted Samel, cracking the reins down to urge the horses through a softer piece of ground. A cloud of smoke wafted over them, momentarily hiding the field from view.

'We have to attack and force a way through,' said Uther, as they cleared the smoke. He scanned the field once more. 'There.' He pointed towards the village. 'If we can get through into the village, there's bound to be a road running along the coast.'

Samel glanced across at him, with a look of concern. 'You want to leave already? We've only just got here!'

'So what do *you* suggest?' cried Uther. 'We're just a little bit outnumbered here. Or hadn't you noticed?' He clutched for the side as they bumped over a grassy hillock, his spears rattling in their holder beside him.

'Well, I liked the bit about attacking,' said Samel, with a grin. He threw back his head and letting out an ululating cry, snapped the reins down once more and turned the chariot towards the wall of screaming Saxons. Behind them, the other chariots wheeled and followed, and the horsemen raced past, screaming their war cries to confuse the Saxon defences and draw attention away from the slower chariots. At least this part was something for which the horsemen had trained.

Moments before they smashed into the Saxon wall with its bristling barrier, the riders peeled away and both horsemen and chariots loosed their first volley of spears and arrows. It was impossible to aim from the platform of a bouncing chariot so, just as on the training field, those in the chariots waited until the last moment, then loosed, inflicting a wave of death that slammed into the bunched Saxons, each spear and arrow seeking those holding the long sharpened poles. A fraction of a moment behind the horsemen, the chariots hit the Saxon line like a hammer slamming through the side of an ale barrel, breaching the shattered defences in an instant. The taunting war cries were replaced by the shrill screaming of injured horses and crushed and trampled men as the chariots jumped and bucked as they struggled over the fallen and tried to get themselves clear. Uther stabbed and slashed with Excalibur, as the Saxons converged on them, cleaving a path as they forged ahead into the mass of screaming humanity.

The world had turned to madness, and it was tainted red.

Saxon warriors rose and fell before them in a moving sea of sharp iron and blood, as one man fell, another snarling, hate-filled face leapt in to fill the breach. As Uther fought, he heard Samel curse and scream beside him, defying the Saxons to come closer. When they did, it ended with him flicking blood from his axe with a practised turn of the wrist as they fell, forever lost from sight as the chariot rumbled and rolled on.

As for the horses, one had escaped uninjured from the poles, while the other had suffered a bloody gash to its right flank. It was snorting, tossing its head in pain and fear, but still moving, doggedly dragging the chariot forward as Samel continued to bellow his defiance.

While Uther fought, he tried to gauge what was happening around him. Standing on the moving chariot afforded him a good perspective of the battle and the Saxon's defences. Only so many could face the chariots at once, but when he glanced about, he could see others running in, crowding behind, eager for their turn. Taking the opportunity to look up once more, he could make out other chariots moving through, some of which were already far ahead, through the fighting, and wheeling round on the opposite side. Others, he knew, wouldn't have been so lucky. Hindered by fallen horses, their riders were quickly overwhelmed by the larger Saxon force.

Uther pulled back Excalibur from where he had just thrust it into a Saxon warrior's chest, and kicked out at another clinging to the side, desperately trying to get on. Beneath him, the chariot lumbered ever forward. Then, with little warning, they were free of the battle and there was a jolt as the horses picked up speed. It knocked them both from their feet, grabbing for the sides lest they fall from the open back. The horses, with noses suddenly filled with fresh air, bolted for the open ground towards the village, frantically fleeing the world of insanity from which they had just escaped.

As they bounced across the grassland, Samel scrabbled up from where he had fallen, dropped his axe, and leapt over the front of the chariot. He landed between the two galloping horses and held on as best he could before gaining his balance and making his way down the yoke-pole between them.

'Samel! Get back here,' screamed Uther, reaching for the reins. He pulled back hard but the horses didn't respond. The left wheel banged hard against a tussock of tall grass and the chariot jumped, flinging Uther to the floor again, one hand managing to grip the rail as he fell.

Between the horses, Samel hung on grimly. Edging slowly forward, he reached out and, taking a good grip of each horse's mane, dragged them round to the right. He strained, bracing his feet against the yoke, bringing them slowly round and under control once more. When they had slowed enough, he shuffled back to rejoin Uther, who merely shook his head at his friend's antics. With this small drama behind them, the horses slowed to a walk, huffing and blowing, and they took their first look back at the battle, it did little to hearten them.

Uther gripped his bow, pulled an arrow from the quiver slung on the back of the chariot, set it and drew. He heard the now familiar creak of the string as his fingers nestled at full draw against his cheek, and then released, watching as the shaft leapt across the distance to slam into the chest of a Saxon, one of several attacking another chariot. He fumbled for another arrow, bracing himself against the side as the chariot jolted heavily again.

'Hold on, lad. We're going back in,' shouted Samel, over the noise of pitched battle. It was already deafening, making him hard to hear.

'Where, by the spirits, is Merlyn?' cried Uther, casting a longing glance towards the Weald. He willed the druid to appear at the head of the huge force of tribesmen, but again the darkness mocked him with their absence. 'We're not going to win this without him,' he continued. With a last glance round at the village, he saw he had been right, there was indeed a road running north. 'If we can somehow get all our warriors clear, we can either take that road, or get back the way we came.'

The chariot was picking up speed again, racing back into the unprotected rear of the Saxon forces. Uther had a chance to throw one spear, saw it miss his intended victim but take another Saxon in the thigh, the scream lost amongst a thousand others from all around, and then they both ducked down and braced for impact. It came with a sickening jolt, the crunching grind of every bone broken by the heavy oak wheels, vibrating up through the wooden frame. The chariot slowed and they stood back up, once more amongst the madness of battle.

Samel let go of the reins and gave the horses their heads. Bending back down, he searched for his axe, caught it just before it fell out, and then jumped up with a roar. With a mighty heave, he swung the axe down, cleaving it through the raised shield of a black-bearded Saxon, dropping him out of sight. More Saxons filled the gap as another stinging cloud of smoke drifted over them and, for a few panic-filled moments, they fought in near blindness.

The chariot lurched without warning as the weight changed and Samel spun around to see that a Saxon had managed to climb up with them. The warrior was euphoric, lost to the fever of battle. Splatters of blood covered his face, his lips drawn back in a drooling smile of killing-madness. His eyes gleamed from beneath a polished helm, the nose guard bent to the side from where Uther had already hit him. The two were struggling, locked together with swords raised, Uther wrestling against the bigger, stronger man who began laughing hysterically as he felt his smaller opponent weakening.

There was no room to swing the axe, so Samel jabbed the shaft into the side of the man's head, feeling it land with a skull-shattering crunch. When, a moment later, they emerged from the smoke, the Saxon was no longer there, but the madness of battle raged on.

Towards the inner side of the fighting, they came across another chariot that had been forced to stop. One horse was down and the other, struggled in panic, its eyes flaring as it felt itself trapped by its fallen companion. Surrounding them was a mob of hollering, screaming Saxon warriors, while standing high above the chaos around them, its occupants, miraculously, still lived. Two big Atrebates tribesmen, both swinging axes, were inflicting more damage than they were receiving, but they were tiring. One warrior fought with his left arm hanging useless by his side, streaming blood from a severe gash. The other remained uninjured as he hacked with great sweeping cuts into the mob around them with an axe in one hand and a sword in the other. Several mounted warriors had joined them and were harrying the Saxons. Uther watched as a horseman jumped down and attempted to cut the dead horse from the chariot's reins.

Samel saw their plight and picked up speed, bringing them in to slam into the knot of attackers, trampling several as the horses forced their way through. As the dead horse on the stranded chariot was cut free, they were able to move away, the remaining horse pulling it, eyes rolling and straining with the effort, its riders cheering in triumph.

'Regroup,' screamed Uther, as they burst free into the centre of the field once more. Samel brought a horn to his lips and blew a long deep note. They trundled further into the central ground and slowed, then Uther turned and counted. Thirteen chariots were moving away with them. He couldn't count the horsemen, but the number had thinned considerably. From all around, the Saxons swarmed towards them and he fought to hold down a moment of despair.

'We have to get through. We can't let them trap us here!' cried Uther, panic beginning to edge his voice. 'Bring us around again. We'll make for the northern road.' The chariots wheeled about, and then to a chorus of yells and curses, the horses were coaxed back up to a gallop behind the heavy chariots.

At the front, Uther braced himself against the side of the chariot, raised his bow, and loosed his remaining shafts. It was as he was drawing back on the last, that he saw Horsa. The black-clad warrior chief was the only mounted Saxon on the field. Uther stared, mesmerized, as his enemy rode up and down the line behind his men, shouting and screaming abuse to drive them on. Another cloud of smoke blew across the field, momentarily obscuring Uther's view. He raised his bow and fired one of his last arrows blind, sending a prayer with it that it would find its mark. However, as they came through the smoke, the Saxon leader was still there, drawing men in from the sides to help form a barrier in front of the charging tribes. Under his direction, they were gathering the sharpened poles, raising them against the oncoming horses, once again; the Saxon wall quickly began to resemble an impenetrable thorny bush.

At the last moment, just before they hit, Uther screamed a curse and helped Samel haul on the reins to bring them round, the chariot almost turning over as it rose up on one wheel. Uther threw himself at the side to stop them turning over, the chariot righted, and then they slammed at an angle into the Saxon lines.

The unexpected manoeuvre caught the Saxons unaware before the poles could be realigned and the chariots crashed through the massed warriors causing havoc, changing what had been the brink of disaster, into a minor victory, before turning back to the open field. Behind them, the horsemen attacked the confused Saxon ranks, thinning them even further, but the tribesmen still hadn't escaped the circle, and it was getting smaller.

The small force of Britons retreated to the open field with the screams and cries of the injured following them. Resting weary arms as they gathered, the riders gazed about at the incredible number of Saxons closing in and tried to remain undaunted. Around him, Uther saw the tribesmen looking to him for guidance, for some hope that he, their King, could find some victory in this bleak defeat.

A Saxon drum began the beat again, and others immediately took it up until the whole field was surging. Uther laid a hand on Samel's arm and the chariot came to a stop.

'This can still be our day!' shouted Uther, to the remains of his force as they drew up and gathered around him. 'The Saxons have us penned here like so many sheep. They believe they are wolves, herding us towards our certain slaughter, but we shall show them we are of the tribes, and we still have our teeth!'

The men roared and raised their swords in salute.

'In those trees over there, are our friends and brothers. They're waiting for us. They promised to be here this day and they will not fail us.' He glanced across to the woodland, the first line of trees now sunlit and more inviting than it had been at any other time since they had first arrived. 'Let us deliver these Saxon dogs to their deaths, for now this battle shall turn!' He slapped Samel on the back and the little Iceni cracked the whip over the horses. The chariot lurched, and the remnants of Uther's warriors charged the Saxon lines closest to the forest.

Both sides knew this would be the last charge of the tribes, and the Saxons swarmed in from every side of the battlefield to meet them. Once the tribesmen had shown their commitment to one direction, the long poles of the Saxons were discarded and they swarmed forward, their bloodlust raised to a peak, to deliver a true and certain slaughter, and they ran quickly lest they miss out.

'I hope you're right about this, Uther Pendragon,' cried Samel, as they rapidly closed the distance. 'But if it's of any consequence, I admire your pluck and wouldn't have the end happen any other way! Pendragon!'

Every tribesman on the field took up the cry, as they descended. The sound of the horses hooves hammering the ground was like thunder, and the cry that echoed around the battlefield again and again was 'Pendragon!'

They hit the first ranks of Saxons with a crunch that was both sickening and deafening, a cacophony of breaking bones and screams, trampling the slowest and slashing out at those that tried to escape to the sides. However, the enemy were too many and, as they were forced to slow, the Saxons swarmed in. The fighting chariots of the tribes were finally brought to a stop some thirty paces from the tree line by the sheer weight of Saxon warriors around them. The shrill cry of the horses as the Saxons slaughtered them rose above the noise of conflict, and the riders now trapped were brought to battle in the tribesmen's last stand.

Wielding Excalibur with both hands, the blade flowing in a blurring dance of death, Uther carved a fighting circle on their right, while Samel fought behind him like a red-bearded war spirit. The battle became a heaving blur of screaming, hate-filled faces, desperate to get at the occupants of the grouped chariots, and the two friends became oblivious to what was happening further than their immediate killing ground as they fought for their lives.

The piercing death cry of a horse rose above the noise of battle just as Uther, for one solitary moment, prepared himself to die, and then, in front of him, a Saxon with a horned helm fell with a scream, but from a blow that he hadn't delivered, and then beside the first, another fell. Other Saxons were turning their backs on him to meet some new threat and he became aware of warriors fighting on foot. As they swept in, he had the chance to rest his sword arm and glance up. Merlyn's tribesmen, a constant flow of warriors, were swarming out of the forest and falling onto the Saxons, turning the tide of the battle in an instant.

The sheer number emerging from the trees forced the fighting further out into the battlefield and away from the stranded chariots, soon leaving the remains of Uther's force standing on their chariots as if marooned upon islands amongst a sea of dead and dying.

Uther glanced to where the battle raged with even greater ferocity, and then to the crows dropping from the trees, celebrating the start of their feast with excited cries as they danced amongst the fallen.

It was as Uther glanced up from the crows that he saw him again. 'Horsa!' Leaping from the back of the stranded chariot, he ran across to a riderless horse, one of the last that was still standing, shivering with shock nearby, and jumped up, guiding the animal through the fallen bodies and after the retreating figure in black. Turning back, he called to Samel. 'Find a mount and some men, and follow me, we have to catch Horsa.' Without waiting for an answer, he cleared the sea of dead then kicked the horse into a gallop towards the village and the northern road that lay beyond.

* * *

Back by the crackling fire on midwinter's eve, the storyteller's audience remained silent as the old man reached down beside his chair and groped about for his mug of ale. Finding it, he drank greedily, the ale running from the corners of his mouth, down through his grey whiskers, and onto his chest. He drained it to the bottom, wiped a hand across his face, and belched softly. 'Aaahhhh,' he sighed in satisfaction, then frowned, and turned his head, staring into the fire as if he had heard something beyond the flames.

Cal looked over, and then smiled as he saw Uther's attention drawn to the crackling logs.

The storyteller raised a hand. 'Soon… the telling is almost done.' He shook his head and charged his pipe for what he knew would probably be a final time. 'That's the trouble with druids,' he murmured to Calvador Craen, 'very little patience with the ways of man.'

Chapter 18

DEATH OF A SAXON

As Uther rode between the Saxon dwellings of Aeglesthorp with the sound of battle receding, the horse's hoof beats and laboured breathing suddenly seemed loud in the comparative silence.

The village was all but deserted.

A few chickens scratched at the dirt, a handcart stood abandoned between the huts, and an old woman carrying a bundle of sticks stood watching them gallop past, offering a vacant, disinterested expression. When a dog shot out between buildings, scattering the chickens to bark savagely at the horse's legs, the horse didn't so much as startle. It had suffered far worse this day on the battlefield, a dog offered little threat.

The only other sign of the Saxon inhabitants was a little girl peering round a skin door. She followed Uther's passing with tear-filled eyes, until a hand hastily pulled her back into the shadows. The sight hit him harder than any Saxon blade had that day... that this brutal race of invaders had children too. It came as a shock, which in turn was cause for concern. That he hadn't thought of his enemy as a people that could have families, loves and fears of their own, that there might be Saxon children awaiting the return of a father or brother, a father or brother that he might have slain.

If Britain is to be a free country, then there has to be a truce, and an end to the war and killing, thought Uther, and it had to include all these people who were now calling it home.

Once out of the village, he headed onto the northern road. It was a proper dirt track, one on which you could feel the earth beneath your feet. Not paved and uncomfortable like the Roman road they had travelled to get to Aeglesthorp. It was wide enough for a single wagon, as the hard sun-baked furrows attested, easier on the horse's hooves than the Roman-cut stone, and felt good to ride on.

The dense woodland of the Weald ran along the left-hand side, while to the right, it was grassy and clear of trees right down to the river estuary, from the horse, he had a good view of the way ahead.

There, in the distance, a black shape moved against the trees... Uther dug in his heels and hung on as the horse lunged forward. As he began to close the distance, the shape appeared to resolve into a group of three riders, possibly four. He felt a pang of annoyance and then uncertainty at his rash flight. Horsa had been the only mounted Saxon in the battle so he had assumed he would be alone... 'Damn!'

He knew he should have waited for Samel and some of the others. Then he glanced back. Surely, they couldn't be too far behind. They couldn't let Horsa get away!

The horse stumbled on the uneven track and began to slow. Glancing down he saw it was tiring. It had carried its rider through a terrifying battle, forced to confront its fear again, and again. Now, after giving its all, it was close to collapse. White foam flowed in long streams from its mouth, trailing along its flanks. Its shoulders slick with sweat, the edges crusting white, dried by the heat of its body.

'Come on, horse, don't die on me,' pleaded Uther. 'If we stop and rest, we'll lose him, and if we press harder, we may catch him before your heart gives in, but then maybe not.' For a moment, he considered his options, gazing along the path with the horse's laboured breathing and hoof beats loud in his ears, but the Saxons were nowhere in sight. The path, stretching away through the reed beds of the estuary, was devoid of any sign of life other than a flight of ducks, circling to land on the water, and a few dragonflies skipping over the bulrushes. With a sigh, he reigned in and the horse slowed to a grateful walk, huffing and blowing hard as it did so. Uther suddenly felt weariness overtake him as the need to push himself passed.

Samel arrived a short while later and approached warily. Uther was lying flat on his back beneath a tree staring up at the sky through the branches. His horse was cropping grass a few paces away, none the worse from its day of battle and mayhem.

'So, are you all right? Or did the Saxon rob us of our king?' called Samel, as the chariot came level. He jumped down and strode over, concerned that the young king had neither stirred nor replied. 'Are you alright lad?' Uther ignored him, even when Samel stared down blocking his view, as he looked him over for wounds.

'It took us a while to round up some horses... Uther... Yer eyes are open, lad, and I don't see anything that could be called a wound on yer body. Plenty of blood, but I'd guess it's nothing more than the taint of battle. What's the matter with yer, can you hear me or what?'

'The killing has to stop,' murmured Uther, his gaze flicking across to Samel. 'We have to build a strong land, but the killing has to stop.'

'One step at a time, lad,' muttered Samel, offering his hand. 'Are we going to chase down Horsa first? Or have you come to some other decision while you were lying there searching for clouds?' He helped Uther to his feet and brushed away the twigs and leaf-mould that clung to the young king's back.

Uther sighed and looked around one final time, at the peace and serenity of the forest. 'No, Samel, there is no other decision. Horsa and I shall meet sword to sword; it's one of the events that, for some reason, cannot be changed. I wish it could, but it will take place.' Uther fixed Samel with a stare so intense that the little Iceni shivered and turned back to the chariot.

'You're starting to talk like a druid,' he mumbled. 'What do yer mean, it has to take place?' Spinning round, his voice rose in anger. 'Why does anything have to take place?'

'I don't know,' replied Uther, 'but this is one meeting that all the spirits are calling to witness, and it's going to happen soon. There's nothing I can do about it,' he added softly.

Two other chariots arrived, rumbling along the track with the riders calling out their greetings, the excitement of victory still upon them as they brought their horses to a stop.

Samel held up a hand, waved, then turned back to Uther. 'Don't underestimate this Saxon. The spirits may well be guiding you, but the Saxons have their *own* gods looking out for their interests.'

'Fear not.' Uther's face broke into a grin. 'I'm in no hurry to die. Anyway, if spirits and gods are truly guiding us, then there's very little we can do about it. We stole a victory from the Saxons today, but in truth, we were very nearly beaten. Uther jumped onto the chariot beside Samel and took the reins, the horses skipped forward in alarm. 'This isn't about a Saxon or tribal victory. It has to be a victory that will include all of us.' He cracked the reins, and the chariot took off.

'Follow us, lads,' called Samel. 'Our King has a meeting with destiny, and he doesn't want to be late!' The three chariots thundered down the path with the whooping battle cries of the riders swallowed up amongst the ancient woodland.

It was getting late in the afternoon when they came across the first sign of the fleeing Saxons, a dead horse by the side of the path with a Saxon blanket trapped beneath it. After a cursory inspection, they continued on and caught sight of their quarry a short while later.

Two of the Saxons were sharing a horse forcing the whole group to travel slower. However, when they heard the sound of chariot wheels behind them, they kicked the horses into action, even managing a short gallop, but the horse's energy faded quickly and the chariots rapidly closed on them.

The Saxons had little choice but turn and fight, with one horse down they couldn't hope to outpace the chariots. Horsa and his men made it to an open area on a curved part of the riverbank before letting the horses loose and preparing for the approaching chariots. The trees of the Weald stood just a little further back at this point, giving them room to fan out and pull blades free of scabbards.

As they got closer, the chariots picked up speed and charged towards the black dressed figure of Horsa, who stood immobile and defiant in their path. Once in the open glade they spread out to make full use of the space and bore down on the four standing men and there were curses and cries as they met.

Uther brought Excalibur down and it clashed with Horsa's upraised sword, spinning the Saxon about while beside him, Samel cleaved his axe through the chest of another, ripping it clear in a spray of blood as the chariots passed.

As Uther looked back, he saw a Saxon squat down before one of the other chariots, and with a swiping slash of his seax, hamstring one of the horses, the sharp blade slicing the tendon of a rear leg. There was a shrill scream from the horse and it collapsed as its weight landed on the useless leg, crashing to the ground in a cloud of dust, dragging the other terrified horse along with it, and the chariot somersaulted over them, flinging its riders high into the air to land heavily some distance away. The riders lay unmoving, while behind them, the two horses continued to struggle and scream amidst the wreckage of the chariot.

The two remaining chariots manoeuvred at the end of their run, trying to turn as efficiently as possible in the confined space. Once they had completed their turns, the two sides stopped and regarded each other some thirty paces apart, ignoring the sound of the panicking horses between them.

'Who amongst you would face me alone?' cried Horsa. 'You chase us down but would any of you fight me man to man?' He said something to his two remaining companions and they laughed.

Uther felt Samel bristle beside him. 'No, Samel, this is my fight, remember?' Samel nodded, but Uther had already jumped down and was walking towards the Saxon chieftain.

'I am Uther Pendragon, war leader of the tribes and king of all the Britons, I will fight you.' He drew Excalibur and, cutting the air with the great sword, brought it up in salute to his Saxon enemy.

'A child leads the tribes? Why, you still have the pimples of youth on your face where a real man grows a beard!' The two Saxons laughed, and then Horsa stepped forward, his face drawing into a frown. 'But I know you, don't I, boy? We've met before, have we not?'

Uther ignored the question. 'I am going to allow your people to remain in this land, to settle amongst us and live as Britons. But you... you I will kill.' He saw a play of confusion turn to anger as it crossed Horsa's face, but went on before Horsa could react. 'You killed the only real friend I had, I know it was you, and then you killed my brother. Most would say, good enough reasons for me to take your life and send you to the shadowland, but the main reason that you will die today, is so that your people can live, in peace, as Britons.'

Horsa roared and swept down his blade, and Uther reacted, raising Excalibur and catching the Saxon's sword as it curved towards him. The two blades clashed, and then sang as they ran together.

'That wasn't much of an effort,' taunted Uther as he stepped back. 'Do you remember killing my brother with a spear in his back? You probably murdered my friend Cal in much the same cowardly way. It must be hard to face me like this.'

Horsa gave another bellow of outrage, and swung his sword two-handed at Uther's neck, putting all his strength behind the blow, but the young king danced back out of range. Recovering quickly, the two fighters exchanged a flurry of strikes, pressing each other in a test of strengths.

'Would it help if I turned my back on you?' Uther asked, swatting aside another cut with ease. Horsa's face had flushed, each laboured breath evidence that he was already beginning to tire.

The fight was moving from where the others waited and was getting closer to the edge of the forest. With a yell, Horsa stabbed forward, and as Uther deflected the flashing blade, the Saxon kicked out, catching him hard in the thigh.

A cry came from Samel as Uther dropped to one knee and gazed up into the triumphant face of Horsa. With one swift movement, Horsa raised his sword, and then brought it down, intent upon taking the young king's head from his shoulders, but Uther wasn't yet ready to die. Thrusting out, he rolled to his left at the same time and felt Horsa's blade slide past, cutting empty air as Excalibur caught his enemy above the kneecap. Uther felt the blade grind as it cut through flesh and slid across the bone eliciting a scream from Horsa who immediately turned, limping into the forest, clutching at his leg with blood pouring through his fingers.

'After him, lad!' called Samel.

He heard a clash of weapons behind him as the two sides met, and then Uther was up and slipping through the trees, trying to see some sign of where Horsa had gone.

Once within the shadows of the forest, it was cool and silent, the memory of the night still hanging heavy through this twilight world, rich in the earthy aromas of life and decay. The sound of a twig breaking under Uther's foot came unnaturally loud to his ears. He stopped, crouched down and breathed deeply, willing his senses to pick up some sign of his enemy's flight. For several moments, all was a soft hush but for the breeze moving through the branches overhead, an unseen whisper of movement of air that never made it to the shadows of the forest floor.

There... a footfall... and again! He scanned the gloom and crept towards the sounds, being careful where he placed each foot. Another noise, like tearing cloth, it was coming from up ahead where a lighter patch lit the forest. The trees had thinned here and the sunlight was able to pierce the darkness, it shone through in bright shafts that danced across the undergrowth, animated by the movement of the leaves high above. As he neared, something caught his eye. He crouched down and examined it, all the while keeping his senses aware of the forest around lest he was surprised, it was a crimson smear of blood on a fern leaf, the red stain, vivid in the dappling sunlight.

Uther crept forward, emerged from the trees cautiously, and was somewhat surprised to see Horsa sitting in plain view on a rock in the centre of the small clearing. The Saxon looked up and smiled at

Uther as he wrapped a piece of cloth, cut from his tunic, about his wounded leg.

'King now, eh, boy? My congratulations to you, that's one mighty leap up from horse thief.' His eyes flickered to the trees behind Uther and the smile returned. 'I tracked you across half this kingdom, captured hundreds of children in my search for you, and then when I almost had you, you gave me the slip at that villa. Of course, back then, I wasn't sure it was you, but I do remember you, and now you've done me the favour of slipping away to die alone... how noble of you.' He pushed himself up from the rock and tested his leg. 'But you still needed to learn so much about leading people. Like how to avoid an early death and when not to stray too far on your own.' To the side of Uther another Saxon appeared from the trees, a big Saxon.

Uther took several hurried steps away from him, his eyes flitting nervously between the two men. Horsa walked slowly towards him while the big man laughed. It came out as a deep guttural sound, making his heavy chest shake. He was huge. Thick red hair sprouted in tufts from beneath a round helm, far too small for the head on which it balanced. The muscles of his massive arms flexed, as if impatient to be unleashed, as he lumbered forward to stand beside Horsa.

'This is Gart,' said Horsa, indicating the huge warrior. 'I sent him into the trees just before you arrived. I do hope you don't mind, it seemed a worthwhile precaution at the time.' He leered at Uther, delighting in the turn of events. 'What do you think... good idea?'

Uther glanced across at the towering Gart. There was a big grin spread across the giant's face, his large fleshy lips drawn back, beneath a thick red moustache, in a smile that exposed the black remains of what had once been his teeth.

'Gart,' rumbled the giant happily, and then ran forward with unexpected speed, swinging a huge rusty sword in a whistling arc as he came.

Uther didn't even attempt to block the blow, but dived to the side, rolled, and flew at Horsa instead. He caught the Saxon chief off guard and attacked, doing his best to keep the limping Saxon leader between him and the giant with a flurry of blows. Horsa stumbled back and just managed to bring his sword up in time to block Excalibur, and then Gart was behind him, trying to get past. The two Saxons stumbled, pushing at each other as Uther continued to attack. Finally, the giant bellowed his frustration and shoved Horsa to the side, his face flushed in anger. Once again, Uther danced away, refusing to clash with him, more intent upon getting to Horsa and delivering a killing blow. As the swords sang, Gart bellowed, trying to get into the fight, then he grinned as, picking up a huge branch, he came between the two and penned Uther in, forcing him to finally face him and defend himself.

Uther could do nothing. While Gart tried unsuccessfully to corner him and land just one blow, he watched Horsa from the corner of his eye as he resumed his position on the rock, a satisfied smirk breaking through the grimace of pain. He was aware of Horsa wrapping a strip of leather round his thigh and wincing when he tied the knot tightly to stem the increasing flow of blood from his wound. More blows came from Gart but he tried to sidestep the huge Saxon to get a thrust into the unprepared Horsa, but the giant saw what he was doing and moved to block him once again.

Gart was big, powerful, and immensely strong but was becoming angry as the tribesman twisted and turned, dodging Gart's blade, still refusing to clash on Gart's terms, it certainly wasn't the battle of strength Gart would have preferred. Uther danced and weaved in intricate circles, leaving the giant bellowing in frustration as his rusty blade repeatedly struck little more than trees or thin air.

Making the giant even madder were the growing number of small cuts and stab wounds now decorating his arms and legs, none of which were fatal, but he was bleeding freely from many and of course, they stung. They were enough to make him furious, distracting him, and therefore making him sloppy in his attempts to kill his smaller foe.

Ducking below another thundering cut, Uther slashed with Excalibur and Gart jumped back with a bellow of rage. Seizing the opportunity, Uther chose not to follow him but changed direction and renewed his attack on Horsa instead, stabbing forward, seeking the Saxon's heart.

'For Odin's sake, kill this puppy!' screamed Horsa, slashing his sword across Uther's path before dashing behind the stone to get out of the way. Drawing back his hand, he threw a knife that missed its target, but distracted the young king enough for Gart to storm in and shove him hard. Uther staggered backwards unbalanced, arms thrashing, as if fending off a swarm of bees, and fell heavily to the ground, the impact knocking the wind out of him.

'On him!' cried Horsa, but Gart needed no encouragement. He ran at Uther and thrust down, letting out a bellow of triumph as the rusty sword stabbed through Uther's thigh, pinning him to the ground.

Uther Pendragon screamed as his world exploded in pain, his vision flared red then blinding white and the surrounding forest erupted with birds flapping wildly up through the canopy in confusion and alarm. A shrill scream forced its way past his lips and he writhed in agony, his lifeblood painting the leaves around him as it pulsed in gouts from the savage wound. With his heart beating loud in his ears, he managed to open his eyes and stare down in horror at the sword protruding from his leg, watching as the blood pumped out around the rusty blade. Throwing back his head, Uther Pendragon screamed and screamed until there was no more and he was only left with a heaving sob. Above him loomed Gart, who smiled and took the sword's crosspiece in both hands. Placing his foot upon Uther's thigh, the giant heaved, ripping the old sword free. Uther screamed again until there was no power left in his voice. He was only vaguely aware of Horsa limping across to stand over him and gaze down at the pooling blood with a sneer of disdain.

'Leader of the tribes and King of all Britons, wasn't it? Well now you die, Uther Pendragon. For this is a mortal wound. You will take with you to the shadowland the knowledge that you have failed your people. Britain will become a Saxon land. Your people will become Saxons, or they shall die.' With a nod to Gart, he stood back and waited for the killing blow to fall. The giant raised his blade and Horsa studied the pain-wracked features of the young king one last time. Then, as the blade fell, he saw the tribesman open his eyes, the pain seeming to dissolve from his face… and a moment later, the blade was stopped a fraction above Uther Pendragon's chest, halted by the intervention of a simple wooden staff, its top hung with shells, leaves, and polished amber. Gart threw back his head and bellowed in rage and frustration while Horsa's gaze travelled along the length of the staff and fixed upon the cold blue eyes of the man that bore it.

The newcomer regarded him calmly from beneath a fine silvery helm decorated with bronze ornate hinges at its sides. It appeared somewhat out of place on the old man, and was in contrast to the rest of his appearance. Dirty brown robes, cinched at the waist with twisted bark, a long grey beard and filthy, matted grey hair that sprouted at angles from the shining helm, surely stolen from some battlefield corpse.

'Who are you?' demanded Horsa, trembling, barely able to keep his anger in check.

The old man reclaimed his staff from Gart's sword with a simple twist. 'I am the druid, Merlyn, and it was once said that my destiny was to save the life of a king… and so, it proves to be true.' He bent down, took a wrap of bark from his cloak, and emptied the contents onto Uther's open wound. The young king stirred from unconsciousness, then groaned and writhed anew. While the Saxons were distracted, Merlyn raised his staff in one fluid motion, and touched Gart gently upon his forehead, the giant collapsed wordlessly to the ground.

A new voice floated across the open glade. 'We are meddling in monumental events here, Merlyn. Are we sure of what we do?'

The sunlight in the clearing seemed to be dimming rapidly, yet there was no cloud hung overhead.

Both Merlyn and Horsa turned towards the speaker as she stepped away from the shadows of the forest. Clad in a white robe, the hood all but covering her face, and mist twisting around her legs spreading out in frail fingers across the forest floor, stood the Lady of the Lake.

Horsa waited, unsure of this new turn of events. The Saxons had little experience of the druids and the only reports he had heard were confused. His initial reaction was to seek escape, but as he gazed about the darkening forest, more appeared, apparently flowing with the mist from between the trees, until a circle of druids surrounded them.

Merlyn inclined his head. 'My Lady of the Lake... am I sure of what we do? No, but then I did not intend to involve myself in these events, it was... unforeseen.' He reached down and helped Uther regain his feet. Uther's face was ashen and he appeared dazed as he gazed about at the assembled druids, and then down at the bloodstained gash in his leggings, as he tested his weight on his leg, he winced.

'Your friend plays the spirits at their own game, and wagers highly, Uther Pendragon.' The Lady of the Lake walked forward, lowering the hood of her cloak.

'Nineve? What's happening?' murmured Uther, his consciousness desperately clawing itself back, trying to find some sense of reality.

She ignored him, studied Horsa for a moment, and then turned once more towards Merlyn. Her eyes closed and the forest became silent. 'They shall fight,' she murmured after a moment, opening her eyes, 'but no mortal may intercede further. The spirits have decreed there shall be cause to forget. The timelines of understanding will become confused; such shall be the cost of this intrusion.

Two shall begin, unsure of their future,

Another will remain, without knowledge of past,

... and the vanquished must walk the shores of the shadowland, without hope of past, present, or future.'

Replacing her hood, she withdrew into the shadows and sunlight flooded the glade once more. As the last tendril of mist whispered back between the trees, Horsa gave a cry and swung his sword at Uther.

Now evenly matched, both warriors fought with a limping gait, the pain of their wounds making the fight a contest of skill and strength, not speed and dexterity. Uther felt stiff and unable to react, as he was accustomed. He could still read his opponent's intentions, but there was no way he could turn and evade as fluidly as he was used to. Horsa was stronger, driving Uther back with a flurry of swinging strikes that threatened to knock the younger combatant from his feet. Seeking an opening, the tribesman twisted on his good leg, crying out with the pain that the move cost him. Excalibur leapt in his hands and Uther saw the shocked expression on Horsa's face as the blade almost reached him, slicing past just short of his throat. Without injury, Uther knew he could easily have stepped forward and driven the blade home, ending the fight there and then... but he didn't. With an explosion of agony, his wound flared, and pain shot up from his leg, through his spine, and with a scream, he dropped to his knees once more.

Horsa was quick to move in, and more than ready to make the kill and be done with these distractions. The boy was on his knees, head bowed in pain. He glanced at the old druid, who was still watching, unmoving and without expression, from the shadows. With a smile of victory, he stepped forward and raised his sword to deliver the final blow... and then the tribesman's sword seemed to leap in his hands and flew out as a blur of silver in the sparkling sunlight. The forest seemed to hold its breath as the blade slipped beneath Horsa's guard, entered his chest, and cut the life from his heart.

Both fighters fell to the floor. Uther Pendragon was still unaware of anything other than the torment of his pain, and Horsa, the final moments of his life ebbing away as his spirit prepared to seek the shadowland.

* * *

The storyteller cleared his throat, and gazed around at the expectant faces. He shrugged his shoulders, and smiled at Calvador Craen.

'I'm getting tired, Cal. I feel... I feel as though I'm fading...'

Calvador Craen rose from the position he had occupied by the fire all evening, and sighed. He turned and glanced round at the audience, and then to his old friend, and nodded.

'With the permission of Uther Pendragon, once King of all the Britons, I shall try and add the final part to his story, so that I can finally take him home.' He smiled at the expectant faces, knowing that most of the listeners still believed there was little more to Uther's story than the imagination of two very old men. However, he decided he would complete the story anyway... for Uther.

'After the death of Horsa, the combined forces of the tribes travelled to Camulod, where they ...' he waved his arm in the air distractedly '... had another battle and eventually formed a truce with the Saxons.'

Uther reached over and grasped Cal's hand. 'Slow down, Calvador, please. Talk about my life after the death of Horsa, what happened? I took a wife, and had a child. I remember his name... Arthur!'

'You had a wife and child, Uther. You married Igraine, which is another long and tiresome story, and had a son, and yes, you named him Arthur. He went on to become one of the greatest kings that this land has ever had, and then while Arthur was still young, Merlyn arrived to complete an old promise...'

Chapter 19

SHADOWLAND

'Where are we going?' Uther leaned across between the horses, and then frowned when the druid remained silent. 'You have to tell me sooner or later... after all, I am king... or I was last time I looked.' Jerking the reins over, he bumped the horses together causing Merlyn to fight for his balance as his horse skittered to the side.

'Be patient, boy,' snapped the druid, once he had managed to regain control. 'I've asked very little of you over the past few years. When we first met, you may recall that I agreed to help you free Nineve, but you may also remember that it was a pact. You agreed that one day you would be beholden to me. If that memory has not escaped you, think of this journey as your repaying that debt. Kindly do me the grace of riding with me, and enjoying my company for a few days. Is it so much for an old friend to ask?'

They continued in silence. It was a warm day, the celebration of Beltane less than a week behind them, with its feasting, dancing and fires of purification now complete. The druids had all departed, satisfied that the land was now reborn and a good harvest season assured, which only left Merlyn with his request for a few days of Uther's time.

'Boy?' said Uther, with a smile. 'You called me, boy. Nobody has called me that in quite some time. Do you call Arthur, "boy"?' When Merlyn didn't answer, Uther continued. 'Well I would wager that you do and that it rankles him as much as it once did me. Does my son progress with his studies?'

Merlyn turned in his saddle and regarded Uther with a sombre expression. 'Arthur is developing well, very well. One day, he is going to make a formidable leader. What's more, he is a good and honest young man.' His face broke into a rare smile. 'But then, Uther, he is your son, I would expect nothing less of him.'

'Thank you, Merlyn, that makes me happy, and it was the most you've said all morning. Maybe, if you're feeling a bit more chatty, you can tell me where we're going, and why the mystery?'

'Just enjoy the day, Uther,' replied Merlyn, pulling the hood of his robe over his head. 'Just enjoy the day. There are no pressures out here. No demands or petitions from your people, just the beauty of the land and, as you say, a mystery to keep your mind occupied, if you so wish.'

When evening began to set in, they made camp on the fringe of the Weald. The sun dipped below the distant hills and the ancient forest became dark and foreboding, sending Uther searching the shadows for firewood to keep the chill at bay. Merlyn watched, clearly amused as the King of Britons blew life into the fire then busied himself constructing a shelter.

'Still remember how it's done then, boy?'

'Stop calling me boy, old man. Of course I remember, and I confess to enjoying the experience more than I thought possible. I forgot about life before I was king. The days when I had to build my own fires and was merely Usher from the village.' He sat back and stared into the flames, lost in the memories of another time, and then glanced around at the shadowy forest and shivered. 'These trees hold many memories and shades of my past. I still remember Horsa chasing us through this forest. And when Cal and I...' he lapsed into a momentary silence before continuing, 'I hope the spirits let me sleep tonight.'

'You will sleep, Uther. Then tomorrow we shall rise early. At dawn we have someone to meet, just a short ride from here, before we enter the forest.' Merlyn gathered his robes around him and refused to be drawn into further conversation when Uther tried, once again, to question him on the true reason for their journey.

It was still dark when they broke camp the next morning, a chill mist hanging to the edge of the trees making for an unpleasant start. For a while, they rode in near darkness along a well-trampled path, and then dawn began to paint the eastern sky with the first blush of the new day, slowly banishing the night and the last residues of sleep from Uther's mind. The sun was still below the level of the treetops as the two riders entered the village of Rudge. There was a general bustle about the place even at this early hour, the good people of Rudge not given to sleeping late when there was work to do in the fields. They rode past the first few dwellings and the smell of cooking reached out to taunt them, and Uther's stomach growled.

'We have a few things to do before we can eat, I'm afraid,' said Merlyn, 'but our first stop is just the other side of the village... not far.' He kicked the horse into a trot and they carried on through the village between the roundhouses and several larger square-built structures, and then on past empty cattle pens and the last few scattered dwellings of the village. Once back out into open country, a narrow path led across a small meadow and down towards a collective of smaller roundhouses in the distance. A boy of around ten summers ran out as they approached, he was hollering and shouting happily, as he waved a stick about his head, closely followed by a small black and tan dog. The boy stopped his game when he saw them, but stood his ground, clearly unafraid of the two strangers as the dog growled protectively at his side.

'Who are you?' Have you come to see me mother? Or is it Tilly, yer after?'

Merlyn smiled down at the boy. 'I don't know. Would your mother's name be Elen, by any chance?'

'Course 'tis, who are you?'

'My name is Merlyn, young man. We met a few years ago when you were... a little younger. I thought I would come to visit and see how you are doing,' The old druid sat upright in the saddle and made a show of searching the trees and bushes nearby, then leaned lower to whisper, '… and this fine fellow here is King Uther Pendragon.'

The boy glanced across at Uther, and then back to Merlyn. 'Is he really? A King?' he gasped. Merlyn nodded and was about to say more, when a woman came out from one of the huts, drying her hands on a cloth.

'Lancelot, come back here!' The dog ran to her, wagging its tail, but Lancelot remained where he was.

''E's a King, Mum. There's a King come to see us!' He pointed up at Uther, a big grin spreading across his face.

'Oh spirits.' The woman's hand went to her mouth as she studied the two visitors, her eyes flitting quickly over to Uther, before coming back to rest upon Merlyn. 'It's you. You were the one… on that day… at his birth in the forest. It was you, wasn't it?'

Merlyn nodded and smiled down at the flustered woman. 'Elen, may we speak with you?'

The sounds of Lancelot attacking trees with his stick and the dog barking excitedly by his side faded behind them as they followed Elen into the largest of the dwellings.

A short while later they were back on the road with Lancelot and the dog keeping pace alongside them as an escort to the edge of the Weald. It was apparently necessary as their young guard and his dog had to defend them from three large bushes and a vicious-looking birch tree before they had made it to the safety of the forest. They left him savaging a holly bush with his stick, daring it to fight back in a loud piping voice.

'What was that all about?' Uther asked, when they were beyond the boy's hearing. 'Who is that boy? And why, by the spirits, did we promise to take him and his mother back to Pendragon Hill?'

'There are many changes ahead, Uther. When Arthur takes the throne, everything must be ready for him. That boy back there was born so that Arthur could become the great leader that this land will need. Remember, there is no such thing in life as coincidence, every-thing that happens, happens for a reason. Unfortunately, most people remain unaware of the clues to life that the spirits leave us, but it's a druid's job to notice when things happen, to untangle the clues and make sense of them… and it's a king's job to listen to the wisdom of druids.'

Uther glanced across and was somewhat relieved to see Merlyn grinning at him. 'Come, boy, we have one more meeting before we get to break our fast.'

The path wove through the woods with the soft light of dawn filtering down through the green canopy. On two occasions, Merlyn stood high in his saddle and peered about seeking direction, and then, each time apparently satisfied, led them from the path, away from the well-trodden route. Uther's stomach continued to complain in gurgles and rumbles, causing him to apologise as the druid frowned in his direction.

'No, it is I who should apologise, Uther. This is taking longer to find than I thought it would. Unfortunately, it was several years ago that I was last at this place and… Well, I wasn't exactly myself at the time.'

'Are you telling me we're lost?' chided Uther. 'I thought that druids didn't get lost?' His stomach growled again. 'I'm sorry. I'm not used to missing a meal.'

Merlyn fished in his bag and pulled out a hard biscuit. 'Stop apologising, and eat this.' He threw it across to Uther. 'We're not lost, we're finding our way perfectly well. It's just a little hard to backtrack after so many years… ahhh, yes, this may well be what we're looking for.'

After a few paces, they could see a large clump of impenetrable brambles looming as a dark shadow through the trees. When they got closer, Uther began leading his mare around on a narrow animal path to the left.

'No, Uther, we're not going round we're going in. This is what we've been looking for.' Merlyn held up his staff, and then thinking better of it, lowered it again and turned to Uther. 'Watch the path for me, Uther. I thought I heard riders just then.'

With a frown, Uther turned and studied the trees; he hadn't heard anything. He strained his ears for any telltale movements that might announce someone coming, but there was nothing. Merlyn coughed behind him, there was a rustle of branches and leaves, and when he turned back, Merlyn was studying him sheepishly. The druid quickly pivoted back to the brambles.

'Oh look,' he cried, 'a path! I hadn't noticed that before... had you?'

Sure enough, slightly to the side of them was a path leading into the brambles. Uther cast a questioning look at Merlyn, which the druid avoided as he disappeared into the dim confines of a thorny passage. Uther followed.

For about twenty paces, they had to be careful of thorns, and then the growth thinned and they emerged into an open glade, which Uther immediately recognised as a druid's circle. He felt a rising sense of unease as they dismounted and allowed the horses free reign to crop the lush grass.

Within the confines of the brambles, large stones were set at regular intervals defining the edge of a circle, each stone rising to about waist height.

'Where are we, Merlyn... and why are we here?'

'You're perfectly safe, boy; trust me. We're going to enter the circle. You may feel a slightly... strange feeling as we do so. Don't be alarmed. It's all perfectly natural and nothing here will harm you, I promise.'

Drawing a deep breath, Uther stepped past the closest stone and onto the rich green grass of the inner circle. A slight tingling travelled throughout his body and a dry whisper filled his senses, it was almost as if the glade had suddenly become host to a swarm of invisible flies. Gathering his resolve, he walked on, taking comfort from an understanding look from Merlyn.

Together, they slowly made their way towards a larger stone that dominated the centre of the circle, the distance taking far longer to cross than felt possible. It was like walking through a fevered dream. Uther raised his eyes to look out at the surrounding trees. They were swaying, and it was hard to focus on them. Light reflected in splashes from the leaves in bright sparkling patterns. It was as if they were moving within a different time and space… and there was no other sound than the whispering of the stones.

In this dream-like state, Uther's mind returned to the day, so many years ago, when he had leapt from a high cliff and down into the deep, green depths of the lake near his village. He had struggled towards the surface, gagging for breath, his ears filled with a hissing rush of bubbles. He remembered gazing up, there had been the same strange patterns of light, reflecting on the surface above him, guiding him to safety, the same lights he was seeing now in the trees around the glade.

The whispering grew louder, drawing his attention back to the central stone. It was of equal height to the other stones, was roughly square, and had a flat top like a small table. Absently, he noticed a strange symbol standing proud on one face. Then, unbidden, he felt his hands reach for Excalibur. He glanced at Merlyn, and the druid nodded as he drew the sword.

'All is as it was meant to be, Uther.' Merlyn's voice echoed loud in his ears. 'This sword was a gift from spirit. It came to you at a time of need, and now you return it for Arthur to claim when his time is right. Strike it deep!'

The whispering vibration within the circle increased to a climax, and Uther felt little more than an observer as, clutching the sword for the last time, he raised it over his head and stabbed down and the blade slid half its length into the centre of the stone. He heard a rasping sound as it entered, but felt no resistance. It was more a sensation of acceptance from the stone as the sword slid home.

Uther found himself, one long moment later, staring at the sword embedded almost to the hilt, as if he were waking from a dream. Glancing about, he realised he could now see and hear properly again, the strange whispering that had filled the glade now replaced by bird song and the breeze blowing through the treetops.

'Try to pull it from the stone.' Merlyn gestured to the weapon, once so familiar. Regarding it closely, Uther now felt detached, as if something more than the sword had gone from his side. There were no feelings of remorse or regret, and he gave the hilt only one small experimental tug, knowing he would be unable to free it.

'It waits now for Arthur. It will be here ready for when he needs it.' Taking Uther by the arm, Merlyn led him from the circle. They walked the horses through the bramble path and only mounted once they were out amongst the trees of the Weald again. They set off and Merlyn began talking of finding some food to break their fast and of the new castle that they should build in Camulod. Uther glanced back. There appeared to be little sign of any path into the impenetrable brambles now guarding Excalibur and his mind immediately began the process of questioning what had happened.

'It's time we built a fortress from stone,' continued Merlyn, breaking into Uther's thoughts. 'The Romans left us plenty of material at Camulod. Of course, the Saxons pulled most of their buildings down when they fought the Iceni, but the stone remains. It would make a fine place for the Pendragons to rule from, and there are now masons among us able to construct it. I happen to know that Berin is very keen to oversee the project.'

As Merlyn chattered happily, Uther rode in silence with a growing feeling that his time was now over. He had brought the land to a relative peace, the tribes united under a ruling council over which he presided. The Saxon invaders had, for the time being, become peaceful settlers. True, their numbers were growing, and there were now Angles, Jutes, and Gauls joining them, but there were representatives from each group sitting at the large round council table, and a peace was holding while they all called themselves Britons.

Then, of course, there was Arthur. The boy had been the centre of his happiness ever since his birthing, one storm-lashed winter night. He had grown, as Merlyn was quick to point out, to be a fine young man who would become a strong, formidable king able to lead and inspire generations, there was nothing remaining for Uther Pendragon to resolve. Maybe it was time for Usher to return and see the land, to run free, and to live.

* * *

Calvador Craen stopped his pacing and glanced round at his audience. 'So there you have the conclusion of this tale. Arthur, as I'm sure you all know, went on to be one of the greatest kings this land has ever known, while Uther decided to slip away and live some time as Usher, the village boy who had once been burned out of his village. However, there was a problem for Usher.'

Cal crouched down and laid his hands upon the old storyteller's knees. 'When Merlyn saved your life, Uther, he interfered with more than just your death. Do you remember what Nineve said before you fought Horsa for the final time? She said that two would begin, unsure of their future... that another would remain without knowledge of his past... and that the vanquished would walk the shores of the shadowland, without hope of past, present, or future.

'Well, both Merlyn and Nineve paid their price for their parts that day, by starting the incarnation of their lives in ignorance of who they really were, the druids had to awaken them. Horsa, even now, walks the shadowland as the vanquished, and you...' He sighed, and then stared into the old storyteller's eyes, searching for the friend he once knew so well.

'The final judgment of the spirits that day was that you would remain in the land you so loved without any knowledge of your past. Uther, you have walked this land now for more than a thousand years, unaware of who you are, or ever were. Arthur and his knights searched for you for nearly thirty years without ever finding a trace of where you had gone.' Calvador Craen stood up and stared into the fire. 'Merlyn entered the shadowland in search of me. I don't know how he did it but the spirits allowed me to return here to find you.' As he turned back, there were tears in his eyes. 'I'm sorry it took so long, Uther... I came here to guide you back to spirit, to those that love you and have waited for you all this time.' Both old men glanced across to the fire as if hearing more than the crackling flames.

'Help me up, Cal.' Uther held up an arm and Calvador Craen gently pulled him to his feet where he swayed for a moment brushing loose tobacco strands from his waistcoat before addressing his audience for the final time. 'My name, is Uther Pendragon… you have known me as Usher Vance. Mine, as you now know, has been a long and some would say interesting life.' Brushing back a strand of long silver-grey hair, the old storyteller gazed about again at the small audience of attentive faces and smiled. 'I'm sorry, my friends, but I must now depart your company. I thank you for listening to my story. I hope that this evening will leave you with stories enough to fill your midwinter eves for many years to come.'

The two old friends turned towards the fire and, as they did, they began to fade. It was as if their bodies slowly changed to grains of sand and, grain by grain, were being blown away upon a breeze. The ghostly figures walked forward, the fire flared as they passed through, and then died back down to nothing as they vanished, leaving the gathering strangely silent before the cold dead ashes.

* * *

Now, so many years later, you can still go back to that village on midwinter's eve and join the villagers as they gather around the fire; it's a tradition. However, just you mind that as they tell stories about that night and the price that Uther Pendragon paid for their land, you don't take to sitting in the old leather chair by the fire. You see; it always remains vacant on midwinter's eve. Out of respect for the old storyteller, and the hope that one day he might just return.

The End.

Printed in Poland
by Amazon Fulfillment
Poland Sp. z o.o., Wrocław